RETURN OF THE PRODIGAL

RETURN OF THE PRODIGAL

MICHAEL CAUDO

ISBN: 978-1-7372988-0-9

Cover design and typesetting by riverdesignbooks.com

For Christine

TABLE OF CONTENTS

NICK DI NOBILE

Nick stood on the balcony and looked out at the Atlantic. He sipped a Lavazza Super Crema double espresso and took in the view. Nick had left Philly almost twenty years ago and made a new life for himself in South Florida. Even now, at the age of fifty and two decades into his self-imposed exile, the view never failed to deliver. Leaning over the balcony railing of his condo on the thirty-first floor of the Bellissimo Towers, he could see his oceanfront bar and grill just a quarter mile down the beach. The Tuscan Tiki (locals called it The Tiki) was wildly popular among tourists and locals alike. Life was good for Nick in Lauderdale-By-The-Sea, so when his Uncle Frank Valletto called and asked to meet him in Miami, Nick started to get that sick feeling in his stomach that usually preceded some crisis. Frankie "The Stone Crab" Valletto wouldn't say what it was about, but it was important enough for him to ask Nick to drop everything and head over to the Fontainebleau.

Grace was still lying in bed, and Nick fixed her a coffee. She was smart, gorgeous and fiercely loyal to Nick. She also had great instincts. So when Nick told her he was going to Miami to meet Frank, her suspicion only highlighted his misgivings. Grace had a place in Pompano, and they hadn't discussed changing that yet. For now, they were both happy to spend most nights together but still maintain their own space.

"I don't understand why he doesn't come to the Tiki if he's only going to ask to borrow more money," Grace said.

"Who knows, Grace. Maybe he wants to take me to lunch."

"More like the cleaners," Grace said.

She's not wrong, Nick thought as he dressed. Frankie the Crab was a great guy, but he was one of those hard-luck cases whose fortunes always promised to turn, and then, at the last second, never quite did. Frank was a regular at the Tiki, and while he wasn't actually Nick's uncle by blood, he was one of Tony Di Nobile's oldest friends, and Nick's closest link to his dead father and the city he'd left behind.

Nick had lost track of the money he'd lent Frank over the years, not that he really cared about the money. As much as Frank could drive him crazy, he loved having the old man around. It was like having a little slice of Passyunk Avenue under the palm trees.

Nick placed Grace's coffee on the night table and kissed her before heading for the door.

"I'll call you on the drive back," Nick said.

"Are you sure you don't have a girlfriend in Miami, Nick?" Grace asked in a manner that could be construed as either a joke or a test, or more likely, a little of both.

Nick didn't miss a beat. "Grace, don't be silly—you know she lives in Delray."

"Asshole," Grace hollered as she threw a pillow at Nick that missed him but startled the oddly marked cat they called Picasso.

OL' BLUE EYES

Nick drove his Bentley Continental GT up the arrivals driveway of the Fontainebleau. He palmed a twenty to a cheerful valet as he exited in front of the lobby's entrance. A doorman gripped one of the iconic gold handles and pulled open a fragrant portal to ageless cool as Nick approached.

"Welcome to the Fontainebleau, sir," the doorman said with a sweeping gesture.

Nick stepped through and strode purposely across the signature bowtie tile floor, the same floor Sinatra and countless luminaries had glided across, both in cinema and real life. An entire hallway was dedicated to Ol' Blue Eyes. His photographs ran its length, chronicling his time and exploits at the resort over the years. Nick took a deep breath and savored the pumped-in signature fragrance, the olfactory component of a potent sensory cocktail. He positioned himself at the lobby bar and took in the visual long pour. The classic lobby had been designed by architect Morris Lapidus, and the place had a way of intoxicating you before you had your first drink.

Frankie The Stone Crab, shuffled down the crooner's eponymous hallway on his way to meet Nick at the lobby bar. He glanced at the Chairman's photo display as he passed by, pausing for a moment to contemplate his favorite: a color still of Sinatra and Jill St. John during the filming of *Tony Rome*. Sinatra, poolside in a dress shirt and slacks, is stretched out on a lounge chair, his hat cocked over his brow. St. John hovers impatiently, hand on hip in a blue bikini, while the grand hotel looms over her shoulder like a jealous mistress. Frank's focus shifted. He caught his unshaven reflection in the glass and looked away. It seemed like only yesterday Frank had strolled through the hotel like royalty, pressing palms and kissing cheeks. Now, he tried to hide inside his oversized, knockoff shirt with rolled-up French cuffs and fade into the background. He wished he could leap into one of those black and white photos and assume the identity of a nameless face in the crowd.

Nick pushed aside a stool, preferring to stand. Frankie was late, as always. He glanced at the Speedmaster on his wrist—quarter after five. The pool crowd was beginning to filter back into the hotel, and a few convention types commandeered the cocktail tables, all name tags and forced smiles. By midnight, half of them would be sloshed and ensconced in a strange room, lanyards intertwined. Nick ordered a Maker's Mark neat. Mid-sip, he saw Frank ambling over, and his heart dropped.

Frank waved weakly and cracked his first genuine smile in months. Nick did his best to reciprocate, but his smile was only half as genuine. Frank had been like an uncle to Nick growing up back in the city. Nick had always proudly introduced him as such and always referred to him affectionately as "Unc." He hadn't seen Frank in a few months. Now he knew why. As he watched the shell of what was once that man shuffle over, he took a deep, hard swallow of his whisky.

Nick cleared his throat. "How's my long-lost uncle?" Nick kissed him on his stubbled cheek and hugged him lightly, sensing his frail frame beneath his shirt.

"I feel like a million bucks, nephew."

"Fucking inflation's a motherfucker," Nick managed to crack, breaking the ice without stating the obvious. Frank even managed a chuckle.

"Whatcha drinking, Frankie?"

"Thought you'd never ask, Nicholas. Stoli Elit martini, up, blue cheese olives."

"Wow, you really have been living in Boca too long."

Frank was one of the few friends from back home who occasionally used Nick's full name. It was a sign of affection and, despite the faux formality, had a disarming familiarity. In the fucked-up, South Philly-South Florida *giambotta* they found themselves knee-deep in, it sent an unmistakable message: *we have a long history*.

Their drinks arrived, Nick having ordered a refill for himself after downing his first upon Frank's approach. Frank raised his glass in a toast.

"Disaster to the wench who did wrong by our Nicky." Frank loved quoting that line from *Gilda*.

"Let's not be so hard on the old gal; she's already paid dearly," Nick quipped predictably.

As many times as they'd playfully recited that tired script, an image of Angie's face still flashed across his mind every single time, even after all those years. He sipped his bourbon without taking his eyes off Frank and wondered if he knew what he was thinking.

Frank played with his olives, swirling the toothpick between his thumb and forefinger and staring at the faint trail of blue cheese it left in the vodka. Nick could see he was searching his glass for something. *Words? Courage?*

"I was so sorry to hear about your father, Nicky. He was a real gentleman. Always treated me like a prince."

"Thanks, Frankie. He loved you too," Nick replied curtly.

"You know, he never judged me, even when I was on the outs. He always had time for me. And when it came to you, Nicky, he was so proud."

"That's enough, Frankie," Nick said sharply. He took a swig and regained his composure quickly. "Thanks, I appreciate it. Honestly, I do. Now, I assume you dragged me here to ask me something, or was it tell me something. Let me guess; it has something to do with my upcoming trip back to the city to settle my dad's affairs?"

Frank looked like he just got kicked in the balls.

"It's not like that, Nicky," Frank almost whispered.

"Oh, it's not? Okay then, Frankie, why don't you tell me how it is. You here to help me?" Nick started to scan the bar now.

"Nick, it's just that *the guy* knows we're friends—"

"Are we?" Nick interrupted. "I must have missed the floral arrangement you sent to my father's funeral." Nick regretted the comment the second it came out of his mouth. It was petty and designed to hit the old man below the belt.

Frank absorbed the blow and gathered all the dignity a beaten dog could muster. "Actually, Nick, I sent a mass card," he snarled back. "You know why? Cause that was all I could fuckin' afford. But I'll tell you what I did do. I went to mass at St. Anthony's, Nicky, and I lit a candle for my old friend. And then I went to the last fucking bar east of Federal Highway that would run me a tab and played all your dad's favorite songs on the jukebox, not that you would know any of them. And I got cockeyed drunk thinking about all the good times we had together."

The pharmaceutical foursome looked over nervously. The old man still had his timbre. The bartender, a seasoned South Beach vet, dutifully set up two fresh drinks without asking. Nick stared straight ahead.

"What … no funny remark now?" Frank was breathing heavily. A pack of Marlboros and a lighter in hand, he turned to the door for a smoke. Nick grabbed his free hand and squeezed lightly.

"Frankie." The old man wouldn't meet his eyes. "I have a serious question, Unc." Frank turned his head and they locked eyes. "There's still a bar in east Boca that will run you a tab?" Frank started to pull his hand away, but Nick held on, firmly but gently. The beginnings of a smile began to betray him.

"Not anymore." Frank exhaled through a mischievous smirk as Nick pulled him close. Frank felt his warm breath on his ear as Nick pulled him in for a hug.

Frank tried to mutter an apology. "I'm sorry, nephew—" but Nick spoke over him.

"No, Unc, *I'm* sorry. Thanks for the card. We all need prayers more than flowers." Frank heard the slightest crack in Nick's voice. Nick let his hand go and cleared his throat. "Why don't you go have your smoke now?"

Instead, Frank pulled out his phone to check a text. Nick could see the screen was cracked. *Probably that fucking junkie whore Jennifer*, Nick thought.

"I have to get back soon anyway," Frank said. "I borrowed a car from the kid at the club and I have to get it back," He seemed agitated. "Listen, Nick, all kidding aside, I did need to talk to you about something. I'm sorry, but *the guy*—"

"The Rose," Nick interjected. "You can say his name, Frankie; Bobby De Rosa. my father's old partner. Don't tell me, he thinks he's entitled to half the Caffé? That's bullshit, Unc, and you know it. My father bought him out thirty-five years ago. It's all on paper, all legit. I have everything from the lawyer: copy of the canceled check, deed, and title insurance. My father might have been a fool when it came to pussy, but he was no fool when it came to business, especially with that snake."

For the first time during their meeting, Frank looked at Nick and said nothing. His face said it all. *I know something you don't.*

"You done?" Frank finally spoke, more firmly now, almost confident.

Nick breathed in deeply and exhaled slowly. His silence was his answer.

"Good," Frank stated firmly. "Cause it's not about the Caffé."

"Well, what then?" Nick was temporarily relieved, but he was getting impatient.

Frank paused for a moment before answering. "The painting nephew. It's about the painting."

Nick almost laughed upon hearing this. "Oh Jesus Christ, Unc. You've got to be kidding me. That old wives' tale? You know better than me how my father fueled that rumor. He fed off it. It was a running gag in my house every holiday. '*Hey, compar, where'd you hide the painting?*' He promoted Caffé Vecchio with that rumor, decorated it with all those reproductions, named the dishes on the menu after the Masters: *Picasso Piccata, Botticelli Bolognese.* You got to admit, Frankie, it was a great gimmick. And the *medigans* ate it up, literally. The food was good. A gimmick only goes so far, but you can't fool the neighborhood when it comes to food. The tourists come once, take their pictures with Dad in front of the paintings and go back to the Main Line with a story. But the neighborhood people kept it going. Now, the neighborhood's changed." Nick finally realized he was rambling and sat back on his stool. Maybe he was trying too hard to reassure himself.

Frank's eyes never wavered. His expression was like granite, inscrutable. In that moment, he reminded Nick of the old Frankie.

"That's where you're wrong, Nicky." For a beaten-down man, his tone was confident. "The neighborhood never changed, not really. Not to us. No matter how many juice bars, yoga studios, or doggie fucking bakeries open up on Passyunk, some things are still the same."

"Okay, Unc, you're right about that, I guess. But that ain't got shit to do with me. I'm flying back, meeting with the estate lawyer, listing the Caffé with the broker, and when I get on that return flight, I'm never looking back." Nick slid three hundred-dollar bills to the bartender without asking for the check, figuring that would more than cover it, and stood up.

"I wasn't finished, Nicholas." *There was the full name again.* Now it was Frank's turn to pull Nick close. He whispered in Nick's ear. "That's not the only thing you're wrong about." He pulled back and stared Nick dead in the eye. Nick gazed into those dark eyes and, for a split second, recognized the Uncle Frank of his childhood—sharp as a tack, handsome, and capable.

"The painting is real, my nephew." Frank stated it like he was reading a headline in the *Inquirer*.

"And you know this how?" Nick inquired weakly. Deep down, he suspected he already knew the answer. Frank confirmed what Nick was thinking.

"Because I saw it with my own eyes."

Nick kept up the front. "Don't tell me, you pulled off the Gardner heist," Nick jabbed sarcastically.

"I didn't say that, so you can stop being a smart-ass, but when the paintings made their way from Boston to Philly, they didn't drive themselves." The old man was firm and more than a little of the old pride was leaking through.

"So *my* father—" Nick started.

"No way, Nicky. Your father never crossed certain lines. His only mistake was always bailing me out of jams."

"I won't argue with that. Unc, so please, the short version if you don't fucking mind."

Frank stared at his drink, collecting himself. Nick signaled for a backup.

"My usual Nicky, I stuck my neck out, drove a fish truck for six hours, pissing in a jug, mind you, with twelve paintings worth five hundred million in the back, and got stiffed."

Nick reflected for a moment. "So how does my father figure into this?"

"I made a beef; we sat down, they paid me five hundred plus gas and tolls and threw in a worthless knockoff for my troubles. I had no use for it, and I knew your father liked art, with all those paintings hanging in the Caffé, so I brought it over. He took a shine to it and gave me five hundred, more out of charity than anything else. He hung it in the Caffé with his other pictures. He loved that picture, kept looking at it, touching it. Then, about a month later, it was gone—just like that." Frank snapped his fingers. "When I asked him about it," Frank said, gripping the top of Nick's hand on the bar to convey the seriousness of his words, "it was one of the few times I heard him raise his voice. He said it was a piece of garbage and had a curse on it so he threw it in the dumpster. I can still see him making the sign of the horns when he said it was cursed." Frank made the sign with his index finger and pinkie to demonstrate.

Nick grabbed his arm, only half joking, and said, "Don't point them at me, Frankie."

Frank laughed. "Still a little superstitious, kid? Good, you should be."

"Okay, so you got stiffed, sold a worthless knockoff to my dad for five hundred, and he threw it in the trash. What am I missing?"

"Turns out," Frank spoke softly, "maybe it wasn't so worthless."

Nick suddenly felt sick. "And my father figured it out."

Frank raised his glass. "You got it, kid."

Now it was Nick who looked like he'd been kicked in the balls.

"Wait, you said twelve paintings, right? I remember reading it was eleven."

Frank's bushy eyebrows perked up. "You read right. Good memory, nephew. Well technically it was six paintings and five sketches, but that's hardly the point."

"My father had newspaper clippings all over the basement. I just figured it was because he considered himself some half-assed art aficionado. Didn't they steal some other bullshit too, a Chinese vase and an eagle from a flag?"

"That they did. Relatively worthless shit compared to some of the treasures they left behind. These guys weren't recruited for their art expertise. I mean, they left a Michelangelo for Christ's sake. And for the record, your father wasn't a half-assed anything, Nicky."

Nick almost blurted out, *I beg to differ*, but thought better of it. Instead, he said, "You said I was right about it being eleven."

"No," Frank responded, "I said you *read* right because that's what the papers said. Because that's the number the museum reported."

"So, the twelfth painting?" Nick looked confused.

"It was actually the first one stolen. It wasn't even in the gallery itself. It was in the basement where they tied up the guards—a workshop-type area where they did cleaning and restoration of pieces for other museums or private collectors, shit like that. And sometimes, they were hired to do, like an analysis to authenticate a particular item. Well, this here piece was there to be evaluated and restored for a collector. They had an idea that maybe it was done by one of Rembrandt's students since the style matched and the paint was the right age, whatever. Well, it turned out to be a fugazi and was in the process of being boxed up before they shipped it back to the poor sucker. Anyway, one of the thieves noticed it; maybe he thought it looked like something he'd seen before, maybe it just moved him the way it moved your father, whatever. In any event, he scooped it up."

Nick shook his head. "I don't understand. Why wasn't it reported stolen?"

"Couple a few reasons. First, no one even noticed it was gone. There were a bunch of paintings scattered all over, leaning against the walls, one on top of the other, and the guards were already blindfolded with duct tape when it was taken. Second, this wasn't a museum piece; it was just some copy of a famous painting. It wasn't inventoried because, as unbelievable as this might sound, the museum was uninsured for theft. They were on the ropes financially, as you may have gathered from the cut-rate security guards. Even the reward money had to be posted by Sotheby's or Christie's or whoever the fuck. I don't remember. Third, and most importantly, the painting had a questionable—*come si dice?*— providence."

"You mean provenance?" Nick inquired gently.

"Yeah, that's what I said. You know, like where it came from. Apparently, it wasn't so clean. The truth is, most of these things have been stolen multiple times over the years. Sometimes by free agents, but usually by armies and governments. But it only becomes a crime when an Italian steals it, naturally."

Nick couldn't tell if he was joking, but he affirmed nonetheless. "Naturally."

Frank resumed. "But I digress. Anyway, this here painting had a particularly dirty history. It was first seized by the Nazis and stashed in some salt mine until the Allies recovered it. Later on, it supposedly got boosted in Ireland by some IRA guys who made the same mistake, and somebody maybe got killed for it at one point. I mean, how would it look if the museum that got robbed had a stolen painting of its own stashed in the basement, with a body attached to it to boot? So the museum, figuring it already had all the bad publicity it could afford, what with the shitty security system and the shady guards, just paid the owner off. After all, it was a *fugazi*, covered in varnish and dirt and hardly worth the canvas it was painted on. The collector, some Russian guy, was content with the payoff, generous as it seemed, and he's long since dead anyway. Personally, I think the museum suspected all along it was the real thing and was looking to rip this guy off."

"Okay, then what's the problem?" Nick asked.

"The problem is, these things are fluid. Experts disagree all the time about this stuff. You know, authenticity. It's every bit as dirty as any other business. Paintings hanging in galleries for decades, even centuries, turn out to be fakes, or if not outright forgeries, maybe painted by a student from the artist's school instead of the artist himself. Your father knew all about this shit. He once told me there was another *Mona Lisa* and the one in Paris was a fake. Anyway, sometimes—sometimes—the opposite happens, and a piece all the experts previously thought was a knockoff turns out to be the real McCoy."

"And in the case of the twelfth painting?" Nick asked, but already knew the answer.

Frank savored the moment. His knowledge filled him with an old feeling as he puffed out his sunken chest. He felt relevant for the first time in a long while.

"Opposite," Frank stated brusquely. The old man was now tapping the pack of Marlboros feverishly against the heel of his hand and it made a sharp cracking noise.

"How can you be sure, though?"

"Somebody's tried to collect the reward from the FBI. The problem is, this painting ain't covered by the reward since it isn't listed as stolen. Shit, it doesn't technically *exist*, and *nothing's* more priceless than something that doesn't exist."

"But how do you know it's the same painting my father bought from you? You said he threw it out."

"Your father would never have destroyed that painting. He looked at it like, I don't know, like he was looking at the face of Christ. Tears were running down his face when he told me he threw it in the dumpster. I thought about this a lot over the years, Nicky. I swear, I think... I think he hid it for you."

Nick tried to process Frank's tale. His mind was firing up flashbacks of information; snippets of conversations he'd overheard years ago; crazy sayings his father would repeat on an endless loop. *Lo spazio tra*—the space between. His father had translated for him. Nick didn't understand it then and understood it even less now. He did remember that the old man would usually recite it when he was listening to music, reading a book, or maybe on a few occasions, looking at a painting. Nick thought of the piles of books that were strewn everywhere. His grandmother, Filomena, was endlessly picking them up and piling them as neatly as she could in their overcrowded rowhome. *God rest her soul.* Tony read all the classics and always encouraged Nick to read. His favorite was *The Count of Monte Cristo.* Nick remembered the dusty, leather hardcover copy of the Dumas classic his father had gifted to him one Christmas many years ago, when every kid on the block wanted a Mattel Electronic Football game. Nick recalled with shame the pained look on his father's face when he asked how the book was going, and Nick responded, with hostile intent, "*What, the one by dumbass?*" Nick still felt that pang of guilt like it was yesterday. He wished he had apologized before his father died, told him how much he loved it, when he finally did read it. Told him how he treasured the loving inscription written on the inside cover. Hell, told him he loved him. Nick silently whispered a heavenly apology. *I'm sorry, Dad.*

He thought of all the art history and reference books his father collected, especially about Rembrandt, Tony's favorite painter. Rembrandt Harmenszoon van Rijn. Tony would use his full name. He remembered his father taking him to the Philadelphia Art Museum years ago for a Rembrandt exhibit. Nick was bored out of his mind. He tried to look at the paintings like his father did, with reverence, but all he saw was pictures of old people.

"So where is it now?" asked Nick.

"If I knew that, I wouldn't be here. Most likely, I'd be dead already."

"Well, I hate to disappoint you—*and* your friend—but I don't know either."

"Nobody thinks you do, but they *do* want you to find it."

"And how am I supposed to do that? As his executor, I've already inventoried all his assets. The only paintings are those dusty canvases hanging in the Caffè. I had them appraised, and the frames are worth more than the paintings."

Frank reflected on this for a moment. "What was that saying in Italian your father was always repeating?"

"Are you fucking kidding me?" Nick responded sarcastically. "He had a hundred of them." Tony was constantly reciting some crazy Italian words of wisdom in his grandparents' cryptic dialect. Nick learned to tune it out at an early age, but a few were indelibly ingrained in his memory.

"*Lo spazio tra,*" Nick offered.

"The space between?" Frank chuckled. "No, not that one. He used to sing this one. Like in a singsong. *Nascosta—*"

"*Nascosta in piena vista.*" Nick finished the phrase in his father's singing voice, which transported him to his family's kitchen table, where his father would hold court. "What does it mean, Frankie?"

"Jesus Christ, Nick, you sounded exactly like him. Fucking hair is standing up on the back of my neck. Hidden in plain sight."

"What's hidden in plain sight?"

"No, that's what it means. *Nascosta in piena vista*—hidden in plain sight."

"Unc, this has been great, seeing you and all, but I gotta get back to the Tiki."

"Okay. I'll see you in the city and we'll pick this up there."

"Wait," Nick said, "you're going to the city? Why? How?"

"On a plane, Nicky, just like you. Well, maybe not just like you. I'm flying Spirit to Atlantic City."

"Spirit flies direct to Philly now, Unc."

"Yeah, but I thought I'd stop by Resorts for old times' sake." Frank emphasized the first syllable—*re*-sorts.

"You do know they opened a few other casinos since 1978?" Nick joked.

"I know, but did I ever tell you about the time I saw Sinatra there?"

"Only a thousand times," Nick responded reliably.

"I sat in the front row with your dad—" Frank began, but Nick picked it up from there.

"And after Sinatra finished 'Mack the Knife,' he raised his glass and winked right at you." Nick finished with a dutiful solemnity, not mocking the old timer's tale.

Frank wasn't offended; he was glad someone remembered the story. "Fucking-A right, Nicky. Anyway, I got a hook up for a full comp, room and meals."

The old man couldn't help boasting a little, but it only caused Nick to theorize about the benefactor behind this unexpected boon for a washed-up, half-assed racketeer. Despite his musings, Nick raised his glass to Frankie's reminiscence and clinked his glass gently. "Salute, Unc," Nick toasted.

"Salute, Nicky," Frank returned the toast, pronouncing it like *ah-zalud*.

The old man hadn't been back to the city in years. He was estranged from his son and daughter and hadn't spoken to them since a regrettable Christmas day four or five years ago. He could no longer remember exactly and had stopped trying. The pain of reflecting on his failures as a father was overwhelming and all-consuming. Frank had done his best to push all that out of his mind and had eked out a hardscrabble existence in south Florida. *Better to struggle here than back home in the cold,* he always said. Still, the sadness hung around his neck like a millstone. They stood there for a long moment, the two expatriates. Nick thought of a quote from Emerson his father had often recited: *My giant goes with me wherever I go.*

They hugged again, kissed on the cheek, and Frank set off for the departures exit, disappearing back through the Sinatra corridor. Frank's *giant* followed closely behind, stalking him like a most patient assassin. Nick stared out the window at the pool. *His* giant stared back through his reflection.

Nick turned to watch Frank's hunched posterior hustle away. His gait was as uneven as the wear on the heels of his ancient Ferragamo loafers. Nick drained the last of his bourbon. He breathed in slowly, held it for a four-count, then exhaled for a four-count. A relaxation technique Grace had taught him. He considered ordering another but opted for a quick stroll around the resort to clear his head before driving back.

Nick pulled an Arturo Fuente Opus X from his breast pocket and rolled it between his fingers. The wrapper pushed back against his thumb reassuringly, a sign to a seasoned aficionado that the humidity level was just right. No surprise, as he had plucked it from an Elie Bleu humidor that contained his premium stash—mostly Cuban, but also some rare Dominican and Nicaraguan blends. Half the "Cubans" floating around South Florida were fakes, replicated right down to the holographic bands. Nick had a trusted source but was partial to the Dominican sticks of late. The Opus was a sentimental choice in honor of the setting. Nick had picked out his smoke as carefully as his wardrobe. Boca was awash in fake Cuban cigars and replica Audemars Piguet watches. They were worn shamelessly and difficult to spot, the men sporting them somewhat less so. They arrived from up north with a story and a pitch, usually a retread variation on some *can't miss, get rich quick* scheme.

The new Ponzi schemes, like the old ones, were heavy on accouterments but light on substance. Some preliminary homework, a call or text back home, usually revealed that the purveyor was fresh out of runway back home and had burned his last bridge. This short con required the charlatan to quickly find a mark "down south" (usually a rich, nerdy kid with access to family money) who couldn't check his story and pedigree. Some cons were more sophisticated and played out on a larger, more intricate stage. These worked out less than half the time, but they usually flamed out, and the scammers returned to their respective northern cities ignominiously.

Nick loathed them and could spot them a mile away. He resented their appropriation of his culture in support of their grift, a rancid, sacrilegious mixture of snake oil and olive oil. He considered it a personal affront and a smear on his heritage, especially when perpetrated by a few who went so far as to assume an Italian name and identity. Those were the worst. When he got a chance to sting them, he relished it.

Nick found himself thinking of all this for some reason, when he should have been sorting out all the information Frank had dropped on him instead. Separating the wheat from the chaff as it were. He planned to take a stroll around the pool and beach, fire up the Opus, and think it all through before he had to strip the second band, but he never got a chance to light it.

Nick's phone buzzed. He looked down at a text from Grace.

All good here. Be careful driving back. 95 is a mess. Love you.

Nick paused beneath a neon sign that read *I Followed You To The Sun*. He started to type a response but got hung up on whether to text back *Love you too*. He hadn't quite realized they had arrived at the "I love you" stage of their relationship, and it caught him off guard. Grace was, well, amazing. She was Nick's biggest supporter and unwaveringly loyal. Grace was also an absolute knockout. Half Italian, half Colombian, she had stopped Nick dead in his tracks when she walked off the beach and up to his bar. They had quickly assumed an easy relationship. It seemed almost a foregone conclusion, and Nick couldn't remember either of them uttering any invitations. They just started drinking and sharing one meal after another until neither could recall a time when they hadn't. She was passionate and fiery, and on some level, it scared Nick more than any demon-filled nightmares from back home.

Still, something stopped Nick short of professing his love for her, even though he felt sure that he did. So far, Grace remained almost supernaturally patient, but Nick knew no matter how saintly her disposition, every woman had her limits. He was touched by her text and had no intention of leaving her hanging. Besides, she was a smart woman, and while Nick didn't doubt her sincerity, he also knew that on some level it was a test.

Nick walked outside onto a small balcony overlooking the resort's vast pool scene as he mentally composed his reply. His focus was soon diverted to one of the oversized, open-air cabanas. It was situated on an island of sorts that extended into the middle of one of the numerous pools. Four men sat around a table as a bottle service girl poured their drinks from an exceptionally large and well-stocked ice bucket. She was leaning over just enough to give the men the slightest glimpse beneath her skirt (which in reality, was basically a pair of shorts masquerading as panties).

The first was a big guy, maybe sixty, full head of hair. Nick thought he recognized him from Lauderdale, maybe Boca. Nick searched his memory. *Rocco—no, Ralph something*. The second man wasn't familiar. Tall, light hair, fiftyish, oversized sunglasses covered his eyes. *Not Italian, Russian maybe?* Then there was Frank, standing just on the perimeter, ogling the waitress. *Naturally*. Nick half grinned. In that instant, it all fell into place. Frank had first approached the bar from the Sinatra hallway, *from the direction of the departures drive*. Nick hadn't given it much thought at the time, maybe figured the old man had come from taking a piss after the long ride. Now, Nick's mind was racing with theories as he watched his *Uncle* Frank click champagne glasses with the fourth man. Someone Nick hadn't seen in years and had hoped he'd never see again; Bobby "The Rose" De Rosa. A younger guy, no older than twenty, sat on a lounge chair off to the side, and Nick couldn't tell if he was with the group or just a straggler.

So, Nick thought as he composed himself, *the Rose is in Florida.*

Nick composed a text message, not to Grace, but Frank. He watched from a distance as the old man reached for his phone, put on his glasses, and read Nick's message. He looked puzzled at first but soon struggled to suppress a smile that spread across his wrinkled face and relaxed his furrowed brow as he turned away from the other men. A silent laugh caused his shoulders to rise and fall rhythmically.

The text read, *Back Stabbers by the O'Jays*

Tony Di Nobile was a devout fan of old school R&B and Soul, especially *The Philly Sound,* of which his knowledge was legendary and encyclopedic. The text was in response to Frankie's challenge. The truth was, Nick remembered all his father's favorite songs—and quite a few things more.

Frankie put his phone away, folded his readers into his breast pocket, wiped his forehead with a linen napkin, and went back to his company.

Three vipers and a stone crab walk into a cabana at the Fontainebleau, Nick thought. *The punch line can't be good.*

EMPTY FRAMES

Isabella Stewart Gardner Museum – Boston
March 17, 1990

St. Patrick's Day was winding down. The last of the drunks had been rounded up and the festivities were coming to an end. It was a long, tough day to be a cop in Boston. Transgressions that would have been met with the business end of a nightstick on any other day were met with indifference or a mild nudge.

Two officers rang the buzzer at the side door of the Isabella Stewart Gardner Museum a little after 1:00 a.m. on March 18th. One of the two guards on duty observed the officers on the security camera and let them in.

By the time the guards realized something about the officers wasn't right, they were handcuffed and taken to the basement, where they were duct-taped and secured to a workbench.

Rembrandt's *Christ in the Storm on the Sea of Galilee* and *A Lady and Gentleman in Black*, along with *The Concert* by Vermeer, were taken from the Dutch Room, while Manet's *Chez Tortoni* was stolen from the Blue Room. In addition to five Degas sketches, the thieves took a Chinese gu and an eagle finial from atop a flagpole after failing to get at the Napoleonic flag secured beneath it. They displayed some lack of planning and discernment by ignoring priceless works by Michelangelo and Botticelli.

The first man to enter the museum wore a fake mustache and took on responsibility for securing the guards in the basement. When he had finished handcuffing them to the workbench, he noticed a painting sitting nearby. It appeared to be weathered and was so dirty he could barely make out most of the image. The face of an old man stood out through the grime. Impulsively, he cut the painting out of its frame, rolled it up as best he could, and carried it upstairs.

In all, thirteen items were reported stolen, including the finial and the gu. The painting snatched from the basement workshop was never mentioned in any of the news reports that followed, so the men figured it was of little value. The initial reward of five million was upped to ten, and the FBI extended an offer of no prosecution for their return.

Theories and wild speculation abounded as the decades passed. Everyone from the IRA to the Italians to a Boston street gang was thought responsible. The guards were scrutinized and investigated to no avail. Countless leads and tips poured in over the years. Some appeared promising but were investigated without success. The empty frames remain on display in a show of dwindling hope.

The one fact that all law enforcement agencies could agree on was that the works eventually made their way to Philadelphia.

FALSE STARS

Nick left the Fontainebleau immediately after spotting Frank. The last thing he needed was a reunion with the Rose, and more importantly, he didn't want them to know he had seen them together. Nick was going to need every advantage he could get to navigate these turbulent waters.

As he pulled out of the departures driveway, he couldn't help noticing a stunning yacht docked directly across Collins Avenue on the Intracoastal. Nick recognized it as a Pershing, having ogled its sister ships on the canals straddling Las Olas Boulevard in Fort Lauderdale. It was metallic silver and magnificent, with the look of a fighter jet. It wasn't the biggest yacht docked across from the Fontainebleau, but it was certainly the most sleek. Nick shared his father's love of boats and everything nautical. It was one of the few interests they did share, although Nick considered his passion to be independent of his father's influence, and thus, purer in a sense. Tony's taste ran toward classic flybridge sport fishing boats, while Nick preferred the new breed of multi-outboard center consoles.

Tony was perpetually restoring a 1974 Bertram 31 he had christened *Tony Rome* after the Sinatra movie of the same name. Sinatra played a private detective in the film, living on a boat and leading a kind of playboy life Nick imagined his father was enamored of. Nick hadn't set foot on it since he was a teenager when Tony forced him to go on fishing trips with him. The whole thing always struck Nick as pathetic, and he resented that the task of disposing of the relic that was now his. Last he knew, the vessel sat rotting on cinder blocks in a New Jersey marina.

Nick glanced at the stern of the Pershing through the rearview as he headed north on Collins and took note of the name on the transom in raised stainless steel letters. *Mishka.*

Grace wasn't kidding; 95 was a parking lot. Nick flipped between the Soul, R&B, and '70s channels on the satellite radio. He paused on a David Ruffin number that had the power to transport him back to a particular time and place, then thought better of it and changed the channel. The meeting with Frank had emotionally drained him. Oddly enough, with all the bombshells Frank had strafed him with, it was that silly *Gilda* toast that lingered like a nauseous lump somewhere between his heart and his throat. Together with the bourbon and lack of food, it was doing a real number on his acid reflux. He searched for a Tums in the console without success. The traffic continued to creep along.

Shit. Grace. Nick had never texted her back. He called her instead and it went straight to voicemail. He didn't leave a message, as he knew she would call back as soon as she saw his missed call. She was essentially running the show at Nick's place. The Tuscan Tiki was a touristy tiki bar with decent bar food and a solid local following that sustained it in the off-season. Nick had never intended to be in the bar business. He had left Philadelphia partly to escape from that whole lifestyle. Well, that and other reasons. Nick stumbled into it somewhat accidentally.

He'd struck up a casual conversation with a guy on a plane—just some informal, friendly banter at first. Nick always drank a beer while flying, no matter the time of day. He asked his neighboring passenger if he would like a drink, and two hours and a few drinks later, they'd become fast friends. Strangers on a plane. It was just one of those moments in life. Amir was from Detroit, about the same age as Nick. It turned out they had a lot in common for two guys from different cities and ethnic backgrounds. Amir was relocating from the Motor City to Fort Lauderdale. His father was sick and needed help running his struggling hotel. They passed the time mostly debating whether Motown or Philadelphia International Records was the superior label and offered examples that at first they recited, but soon sang out loud, much to the dismay of the middle seat passenger separating them. The man quickly gave up his seat.

Amir didn't know anyone in Lauderdale, or South Florida for that matter, so Nick introduced him around to the fellas. Amir was an exceedingly likable guy and could frankly pass for Italian. Many casual acquaintances made that assumption. In truth, he maintained a connection to his Muslim faith, but like many second-generation Americans, adopted a somewhat relaxed adherence to its tenets. The way he'd explained it to Nick made a lot of sense.

"Look, you're Catholic, right? Do you attend church every Sunday? Do you have premarital sex, use birth control? Yet, I bet you observe Lent and go to church on Christmas and Easter. Well, it's not that different for me. I fast for Ramadan and give up alcohol but enjoy a drink the rest of the year. Technically, alcohol is *haram*, forbidden, and my parents and grandparents abstain. For me, I consider it a minor sin, and I have made my peace."

"Funny, my grandmother never observed Lent. She believed 'God cares more about what comes out of your mouth than what goes in it.' At least that's what I remember her saying."

"Good for Grandmother," Amir exclaimed as he raised his glass.

That's how it had begun.

Amir had tried his best, but his heart wasn't in the hotel business. Luckily, Nick connected him with some hedge fund guys from New York who were buying up hotels after the recession, and Amir's family made a tidy profit. Nick's commission came in the form of the liquor license and a highly favorable long-term lease to the oceanfront bar and grill. It was little more than a tiki hut, but the view was priceless. Amir's father had mainly utilized it as storage for beach chairs and watersport equipment rental, as he eschewed serving alcohol, but Nick saw the potential. He spruced it up, ran plumbing, and breathed new life into the adjacent grill with a few of the old man's recipes. That's how he found himself the unlikely owner of the world's only South Philly Italian Tiki bar.

Grace managed the bar during the day shift, and Nick had come to rely on her more and more. After her shift, they would usually have dinner together before Nick took over for the evening. They always did something fun on

Mondays and quickly settled into a comfortable routine.

The traffic gradually let up as Nick approached the exit for Commercial Boulevard. He decided to give Gary a call at the Caffé.

"What's up, slick?" Gary's voice boomed over the Bluetooth.

"Hey, big man," Nick responded. Just hearing that voice gave Nick some hope maybe this whole twisted tale was a figment of an old man's yearning for his glory days. Gary could always cut through the bullshit and set Nick straight. He had been working at the Caffé for as long as Nick could remember and, since Tony's death, was keeping the place going. It was on fumes, but at least the bills were getting paid.

"When you get in, pretty boy?" Gary asked.

"Tomorrow afternoon, pal, four-thirty. You picking me up?"

"I'll be there. You okay?"

That wasn't good, Nick thought. *He sounds worried.* Gary's next words confirmed his suspicions and dashed Nick's naïve hopes.

"Some boys been coming around."

There was a long pause and the conversation stalled. Nick broke the silence.

"See you tomorrow, big boy."

"Safe flight, pretty boy. Text me when you land. You checking a bag?"

"Never pack more than you can fit in a carry-on. My old man taught me that."

"Indeed," the big man responded, then the call went dead.

Nick turned onto A1A. The season was in full swing, and the rubbernecking snowbirds were causing gaper lock. An eighty-year-old driver had turned left into oncoming traffic. It happened at least once a day. Nick wanted to stop by the bar and relieve Grace, who had been there since ten. He still needed to finish packing but had to make sure Ethan was okay to close up, and he needed to decompress and stare out at the ocean while he sorted everything out. Nick parked at his condo building a few blocks down from the bar so that he could walk up from the beachside. He took off his Tod's driving shoes, carried them with two fingers, and took in the calming sensation of the cool sand on the soles of his feet.

Grace was always preaching to him about the importance of living in the moment and mindfulness or some such nonsense. *Maybe this is what she means*, he thought as he simply accepted the pleasant sensation and stared out at the ocean. A waning gibbous moon illuminated the water, and he felt an overwhelming desire to wade out into the sea and float there for a while, suspended in time, free from the past.

It wasn't for long, though, as his mind started to race with theories and scenarios. He could see the lights of the Tuscan Tiki up ahead. The distance distorted the sound of the jukebox somewhat, but he could make out Marvin's distinctive voice on "Come Get to This." He plodded forward through the deep, coarse sand until he reached the bulkhead and paused to gaze for a moment at Grace before she could notice he was there.

He sensed that maybe their relationship was coming to a tipping point. Nick recognized that point all too well. He had spent a good deal of his adult life teetering on that fulcrum.

Nick considered himself a fairly evolved person. At the very least, a few stages progressed from the philistine who first ventured to these shores all those years ago. He thought of how cruel life can be in that regard. You finally figure out your true self so late in life you hardly have time to enjoy it. In hindsight, that little voice was always there and was unerringly accurate. It's as if, he thought, you set out on a long voyage with a compass, but instead of trusting your instrument, you keep chasing stars on the horizon instead, zigzagging from tempest to tempest. Nick had left most of those false stars in his wake, yet he still occasionally glanced over his shoulder at Sirius, the brightest star in the night sky. The further he ventured, the brighter it seemed to shine. Even now, he felt her gravity pulling him back.

Nick recovered from his ruminations at the sight of Grace behind the bar. The big-screen LEDs and Christmas lights flickered in a happy dance. Nick could make out the outlines of a few reliable regulars at the end of the bar. Grace was laughing, at some corny joke, no doubt. For that second, looking at her, Nick felt blessed. He tried hard to live in that moment, but his lofty thoughts inevitably devolved to the trip, his father, the Caffé, and now, the painting.

Nick stepped behind the bar, and Grace greeted him with a peck on the cheek that was somewhat less passionate than the Stone Crab's kiss. He hugged her from behind as she was working a blender and said, "I missed you," close enough to her ear to be heard above the whirring of the blades, but she pretended not to hear. Her intuition suggested that Nick was about to embark on a path that would determine the future of their relationship, and of course, she was right. Grace was a proud woman and had experienced her share of heartache; she wasn't going to sign up for a fool's errand of trying to change a grown man. It would be what it would be, and she was at peace with that. It was this strength of character that drew Nick to her in the first place, and he had to admire her for it.

Nick took a seat at the end of the bar and pretended to watch one of the many games playing on the flat screens circling the hut. He sipped a Funky Buddha Floridian and tried to sort out the events of the day. He wished he could tell Grace all about it, but he knew what her reaction would be and was afraid it would drive her away. Right there and then, he vowed to handle his business in the city as quickly as possible and return to Grace. He could only hope she would still be there when he returned.

The next day, they had lunch on Las Olas before she drove him to the airport. They had made love the night before, and the uncertainty of their future only added to their passion. There exists a heightened plane of connection between lovers when the possibility exists it might be the last time, and although neither would admit it, that was exactly how it felt. As Nick held Grace's hand across the table and considered just scrapping the whole trip, his phone vibrated once in his pocket, signaling a text message. He glanced at it in his lap. It was from Frankie. *Meet me at The Paradise tonight.*

Let's get this business over with, Nick thought, and texted back, *see you at ten.*

Grace drove him to the American Airlines terminal. She pulled over to the curb and leaned over to kiss him deeply. "I love you, Nicky," she hollered after him as he walked to the terminal door.

Nick turned and saw her smiling through tears. "I love you, Grace," he hollered back.

How cruel, he thought, that he was never so sure of anything in his life. He pulled his carry-on behind him into the revolving door and headed toward security.

Grace watched until he disappeared from her sight.

THE HOMELESS BON VIVANT
OF BOCA RATON

Royal Palm Club and Resort, Boca Raton, Florida
The Previous Day

One foot still in the ooze of the dream realm, that split second before Frank was fully awake. The space between the conscious and the subconscious where truly vivid dreams occur. Time has no dominion there. It could contain a millisecond or a lifetime. More often than not, Frank was a sojourner in a lost time, a leading man in his own personal Gilded Age. But like an ancient studio actor in a Hollywood that no longer existed, the phone had long stopped ringing for Frank.

The phone. That piercing, clanging, rotary ring. It spat its insulting refrain in his face.

He hung on to the dream world like a crab grasping a piece of bait, felt himself pulled to the surface. Mercifully, the ringing faded. His subconscious struggled to find its place. *Where am I? Fuck. What decade?* A laser of light slashed at his eyelids as a projector sputtered inside his skull. He walked through a nightclub. Faces all around, spinning wildly, hands outstretched, rocks glasses extended in a toast. His clothes draped regally upon him. *What was that fabric? So decadent.* Gatsby never possessed such a shirt. And the women, my God, their hair. It brushed his face as he cut a path through a pulsating tunnel of disco-era élan. Their perfume swirled in his wake. It smelled like exclusivity, with lingering notes of unattainability. He moved with purpose, gliding across the whiskey-soaked floor. What divine creature awaited his arrival, perched perfectly on a Naugahyde stool, legs elegantly crossed, sipping from a highball glass, spinning to greet him? But of course, he knew. It could only be her.

He made his way along the perimeter of the horseshoe bar, catching his reflection in the mirror. He was the type of accidental handsome men never really think about and generally took for granted—until it was gone. The lights flashed neon, blinking diamonds, spinning clockwise and then reversing course to the relentless bass beat that hummed through the walls, whomped beneath the floor, and resonated in his molars.

The music downshifted. "*Last call, sucker.*" That dreaded last song of the night, "I Think I'll Tell Her," by Ronnie Dyson. He had to find her. The fog from the dance floor mingled with the smoke of a thousand cigarettes to create a sea of dark matter. His left arm parted the haze. He cradled a drink close to his chest with the right as he sidestepped through a slow dancing mass of bodies. She had to be here. And then, as always, as ever, the lights came on.

The realization landed like a punch to his solar plexus. It felt like an elephant of uncertainty sat on his chest. The electricity traveled up to his head as the disco lights intensified. They weren't lights at all. Sunlight slashed through the slats of the cabana door. It reflected off the bottom of an overturned bottle of Stoli Elit, projecting onto the walls like a disco ball of regret. That ridiculous rotary ring tone was back, jangling in his skull like a jackhammer. Before he could adapt to this particularly exquisite pain, a more insidious demon launched a left hook of panic that landed squarely on the button. Frank knelt on the canvas, then staggered to his feet. No longer the dashing figure in the dream. He was old, and worse—much, much worse—he was broke.

Frank only had two states of existence of late, regret and panic. He vacillated between the two, but if he had to choose, panic was easier to take.

There was that rotary ring again. Jennifer had set the ringtone on Frank's cell phone to an annoying old-school ring. She probably meant it as an insult, but Frank didn't give a fuck. He kept meaning to change it but could never quite find the time. He would occasionally put it on silent, but if he ever missed Jennifer's call, well, her punishments could be grueling. Unable to locate his glasses, he looked through blurry eyes at his missed call log. It was just Ralph. *Thank God.*

He looked around the cabana, taking stock of his surroundings and circumstances. It felt like Thursday, he thought, as he opened the calendar on his phone. It was Friday, December 28th. Christmas had come and gone in a blur. His calendar had one entry: *Meet Ralph at Roberto's.*

The cabana itself was plush, as cabanas go. It was the approximate size of a New York studio apartment and tricked out with every amenity a member of the Club could desire, except Frank wasn't a member, not even close. Frank had been crashing at the cabana most nights when he was fighting with Jennifer. And he was always fighting with Jennifer.

There was a light knock at the cabana door. "Hello?"

"Come in," Frank said to Eduardo, the cabana attendant, like he was inviting him into his oceanfront estate.

Eduardo came in with a fresh fruit tray, replacing the previous day's untouched tray. A new one arrived each day, no matter what, just like the spring water, towels, and premium toiletries that Frank hoarded. The cabana belonged to Rochester Benny, who used it about twice a season and had neither the time nor the concern to track its expenses. It was only the tip of the iceberg of discretionary spending Frank had leveraged and appropriated to help him eke out an existence in Boca. Frank Valletto had the undoubtedly singular distinction of being the Royal Palm Club and Resort's only housing insecure denizen. Ralph had unceremoniously christened him "The Homeless Bon Vivant of Boca Raton."

"No bueno, Mr. Frank," Eduardo remarked as he surveyed the cabana.

"Sorry, Eddie," Frank said. He handed Eduardo a twenty-five-dollar Dunkin Donuts gift card as a tip.

"That's okay, Mr. Frank. I just don't want to get in trouble. You're not supposed to be sleeping here."

"I know. Just been fighting with the old lady. You know how it is."

"Okay," Eduardo assured him. "No problem. I don't see nothing."

"Thanks, Eddie." Frank tucked a Protocol Blue cigar in Eduardo's breast pocket for good measure as he left. A bold toro crafted in Esteli, Nicaragua, it was Frank's go-to stick, when he could get his hands on one.

Frank took a quick shower, luxuriating under the rainfall showerhead until he could think clearly and the panic receded just enough for him to function. He dried off and dressed in the same clothes, then left the cabana and made his way through the resort. He passed the poolside bar and waved to the barbacks packing the coolers and cutting limes.

They waved back cheerfully. "What's up, Mr. Frank?" The waiters, doormen, and barbacks were unanimous in their opinion that Frank was one of the friendlier and more respectful guests. They never suspected maybe it was because he was so much closer to their lot than they imagined.

Denroy held the lobby door open for Frank and brought him a plastic cup of water from a large jug filled with orange and lemon slices. Frank ordered an Uber on his phone. The payment method for his Uber account was Ralph's Amex. Ralph didn't mind but would occasionally feign distress over the charges just to break his balls. Most of the trips were running around for Ralph anyway, and Frank's car was too unreliable these days. The second time Frank broke down, Ralph insisted he start Ubering everywhere. Frank tipped Denroy with a gift card for The Pier Lobster House. Frank had a pretty nice collection of gift cards he had scored from Sean, the accident lawyer Frank provided with his monthly oxycodone prescription. Sean had personal injury billboards all over I-95 from Palm Beach to Miami. He hung out at the cigar bar and was a decent enough guy, but he was gut-hooked on the painkillers of late. Frank knew it wasn't going to end well.

Denroy helped Frank navigate the occasionally tricky labyrinth of the Club. Frank generally managed to move freely and could recite Rochester Benny's member number by heart when challenged by some new or nosy employee. Still, Denroy would slip him a non-member guest pass on busy weekends during the height of the season, when management tended to crack down. Frank and Denroy had formed a genuine friendship, and Denroy looked up to him as a kind of uncle figure. Denroy liked hanging at the cigar bar, and Frank was happy to reciprocate the hospitality at The Ambassador.

"See you later, uncle." Denroy smiled cheerfully as Frank got in his Uber and headed for Roberto's Bayview.

"Later, nephew." Frank waved back.

THE ASSIGNMENT

"Frankie, you gotta listen to me. This is no way to live." Big Ralph swirled his wine glass clockwise absentmindedly, gripping the stem at the base between two downturned fingers. The generous pour of Tignanello surged like a tempest, climbing precariously up the sides of the glass. Ralph stared up at one of three big-screen TVs as his horse faded down the stretch. The bartender dutifully wiped up the spilled wine before the rivulet could meander down the bar toward Ralph's cell phone and Marlboro reds. He carefully placed the phone and cigarettes on a black linen napkin, just in case. The remaining contents were transferred to a new glass, topped off, and set upon a fresh coaster before Ralph's horse crossed the finish line—fourth.

"Cocksucker." Ralph snatched up his lighter and Marlboros. "Sorry, Chanel," Ralph apologized.

"No problem, Mr. C." Chanel smiled.

"Thank you, Brian." He handed the bartender a folded hundred-dollar bill.

"No problem, Mr. C. That's not necessary, but thank you."

This scene played out at least three times a day at Roberto's Bayview, an upscale bar and restaurant on the Intracoastal in Pompano Beach. Frank and Big Ralph sat at the inside, open-air bar and bet horses while the tourists watched the yachts cruise by, and Ralph filled an invisible swear jar. The lunch crowd generally stuck to the outside bar and waterfront tables, so Ralph and Frank and the crew had the inside bar to themselves. They liked it cool and dark, just like the bars back home. Brian and Chanel made more in tips on any given weekday afternoon with the crew than the others earned on a busy Saturday night. Management took Brian off days once. The crew summarily moved across the Intracoastal to Full Moon Brewery. Ralph would call each day to politely inquire whether Brian was working. Management relented. It only took a glance at the weekly receipts for the inside bar. The crew still occasionally switched over to Full Moon for a day or two, both as a courtesy to Charlie at Full Moon for the hospitality and to keep Roberto on his toes.

"I'm serious, Frank. Listen, you're welcome to the condo as soon as that jerk-off son of mine wises up and goes back to his wife, but in the meantime, you can't live like this." Ralph lowered his voice, not wanting to embarrass Frank in front of Brian and Chanel. "This is crazy, Frankie. You're fucking homeless."

"I'm not homeless," Frank retorted indignantly.

Ralph hovered over Frank's stool and draped a beefy but loving arm around him. The light refracted off his Hublot Big Bang, flashing a kaleidoscope all around the bar. The effect was at once both startling and intimidating. It was just a random byproduct of charisma colliding with physics.

"Frankie." He paused as he lifted Frank's slightly dirty martini, for which Ralph would graciously pick up the tab. "See this? This is a home." He gestured to the sweaty glass. Ralph gently pinched a blue cheese stuffed olive between his freshly manicured thumb and index finger, plucking it from its liquid abode. "This is you." Ralph held the olive to Frank's eye like a monocle and then rolled the olive down the bar. It wobbled toward an unsuspecting young lady filling out what looked like an employment application. "Homeless," Ralph needlessly punctuated.

Brian, expressionless, intercepted the newly evicted olive.

"Sorry, Brian. Sorry, Chanel." Ralph glanced at the unsuspecting applicant, noticing just then that she was quite stunning. "Sorry, Miss." He peeled a crisp hundred off a hefty wad. Ralph used a thick rubber band from an asparagus bunch as an Italian money clip, and it made a sharp snapping noise as he stretched it back around the stack. He slid the bill along the bar to the new girl.

"What's this for?" she whispered to Brian.

"It's a tip," Brian answered.

"But I don't even work here yet," she responded sheepishly.

"You do now," Ralph boomed over his shoulder as he walked out to the parking lot for a smoke.

Frank excused himself to the men's room. He stood before the sink and splashed his face with cool water. He squirted a measure of mouthwash from a pump bottle into a tiny paper cup and gargled, wiping his face with a thick cotton hand towel. Frank liked the feel of it on his skin. It was luxurious, yet wasteful for a lowly bathroom towel. That's how people measured one another's wealth in South Florida, not so much by how conspicuous their consumption was, but by the conspicuousness of their waste—a barely smoked Cuban abandoned poolside; a mega-yacht sitting idle, awaiting her owner's infrequent visits. He tossed the towel into a wicker basket and stared at his reflection. The mirror had an infinity lighting effect and, together with the martinis, gave Frank a feeling of lightheadedness. Frank stared into the abyss of that mirror for a long time looking for an answer, some escape hatch from his never-ending predicaments.

His indulgence was interrupted by Ralph barging through the door. The room felt a good deal smaller as Ralph joined him at the sink. Ralph took a swig of the mouthwash and crumpled the paper cup before tossing it carelessly into the wicker basket instead of the trash can. He smiled broadly at himself in the infinity mirror, and his veneers gleamed back like obedient stars.

"I've got a proposition for you, Frankie."

There are certain moments in a man's life that have nothing to do with his ambition, merit, or sins. They simply present themselves, and cumulatively, they form the trajectory of his existence. In hindsight, they're always easy to single out; an unexpected meeting, a missed opportunity. They could seem either a blessing or a curse at their inception, but usually ended up being the opposite—a seemingly random confluence of events that were too coincidental to be orchestrated and therefore attributed to fate. For Frank, this was just such a moment.

Frank and Ralph walked out of the men's room together, and Ralph said his goodbyes at the bar. Frank downed the remnants of his now warm martini. It didn't mix well with the lingering minty mouthwash taste. Ralph didn't require a ticket as they walked outside to the valet stand. He would just pull the Wraith up in front upon arrival, and Raymond would move it less than fifty feet into its designated spot. Raymond offered to drive it back to the front door, but Ralph waived him off and palmed him a fifty as Raymond handed him the key fob.

Frank loved the feel of entering and exiting the suicide doors. It reminded him of a certain '67 Lincoln Continental, and of course, Maria. He savored the idea of stepping out of the Wraith at the Club and secretly hoped that pain in the ass assistant manager, Josh, was there to witness it. Frank needed a fresh shot of cachet. He was running on fumes, and the smoke and mirrors routine was wearing thin at the Club.

What Ralph proposed on the ride over was about to change all that. A solution to all his problems, and a shot at redemption.

THE RIDE

"Let's take a ride."

That phrase had preceded more trouble, mischief, and doom than any other phrase in the English language. "Don't ever go for a ride with anyone." Frank's father had imparted that puzzling nugget of advice. Together with "Don't ever write a letter, and don't ever throw one away," they composed the worthless exacta of advice dispensed by Frank's father. His angelic mother, Rita, had died when Frank was seventeen. After the funeral, Frank retrieved his father's leather belt from its perch draped over a chair in the ogre's bedroom, where he'd regularly terrorized Frank's mother. It was worn bare along the length of the holes that tracked his expanding waistline, and Rita's sad existence.

Frank had just planned to humiliate his father, the man they called Fuzzy, give him a little taste of his own medicine. What followed instead was a beating as severe as Frank had ever witnessed, much less administered. He realized much later in life—the time when men revisit the formative events of their lives—it was as much those pathetic wear marks that drove him into a rage as it was the relentless abuse of his mother. Frank stopped only, and precisely, when he heard his father's infantile wailing and saw the snot running from his nose like a spigot. He walked out of the house that day with the clothes on his back. Tony Di Nobile's family took him in for a time, but he soon threw himself headlong into the business of the streets, and for a brief, shining moment, he prospered. Frank had spent the rest of his life striving, yearning to recapture that golden hour.

Now, at sixty-seven, he was struggling for basic sustenance and his very survival. Frank had visited a few old transplants who withered away in South Florida hospitals and nursing homes, alone and abandoned like old muscle cars in a junkyard. It wasn't a pretty sight, and Frank vowed to end his life on his own terms before he ever came to that pass.

Frank looked down at his shoes. They were freshly polished, but the soles and heels were worn. He started to feel that old rage, but now it was directed at himself. He stepped through the suicide portal, then pressed the button that closed the door and settled back into the indulgent seat for the ride back to Boca.

Ralph moved to the right lane on Commercial in anticipation of circling back to Federal Highway, but Frank suggested, "Let's take the beach, Ralphie."

"You and that fucking beach." Ralph balked but accommodated him. It was a prettier ride for sure, and truth be told, he loved it as well. But he also couldn't help thinking that, just maybe, it could be Frankie The Stone Crab's last time enjoying the view.

Once they got to Hillsborough, the traffic eased. The gated mansions on the right side of A1A, together with the

Intracoastal on the left, never failed to deliver. You get to a point where any notions of outrageous fortune you may have entertained in your youth were just that—notions. Still, Frank thought, maybe there's still a little piece of all this reserved for me, some sliver of dignity. What Ralph proposed to Frank on the way to Boca fueled that fading hope and resuscitated all those foolish notions.

As they reached the gatehouse of the Club, the acid in Frank's stomach had made its way to his esophagus, and Frank was spitting out the window while scrambling for a precious Tums or Rolaid in the messy detritus of his pockets. Ralph's proposal didn't mix well with the martinis. Frank found only a crumpled prayer card in his pocket—St. Michael the Archangel, his foot on the devil, sword raised. He flipped it over.

> *St. Michael the Archangel, defend us in battle, be our protection against the wickedness and snares of the devil. May God rebuke him we humbly pray; and do thou, O Prince of the Heavenly host, by the power of God, cast into hell Satan and all the evil spirits who prowl about the world seeking the ruin of souls.*

Frank had carried a similar card all his life. He had lost many and couldn't recall where he picked up this one. He did remember that the first one was given to him by his poor mother. Frank could still hear her words. *Pray to him, Frankie. He will never abandon you.* Not that St. Michael did *her* much good. And he wondered, when did *I* become the evil spirit prowling the earth?

The gate lifted as Ralph approached. Ralph was neither a member nor a guest. Still, the gate moved, reliably as Galileo's earth. Ralph pulled over just ahead of the front door, waving off the valet. He handed Frank an envelope. "There's five thousand in there, Frankie. Clean out your cabana and get yourself a room. I'll pick you up at eight."

Frank held the envelope in front of him for a moment. He stared at it on his lap. "I haven't agreed to anything yet, Ralph."

Ralph flipped down the visor, smiled broadly in the vanity mirror, checking his veneers. "Sure you did, Frankie. A long time ago."

Frank folded the envelope in two and jammed it in his pocket, right next to St. Michael.

"One more thing, Frankie, just to be clear. This was *my* idea. I know how things have been for you, and I figured this was a good break. I mean, honestly, how's this whole cabana thing working out for you?" Ralph gestured with a sweep of his arm.

Ralph had a point, Frank thought.

"I'm a stranger in a strange land," Frank said.

Ralph thought about it for a second. "We all are, Frankie. But we came out too far to swim back, and we'll drown if we try."

Frank got out of the car. A fleeting image of him doing the dead man's float in Lake Boca flashed across his mind. The massive car door closed behind him, and he stood in front of the valet stand as Ralph began to pull away, his beefy arm draped over the driver's door.

"And don't be late!" Frank barked out sarcastically in front of Denroy.

"Frankie-motherfucking-Stone Crab." Denroy shook his head in amazement. "I don't know how you do it." Josh, the milquetoast assistant manager, looked on in a combination of suspicion and jealousy.

That makes two of us, Frank thought.

As Ralph drove away, his arm rotated 180 degrees, middle finger raised in a departing gesture. The bezel sparkled in the low sun.

Frank took out the envelope and peeled off a crisp hundred for Denroy, rubbing it between his thumb and forefinger to make sure two bills weren't stuck together.

"Thank you, my uncle."

Denroy was a good kid. He maneuvered above the politics of the Club and its members, respectful, deferential, but keenly observant. He was painfully aware of the value of money, having come from a childhood of suffering and abject poverty in Kingston that the members, with a few notable exceptions (like Rochester Benny), could never imagine. Maybe that's why he genuinely liked Frank so much. He pretended to go along with Frank's masquerade, and truth be told, actually promoted it, propping him up when he needed it. He knew about the cabana and shielded Frank, as best he could, from prying managerial eyes. Denroy sensed a goodness in Frank. He reminded him of his Uncle Winston back in Trench Town, flawed but with a good heart.

Frank returned the envelope to his pocket as Denroy held the door. As he did, the prayer card came loose, and St. Michael fluttered to the ground.

THE STONE CRAB SHUFFLE

Frank managed to get a few hours of sleep. Somewhat rested, he retrieved a bag from the cabana that contained some clothes, toiletries, and medicine. His back was killing him, so he skimmed an oxycodone from the prescription bottle earmarked for Sean.

Lately, Sean was getting worse and spending more and more time at the Ambassador instead of the office. Frank had decided to have a talk with him and cut him off after this month. Frank had also spotted Sean's wife in a dive bar off McNabb in Pompano. She was with some seasonal scammer from Springfield Frank vaguely recalled meeting at the cigar bar. He decided he would keep this little tidbit to himself for now. He may have run low on conventional funds, but he was rich in the currency of information, and sometimes that was just as valuable.

He decided to check in with Jennifer and regretted it the moment she answered. She was screaming about something, hardly mattered what. It was all just a prelude to her shakedown. Frank had met her on a midweek day shift at a strip club in North Miami. The relationship started as a quid pro quo arrangement, and like all such relationships, the early precedents never changed.

Jennifer was ranting about the rent, and her broken-down car, and clothes for the kids. What she really wanted was money for her and her biker ex to get high. Frank had grown to care for the kids, and it killed him to see the chaos they were growing up around. He did his best to provide a little stability, but if he was honest with himself, they were probably fucked for life. Still, people can rise above their upbringings. But if that was the case, why hadn't *he*? Frank dismissed those musings. Jennifer was still screaming. This was the point where Frank usually caved and figured it was easier to give her some money, anything as long as she would just shut up.

Why the fuck do you subject yourself to this shit? Ralph would chide him. *She doesn't even suck your dick anymore, am I right?* Ralph was right, of course, but Frank wasn't much better than most men when it came to making rational decisions concerning the fairer sex.

"I'll stop by tomorrow and take care of everything," was his response to her diatribe. Unsure of whether she heard him or not, he hung up.

He thought about her kids, Billy and Amber, and resolved he would find a way to make their lives better somehow. *Who am I kidding? I haven't even been a father to my own children. How am I gonna save them?* How the fuck he had gone from an angel like Maria to this skank was the story of his life. It crumbled the same way everything else in his life had deteriorated—gradually, and then suddenly.

Maybe it was neglect, perhaps it was rust, but the Stone Crab had fallen a long way. Letting Maria slip away, well, that was all his doing. If he had to pick one moment when everything shifted and he began the slow descent into his present straits, it would have to be the day Maria left him for good. Frank could have stopped her; she wanted him to stop her. She begged him not to go to Florida. He tried to convince her that he was only trying to set up a better life for the two of them away from the city. But in the end, he got on that plane and lost her forever. Frank had thought about that day a lot over the years. Replayed it and reworked it. Imagined a life where they stayed together and raised a family. He realized it was bitter regret and self-flagellation, but he took comfort in knowing he deserved the punishment and suffered it like a willing penitent.

The room in the Admiral's Wing of the resort was plush even by Club standards. A fifty slipped to the desk clerk had secured the upgrade that otherwise probably cost another three hundred a night. Frank realized he hadn't slept in a real bed for over a week. He wanted nothing more than to sleep until the next day, but Ralph was picking him up at eight to go God knows where. In all likelihood, they would eventually end up at the cigar bar, so he texted Sean to meet him there around midnight. Frank showered and shaved and rode the elevator down to the lobby. He stopped at the Safari Bar for a quick taste, and the bartender automatically put the drink on Rochester Benny's tab.

Benny Barone was actually from Utica, but that didn't sound as good, and a little thing like the truth seldom got in the way of a good nickname. Frank asked the bartender to break a hundred and left a thirty-dollar tip before walking over to Bradley at the concierge desk. Frank placed five hundred dollars in an envelope embossed with the resort coat of arms, wrote *Benny Barone* on the front, and asked Bradley to get it to him. It had been a while since Frank had last settled up with Benny. The man didn't expect it, didn't even keep track, but he would appreciate it. It certainly made Frank feel better, and he was beginning to get back to his old self. Funny how a little money can do that.

Ralph was a fixture at the Club but wasn't a member. He refused to pay the initiation fee of forty-five thousand on principle. Ralph also used Benny's member number to charge food and drinks and frequently stayed overnight in one of the Bungalows. Some members who didn't know any better balked and raised the issue at member meetings, but seeing as Ralph had the highest spend (via Benny) of any *member* by far, management just mollified the complaining member and kept kicking the can down the road. Occasionally, said members would receive some complimentary perk or swag, which would cool things down for a while. If that didn't work, valet would start misplacing the member's car for hours at a time. Then maybe someone would sneak into their cabana and take a shit in their ice bucket or something like that. That usually resolved things.

Frank walked out to the valet stand and lit a cigarette. He stood off to the side a bit but still got a dirty look from a fossilized socialite waiting for her car. She had the Palm Beach special—a combination of plastic surgery, theatrical makeup, and a strategically placed Hermes scarf that made her age undecipherable, absent carbon dating. Ralph pulled up short of the portico on the other side of the roundabout, not wanting to get caught up in the valet bottleneck. The fossil's Bentley had arrived, and Frank discretely extinguished his Marlboro on the *boot* as he walked around to meet Ralph.

They headed west on Glades to Primo Bar and Grille.

PRIMO BAR AND GRILLE

The front line at Primo was packed with Rolls-Royces and Bentleys. Ladies night was a huge draw at the upscale steakhouse. There were the Palm Beach fossils, the con men up from Broward, some newly minted divorcees from West Boca, and a few pros from Miami perched up at the end of the bar. It was like the opening scene of Central Park in *The Warriors*, except there was no unifying warlord, unless you counted the ever accommodating but no-nonsense maître d', Billy G.

Billy greeted Ralph with a kiss on the cheek and set them up at the bar while their table was made ready. Ralph liked to hang at the bar for a while anyway, and Billy knew it. By now, ladies night was in full swing. Not some cheesy promotion, Primo put out a top-shelf spread. As a result, the place was packed with women, and a pack of hyenas circled the perimeter. Not all of the women reeked of desperation either. There were a few who definitely occupied the top of the food chain. They sat at the bar and rebuffed the nipping horde with dismissive eye rolls. A particularly striking brunette sat at the turn of the bar, buffered by her entourage. Frank watched with amusement as a deeply tanned lothario approached her.

He wasn't a bad-looking guy and was dressed expensively, but his approach was all wrong, and he looked like he'd walked into Neiman Marcus, pointed at a mannequin, and said, "I'll take that." Frank could smell his cologne from the other side of the bar. All the brunette could smell, though, was desperation. The mannequin managed to get close enough to whisper something into the back of her head while placing a business card on the bar in front of her. Whatever it was, she didn't even dignify it with a head turn. She just raised one brow and looked at him out of the side of one eye like he was some invasive lizard species. She slid the card into the drain tray, and he skittered back across the tile floor like an iguana.

She looked up at that moment, her tongue delicately searching for her straw, and caught Frank staring at her. She must have realized Frank witnessed the exchange with the mannequin and smiled at him. She was even more beautiful than he first noticed. Frank nodded in her direction and raised his glass slightly. She reciprocated with her glass. *Great*, he thought. *Women used to smile at me like that because they wanted to sleep with me. Now, they just figure I'm harmless, like a stone crab missing a claw.*

Frank heard him before he saw him. "Still flirting with the girls." The Rose's obnoxious voice boomed above the din. He placed a hand on Frank's trapezius in greeting but squeezed just a little too hard. Frank turned and grudgingly exchanged a kiss on the cheek. Ralph signaled to Billy G, and they headed to their table in the center of the restaurant.

A DJ/singer was doing a keyboard karaoke combination to the delight of two Pompano pumas. They performed what they presumed to be a seductive dance, but the result was a cringeworthy attempt at mimicking moves appropriated from their kids' TikTok videos. The aforementioned mannequin was filming them with his iPhone under the guise of a fake sizzle reel for a non-existent reality pilot. He had handed them a business card for a vanity production company that named him as CEO. To his credit, it actually had a website, Instagram, and Google business pages, with an address in a shared space office building on Palmetto Road. Good thing, because puma number one Googled it in the ladies room. The gyrations paused for a moment when their feverish grinding to a Barry White song caused their designer belt buckles to interlock. Mannequin rushed over to disengage the YSL buckle from its Gucci counterpart. It seemed like an awful lot of trouble to go through for a parking lot blowjob. That's what Frank was thinking as he looked over his shoulder to see if the brunette was sharing his view of the floor show, but she was gone from her perch.

Billy G sent over a bottle of Stag's Leap, and Frank joined Ralph in a glass. The Rose was drinking Dewar's and water. He wasted little time and launched right in on Frank. "It looks like life really agrees with you down here, Crab. Ralph tells me you're doing pretty good for yourself." He said this while gripping Frank's left upper arm. He feigned inadvertence and withdrew his hand, smiling the whole time. "Sorry, Frankie, how's the old arm?"

This was some pretty thin sarcasm, of course, as Ralph had said no such thing, but the Rose was the type of guy who wanted to establish the hierarchy right off the bat. That was unnecessary in the current setting, as the three men had known each other since childhood, and everyone at the table knew about Frank's genetically defective left arm. But old habits die hard, and the Rose never missed an opportunity to be mean-spirited, even when he needed something from you. Especially when he needed something from you. It was his way of establishing dominance.

If the years had been tough on Frank, going by looks alone, they had been brutal on the Rose. He was never what you would call a handsome guy, but all that malice and venom had carved a road map on his face. He had the pallor of an albino crypt keeper, and his jowls sagged like a malevolent bulldog. A lifetime of scheming, plotting, and dissembling had taken a toll. Those steely eyes hadn't changed, however. *They say your eyes never change from birth*, Frank thought. *Well then, the Rose must have been one evil-looking infant.* Frank set aside his observations and raised his glass in acknowledgment instead, making a perfunctory toast. "To the good life." Ralph echoed back in Italian, "*La dolce vita*," and they all clicked glasses. The Rose threw in a dismissive, "Yeah, *cent'anni.*"

Frank took a deep, satisfying sip of his cabernet. Beneath the linen, he made the sign of the horns with his left hand and pointed them straight at Bobby DeRosa. *It's still good for one thing motherfucker.*

Frank always wore long sleeves. No matter how hot, no matter how humid. At Roberto's, the Club, even poolside, Frank kept the deformed limb covered. People always assumed the Stone Crab nickname came from some affinity for the pricey delicacy. Stone crabs are harvested by taking only one claw at a time, allowing the crab to molt and regrow the appendage. It takes several molts for the claw to regenerate fully, and if incorrectly removed, it never grows back. The practice is somewhat controversial, and critics maintain it leaves the crab unable to defend itself and jeopardizes its survival. The *Frankie Stone Crab* nickname had evolved from simply *Frankie Crab* back in Philly. Labels affixed in youth tend to stick. Frank didn't mind the name. When used by his friends, it was stripped of its original connotation and replaced with affection. Only very few (like the Rose) still wielded it like a schoolyard weapon.

They ordered, and the Rose insisted on some colossal claws for an appetizer. He made a big production of cracking each one as he stared at Frank. Ralph noticed and was growing impatient with the Rose's tired routine. They had business to discuss and the act was getting in the way. If De Rosa had some other agenda, he needed to let it go. Ralph decided to take over the conversation in an effort to derail the tension.

"Frank is headed back tomorrow. Everything is in place," Ralph said.

"It fuckin better be," the Rose said in between bites of a well-done tomahawk steak reduced to the consistency of a hockey puck and slathered in sacrilegious A-1 steak sauce. His ridiculous toupee was in danger of becoming dislodged by his vigorous chewing.

Fucking gavone, Frank thought. *Ruining a beautiful piece of prime meat like that.*

Ralph made the same observations, but with his broad smile, he remained inscrutable. Instead, he asked, "How's your steak, Bobby?"

"Fucking fantastic," the Rose replied.

Frank was so repulsed, he took the napkin from his lap and placed it on the table in surrender. "I'm going out for a smoke," he said, excusing himself from the table and walking toward the door, cigarettes and lighter already in his hand.

"Fucking derelict. Him *and* his fucking nephew," the Rose muttered as soon as Frank was out of earshot.

Frank walked a respectful distance from the door before lighting up. The brunette was leaning against a Bugatti, one ankle crossed over the other, texting delicately, balancing an unlit cigarette between her fingers. She looked up at Frank as he was walking by.

"Got a light?"

Frank was startled but recovered quickly and extended a light, cupping the lighter with his other hand purely out of habit since there wasn't a breath of wind. It was another in a series of the hot and still nights Frank had become accustomed to. Frank was also used to being in proximity to a multitude of beautiful women, but the brunette was genuinely stunning. She exuded a casualness honed by a certainty that men found her irresistible. She took a drag, and her perfect manicure gleamed under the parking lot lights. He noticed her distinctive necklace. It displayed three intertwined gold rings of varied shades.

She exhaled out of the side of her mouth but kept her eyes straight ahead as she extended her hand. "Donna."

Frank took her hand delicately, but she gripped back firmly.

"Frank."

"I know." Her response caught him off guard, and she laughed a little as his eyebrow went up. She let him off the hook quickly. "I heard Billy G say hello to you at the bar." She kept looking at him as she finally let go of his hand. "I think I've seen you around the Club too. Are you a member?"

"I'm sure you have, and no, I'm not," Frank answered.

"I didn't think so," she said. Then, perhaps to correct any false impression, she hurriedly added, "You don't look like a snob."

Frank appreciated the effort. "Thank you, Donna." He felt good just using her name. He didn't ask her if she was a member. It would have made as much sense as asking a great white if he had a beach tag.

"This might sound like a stupid question," Frank ventured, "but what are you doing here?"

She smiled. "You mean, what's a nice girl like me doing in a place like this?"

Frank realized how silly he sounded and explained himself. "That's not what I meant. Primo isn't exactly a dive."

"I know," Donna responded. "And maybe I'm not exactly a nice girl." She punched Frank lightly on the shoulder and flicked her cigarette across the parking lot as she started to walk back to the restaurant. "Nice meeting you, Frank. See you at the Club."

Frank was speechless for a moment but managed to reply, "See you at the Club," before she disappeared back into Primo.

By the time Frank arrived back at the table, Ralph had already paid the check and taken the liberty of ordering

Frank a coffee and Sambuca. Frank poured the Sambuca into his coffee, and Ralph did the same. The Rose was now drinking an espresso martini.

The Rose wasn't drunk, but he was definitely getting fired up, as was his reputation. He was going on about Tony and Nick and the Caffé. He laid out a rough outline of the plan, but Frank could sense he purposely left certain things out. His hatred for Tony, Nick, and "that *mool*" Gary was all-encompassing and threatened to overshadow the painting, which was supposed to be what all this was about. They made a plan to reconvene the next day at the Fontainebleau, where they would meet up with the Russian. Billy G came over and they all said their goodbyes.

As they walked toward the door, the Rose draped an arm around Frank's shoulder. It made Frank feel dirty. The Rose had to shout over the music as they were walking past the speakers. "When's the last time you marched in the parade, Crab?" he asked, and with that, the Rose broke into a Mummer's strut toward the door, looking like a demented jackal. The DJ was mangling the vocals to a Lady Gaga song as one of the pumas broke out into a full-on twerk while puma two pantomimed smacking her ass.

"We've come a long way from 9th and Morris, Crab." Ralph spoke close to Frank's ear as they walked side by side. He tousled Frank's hair just like they did when they were teenagers on the corner.

"I'm not sure if I ever told you this." Frank replied, "but sometimes I really fucking wish we were back there." He was referring to a time as much as a place, something he didn't have to explain to Ralph.

"Me too, Frankie," Ralph said. "Me too."

THE PHONE BOOTH

They drove south on 95 and exited at Atlantic. "Where we headed?" Frank asked from the back seat.

"I need to make a phone call," the Rose answered, turning to Ralph with a grin.

Ralph caught Frank's eyes in the rearview and gave a kind of eyebrow shrug meant to convey that everything was all right. The Rose was giving directions to Ralph, and they drove west to Powerline Road to an out-of-the-way "gentlemen's club." They were in an industrial area somewhat off the beaten path of the chain restaurants and stores that proliferated Federal Highway. A purple neon sign with the name Total Titanium hung over the entrance. A large, bald bouncer gave the Rose a familiar hug after unclipping a red velvet rope bordered by two searchlights that all seemed like a bit of overkill. No one was going to confuse this place with some Hollywood premiere party.

It took a few seconds for Frank's eyes to adjust to the light, and he almost tripped over the extended foot of a patron receiving a lap dance in a swivel chair next to the stage. Kamal, the bouncer, led them to a table that was slightly elevated above the others and cordoned off with another red velvet rope. A menu was propped up on the table, promoting obscenely overpriced champagne, vodka and tequila.

This was the Rose's show, and he ordered a bottle of Don Julio 1942. A humorless bottle service waitress poured their drinks. Frank couldn't tell if she was a former stripper past her prime, or just a displaced office worker making ends meet. She left the cheerfulness to the three dancers Kamal sent over to keep them company. They introduced themselves by their stage names, and Frank pegged them for a Russian and two Cubans. They poured themselves drinks and engaged in the obligatory flattery. Frank recoiled a bit as the girl who introduced herself as Blanca ran her hand over his bad arm. Her English was pretty good, and she wasn't pushing a lap dance or champagne room or some other hustle. The Rose obviously wasn't a stranger here, and Kamal must have been sufficiently greased.

After a couple of drinks, Blanca stood and took Frank by the hand, gently urging him to stand. Frank resisted at first, feeling awkward and not a fan of the whole strip club experience. The desperation in these places was palpable on all sides, and Frank usually eschewed the small talk and head games that went along with it. But he was technically here on business, Ralph gave him an encouraging nod, Jennifer hadn't slept with him in ages, and Blanca was gorgeous. These thoughts and all the other justifications men construct for themselves propelled Frank toward a row of curtained rooms that resembled phone booths. More ropes separated the booths from the rest of the club, and a solemn man, even larger than Kamal, stood like a silent sentry, his hands crossed in front of him until Kamal signaled him to unclip the rope.

Blanca closed the curtain behind her, and the two panels met in the middle. She retrieved three large binder clips from her bag and used them to seal the panels shut, blocking out the bright stage lights and any prying eyes. Frank was seated facing out, and Blanca knelt before him. He made a halfhearted protest, but the tequila and Blanca's hand on his chest conspired to hold him in place.

"How was your call, Frankie? You didn't have a bad connection, did you?" the Rose jabbed at Frank. In compliance with the unwritten stripper code that all dancers adhere to, Blanca sat close to Frank and put both arms around his neck in response to the Rose's query. It was all part of the act, but Frank appreciated it nonetheless. Once all the men had made their phone calls and were ready to leave, Frank folded three hundred-dollar bills and slipped them to Blanca by grasping her hand in both of his and pressing them into her palm. She resisted while shaking her head, her eyes cast down. Frank pushed back just a little bit harder, and she put them in her bag.

They all thanked Kamal for the hospitality, and Frank detoured to the men's room to take a piss. The Rose followed behind him, taking a place at the urinal next to Frank even though there were two others open, breaking a cardinal rule of men's room etiquette.

"That Blanca is some piece of ass, no, Frankie?"

Frank answered quickly, trying to end the conversation before his piss ended. "She's a beautiful girl, no doubt about it." Frank zipped up and moved to the sink. The Rose was still talking to him over his shoulder. "Yeah, I usually keep her for myself, but I figured I owed you one, Frankie."

"Thanks, Bobby."

"No problem, Frankie. I figure that's the least I could do. No hard feelings, right?" The Rose extended an unwashed hand. Frank shook it anyway. He knew what he was referring to.

After Frank first moved to Florida, the Rose started going with Maria. Frank had been madly in love with her and had planned to send for her as soon as he got on his feet. Of course, things didn't quite work out as Frank had planned—what ever did?—and the Rose moved in. Frank never spoke to her again. It was one of those things that no one ever mentioned, but it always hung there like a stench. The fact the Rose would suggest this evened the score was a greater insult still.

Frank dried his hands under a turbo hand dryer that sounded like a jet. The Rose shouted over the noise, dispensing with the friendly act.

"One more thing, Frankie."

Frank turned toward him, still wiping his hands off on his pants.

The Rose continued at the same volume even as the dryer shut off automatically. "If you fuck this up, you're dead!"

"Don't worry, I won't," Frank said with conviction as he walked out the bathroom door.

He knew full well the Rose wanted him dead either way.

THE AMBASSADOR

Frank asked Ralph to drop him off at the cigar bar. The Ambassador Cigar Bar was the central meeting spot for gentlemen of leisure in Boca. It had all the trappings that cater to Northeast transplants, young and old. Some were true cigar aficionados, but most just came to hang out in the clubby atmosphere. More business was transacted at the Ambassador than in any conference room in Boca. You could borrow a Richard Mille luxury watch, lease a low-mileage Rolls-Royce and rent a high-mileage girlfriend all in the course of one night. If Boca were the Serengeti, this would be the watering hole, except you couldn't always tell the predators from the prey.

Sean was sunk low in a butter leather chair that threatened to swallow him whole. He looked like he was about to jump out of his skin. He was smoking a Davidoff Double 'R' that seemed out of place in his awkward grip. In between puffs, he chewed on the nails of his other hand. He started waving wildly as soon as he saw Frank walk in, even though the place wasn't that big and he was only sitting about twenty feet away from the door.

"Hey, Frankie." Sean stood to greet Frank with a hug, almost burning the Crab with the cigar in the process.

"Have a seat."

"How's it going, Sean? You okay?" Frank couldn't help asking. Sean looked manic and disheveled. He was usually impeccably dressed, and while his outfit was undoubtedly expensive, his clothes had that wrinkled, slept-in look that Frank knew all too well.

"I'm good, Frankie. I'm good."

A waitress walked over to take their order. Frank knew her from hanging around the cigar bar and maybe the Bayview. She was a sweet, gorgeous kid and was always went out of her way to be nice to Frank, even when he was broke, which was pretty much all the time.

"Two Don Julios," Sean ordered for both of them.

The waitress, Brianna—Frank now remembered her name—looked at Frank for a signal the drink order was okay. Frank squinted and nodded slightly to indicate it was.

"How about a stick? Get him a Double 'R.'"

"No, I'm not staying that long," Frank protested.

"I'll pick something suitable," Brianna stated with surprising authority and walked away without waiting for an answer.

Frank watched her as she walked away. Any semi-conscious, straight man would. She was perfect in every way and clearly destined for a bright future beyond the smoky confines of the Ambassador. She was at the beginning of a journey Frank had squandered and was approaching the end of. "Good luck, kid," he caught himself whispering under his breath as she walked away.

"What did you say?" Sean asked.

"Nothing, Sean. How you doin? What's up?"

"Not good, Frankie. Not good."

Frank cut him short. "Listen, Sean, my doc cut me down. I don't have anything for you."

Brianna returned to the table with a cigar on a small silver tray. "It's called the 'Work of Art.'" She smiled at Frank.

Frank was familiar with the small, oddly shaped perfecto from the Arturo Fuente Hemingway line. The tapered stick developed a surprising complexity the longer it burned. At least that's what the tasting notes claimed. The wrapper was a dignified Cameroon that had grown out of favor of late. Just like Frank.

"Thank you, Brianna, it's perfect."

"Would you like me to cut it for you?" she asked.

"No, thank you." Frank placed it in his breast pocket. "I'd like to save it for later."

"Okay, Frank, if you say so. Just don't wait too long."

"I won't," Frank said as he reached in his pocket to peel off a hundred for Brianna.

She shook her head and raised her palm. "That's on me," she said, before hurrying off to another table.

"What was that all about?" Sean asked.

"I have no idea."

"I've been trying to get in her pants for months," Sean said.

Frank was disgusted by the comment. He was a street guy and no angel when it came to women, but he didn't engage in that kind of talk. Frank got right to the point. "What's the problem, Sean? You wanted to see me?"

Sean leaned forward, his eyes a bit crazy. "It's Colleen, Frankie. I think she's seeing someone." Frank thought back to the dive bar on McNabb. He knew Sean was correct.

Two young women walked over to the table. One of them helped herself to the chair next to Sean and crossed her legs. Every night, a few would pass through. Some were looking for a boyfriend, some straight-up hooking. It was often hard to tell the difference. They were referred to collectively as Cigar Bunnies.

"I'm Jade." The seated bunny elegantly extended her hand to Sean, who readily took it.

"I'm sorry, ladies," Frank said, not wanting to appear rude. "We were just wrapping up a conversation. Would you mind if we took this to the bar?" Frank caught Brianna's attention. "Brianna, could you please set these ladies up with a drink at the bar?"

Brianna smiled and extended her arm toward the bar like a kindergarten teacher guiding her students out of the playground and back to class. She winked at Frank as the bunnies walked to the bar.

"So," Frank resumed, "I'm sorry to hear that, but what's it got to do with me?"

"I think the guy's from Springfield, and I figured maybe you could ... you know ... do a Stone Crab number on him."

"A what?" Frank snapped. "No, I don't know. Who the fuck do you think you're talking to anyway?" Brianna looked over in concern from the bar. Frank lowered his voice in deference to her. "And another thing, you don't get to call me by that name. You don't know me like that."

"Sorry, Frankie."

"Forget it," Frank said. "Just do me a favor and lose my number."

Frank got up from the table and stopped by the bar on his way out the door. He placed two hundreds on the bar in front of Brianna. "This is for their drinks." He touched one bill while glancing over at the bunnies. "This is for you." He pushed the other bill gently toward Brianna. "I insist."

Something in Frank's demeanor told her not to protest, so Brianna smiled and touched the top of Frank's hand lightly. "Thanks, Frankie. You're a class act."

"I used to be," Frank said and walked out into the warm Boca night.

PASSYUNK AVENUE

Passyunk Avenue (pronounced *pashunk* by the locals) cuts a rude swath across an otherwise orderly grid of streets in South Philadelphia. Except for Passyunk (and Moyamensing) Avenue, the neighborhood is composed of a uniform matrix of numbered and named streets—one big street followed by two little streets. Viewed on a map, they form ninety-degree angles and predictable intersections. Passyunk Avenue, or simply Passyunk, is the great disruptor of this comforting geometry. Irregular and meandering, its slashing path intersects with the more obedient byways. Together they form a unique gridwork of inconvenient crossings and odd angles. The cumulative result is one of strangely shaped buildings. Their pointy corners puncture curious cells of dead space—the spaces between. While born of necessity, the resulting architecture created by these acute angles also manages to be strangely beautiful, an exotic visage in a sea of pretty faces. If you've ever seen the famous photo of Sophia Loren giving the side-eye to Jayne Mansfield, that's Passyunk—South Philly's middle finger to white bread Center City. At least, that's what it had always been.

The Lenni-Lenape people initially inhabited the neighborhood and city. The name Lenape roughly translates to "original people." *Passyunk* is a Lenape word meaning "in the valley." Those indigenous people lived there, peaceably, for over ten thousand years.

In 1682, their leader, Chief Tamanend, entered into a treaty with William Penn. They were to live together in harmony as long as there were stars in the sky. Or at least that's how the story goes. While Penn treated the Lenape fairly, they were renamed the Delaware Indians and displaced to the west within a generation after being screwed over by Penn's son Thomas. Few survived the trek. So much for the stars in the sky. That's the funny thing about treaties and truces; they're only as honorable as the virtue of their heirs.

Today, there is a different migration and a testy exodus of another type of "original" people. There are no treaties, only Agreements of Sale. East Passyunk had become one of the hottest restaurant and lifestyle neighborhoods in the country, and property values skyrocketed accordingly. For those who choose to stay—or can't leave—tensions build with each new hipster watering hole and every evaporating parking spot. If you think South Philadelphians are passionate about their sports teams, you haven't seen a South Philly girl circle a block ten times looking for a spot. Parking isn't an amenity in South Philly, it's a birthright.

Not infrequently, a few empty nesters return to the old neighborhood from the suburbs. Seeking to downsize and get in on the burgeoning scene, they return to renovated rowhomes, resplendent in quartz, hardwood, and colorful front doors.

It is this *Nouveau Passyunk* that Nick returned to from his self-imposed exile.

FINAL DESCENT

Nick tossed his carry-on up into the overhead and took his window seat in first class. He propped a neck pillow up against the closed window shade once they made altitude, closed his eyes, and fell asleep.

He dreamed he was on his father's boat. They were on one of his epic fishing trips, and Nick was just a teenager. He was steering as his father set out a spread of trolling lures and ballyhoo. Tony spoke as he worked, both to instruct Nick and remind himself of the old techniques. He ran lines through the outrigger clips, long and short, and staggered them in length to resemble baitfish separated from the pod. "How they looking, Nicky?" his father asked. Nick glanced back at him for a moment. He was smiling as he set the last line and sat on the gunwale, admiring his handiwork.

Nick turned back to the wheel and realized he had strayed from his course. The compass was spinning wildly, and he was oversteering to compensate. At that moment, the sky grew dark, and the seas began to build. He expected to feel his father at his side at any moment, taking the wheel from his death grip, making everything right, but he never came. A rogue wave struck the boat on the beam, capsizing it and hurling Nick into the water. He swam to the surface, grasping a sheet of plywood floating there. Waves crashed into his face, and he swallowed saltwater as he gulped for air. His father was nowhere to be found, and Nick cried as he realized he was gone.

As he clung to the wood, he realized it was, in fact, a painting. His grip began to give out as the paint leached out from the saltwater. His palms turned red as the paint became blood. He tried to pray, but remarkably, he couldn't remember the words to the Lord's Prayer. He cried out to Jesus to save him, as a memory of the image of Christ in the storm played in his head. He looked up to see two massive fins circling him as he clung to the painting. Presumably, this was God's response to his prayer. He let go of the painting and slipped below the surface, falling through the depths as he watched the light fade above him.

The sharks crashed into the painting, tearing it into shreds. In their frenzy, they tore pieces of flesh from each other and the water turned dark crimson.

Nick heard a dinging sound and was jolted awake by the flight attendant's voice. "We have now begun our final descent into Philadelphia." Nick sat up in his seat, covered in sweat. The businesslike manner with which she recited this announcement, probably for the thousandth time, struck Nick as ominous. His seatmate was looking over at him like he was a lunatic. He composed himself as best he could, wiping his face with his sleeve. He slid up the window shade and looked out to the east at a frigid, unforgiving Atlantic.

Nick's father had prearranged his funeral, which had taken place at Our Lady Star of the Sea Church in Atlantic City. Nick spread his ashes in Absecon Inlet from the end of the jetty on the Brigantine side. A northwest wind carried them toward the sea, just as Tony had instructed. He'd eschewed the City, the Avenue, and the Caffé for the entirety of that short visit, staying at the family shore house in Brigantine instead.

At the time, he hadn't set foot in the city of his birth in over nineteen years, not since Jimmy's funeral in '99. *Jesus, had it really been that long?* His mother had died when he was six, and Nick no longer felt anything keeping him there. But if he was being honest with himself, which he was striving to do of late, it was Angie breaking his heart that had driven him to pack his bags for good. Nick had sensed the distance growing between them, and surely he must have been a handful to deal with after Jimmy's death. He had to remind himself of his own advice: *nothing lasts forever.*

Finding Jimmy in the bathroom of the Paradise had caused something inside him to snap. Jimmy might have looked like he was simply drunk and curled around the toilet if it wasn't for the blood that was pooled beneath his head. The blood had trickled between the black and white tile squares, forming rivulets in the grout lines that carried his life away to the point drain. He was clearly dead, but Nick got down on the floor and cupped his head in his hands, hugging him as best he could in the small bathroom. He remembered the stickiness of the blood as he lifted his face from the cold floor and thinking he must have been there for some time.

Angie had called him at 4:00 a.m. and told him he needed to get over there. Her best friend, Tina, was bartending at the Paradise and was counting the receipts after locking up at two. Jimmy was keeping an eye on her and was going to drive her home. They had been seeing each other for a few months, and Jimmy was crazy about her. The story was that he went into the bathroom and shot himself after Tina told him she was breaking up with him. Jimmy had his demons, but Nick never pegged him for a suicide. Tina's story never made any sense, and Nick didn't buy it for a minute. The chronology was off, for one, and though Nick knew Jimmy carried a gun from time to time, the pearl-handled Saturday night special next to him wasn't one of them. Still, what good would it do? He was no vigilante. Nick hated guns.

Most importantly, nothing was going to bring Jimmy back. Nick knew Jimmy's heart well. If he could speak to Nick from the grave, he would tell him unequivocally, *leave it alone*.

Nick wasn't surprised when he found out Angie was seeing someone else. Still, he was crushed. The pain was downright physical, and to this day, if he allowed himself, he could go back there in his mind and conjure it up fresh. He'd sat down at the bar in the Caffé and drank for almost a week. Gary had sat with him, drank with him, cooked for him (what little he ate), and carried him upstairs to a futon when he would finally pass out.

After a week had passed, he got to work. His mind was racing as he strategized and made plans. He rounded up all the money he had, collected as much of what was owed to him, and kissed his father goodbye. Gary drove him to the airport in the Fleetwood, and Frank picked him up in Fort Lauderdale. He hadn't spoken to Angie since.

Over the years, Nick would think about it often, recon-struct the events—Angie's call, Tina's story—but it wasn't until years later that he put it all together. He thought he knew who killed Jimmy.

Unlike most people, Nick usually enjoyed flying. Sure, he understood why people complained about the inevitable delays, cancellations, and cramped quarters, but he savored the time aloft. Free from gravity, neither departing nor arriving, Nick would think what it would be like to remain simply suspended. Looking out from his window seat, he often fantasized that time no longer existed. Perhaps he would land in a different era, deplane into an unknown city, and walk out of the terminal as another version of himself.

The sound of the tires screeching on the runway of Phil-adelphia International Airport dispelled him of any such notions. The dream had left him with a sickening sense of dread he couldn't shake. Nick powered up his phone, and the notifications from the past two hours and forty-five minutes announced their presence. They mainly consisted of the usual bullshit emails and social media conceits. The drudgery of deleting the self-inflicted intrusions of the modern digital realm confirmed his return to terra firma.

Finally, a text bubble popped up. It was from Gary. *I'm on 95, see you outside Terminal C.* Nick pulled up a picture from his downloads. It was a photo of his father Anthony, that big smile on his face, his arm around his old friend Gary. They are in his beloved Caffé Vecchio, standing in front of the bar. Nick loved Gary as much as anyone in his family. God knows, he trusted him more than anyone. Big Gary had been a steady, calming presence during Nick's wilder days and was often the only voice of reason in the sometimes chaotic chorus of the Caffé. Still, Nick felt a pang of hurt as he looked at that picture and saw the genuine bond between the two men, the effortless ease of their friendship. Nick knew better than to indulge the old hurt, but couldn't help picking the scab off the wound. He conjured up the ache until the cut was reopened and shone bright red. Like the apostle Thomas, he found a macabre comfort in exploring its contours and plumbing its depth.

Caffé Vecchio was a rare double storefront on Passyunk Avenue. Gary had been running the Caffé since Tony passed away a year ago. Technically, it was owned by the Di Nobile Family Trust, of which Nick was the named Trustee. The bills were getting paid, but Caffé Vecchio was a far cry from the halcyon days of the Passyunk Avenue restaurant renaissance it had once heralded. Tony hadn't planned on sparking a cultural revolution, he was just in the right place at the right time.

The Caffé was initially little more than a social club. Tony would cook for his friends and regulars, and eventually, it morphed into a "real" restaurant. The Caffé served as a sort of linen tabled centerpiece around which the burgeoning scene revolved. That scene had slowly evolved into an edgier, allegedly hipper vibe. More eclectic shops and restaurants opened—and closed—with regularity. The cuisine ran the gamut from banh mi to Scandinavian. The grand dame of the avenue gradually fell out of favor, and the changing demographic didn't help. It seemed the craft beer crowd had little taste for risotto. There were still the stalwart regulars who remained loyal, and to his credit, Tony actually made some concessions. But if he didn't own the bricks, the Caffè would have been shuttered long ago.

They tried to adapt. Tony added some panini for convenient take-out, and Gary hired a neighborhood kid to do some social media marketing. The kid, Joey, did an excellent job, signing the Caffé up to the online reservation and delivery apps and wrestling Vecchio into the millennium, occasionally kicking and screaming. The kid also started to hang out, cleaning up, running errands, and promoting the restaurant. Mostly, he begged Gary to allow him to begin a music promotion to showcase his DJ skills. Joey was so relentless and passionate about the idea that Gary eventually relented. In truth, the kid had made himself such an asset to the Caffé they couldn't afford to lose him. Tony begrudgingly gave his blessing to an old school, vinyl, R&B night—it took off like a rocket.

Between the Joey's self-promotion and Tony's dishes, the Caffé had found a new audience and some much-needed revenue. Joey wisely snuck in some more contemporary cuts as the nights wore on, and Gary started a late-night menu. Joey added different theme nights and occasionally brought in a guest DJ with his own following. Things were looking up with Joey the Kid (as Tony had named him) promoting and Gary kicking out the grub.

Then the worst thing that could happen did. Tony died suddenly. The Caffé began to slip. Ever so slightly at first, but without Tony at the helm, the slide was inevitable. Gary and Joey did their best to keep it going, but despite their best efforts, revenue plummeted. Nick had taken a largely hands-off approach in his trustee role, mostly delegating the financials to Tony's lawyer and accountant and leaving the day-to-day running to Gary. Now, Nick had to make the tough decision to pull the plug on the old girl, and break the news to Gary. The numbers didn't lie, that's what the accountant said, but Nick still couldn't help feeling like he was taking the last vestige of his childhood out behind the barn.

On the upside, the real estate market was scorching hot, and a double storefront on the avenue would likely get multiple offers above asking on the first day it was listed. Nick planned on taking care of Gary out of any sale, but no amount of money would fill the void left by the Caffé's absence from the big man's daily routine. *Nothing lasts forever*, Nick thought, but that notion that had got him through many personal travails was of scant comfort when it impacted the people you love.

Nick was thinking of all this when he saw his father's vintage Fleetwood gently crest a speed bump and swerve in front of a rideshare Prius as Gary masterfully maneuvered the mammoth to the curb. Gary rocked his heft out of the driver's seat to help Nick with his bag. Gary wrapped him up in a bear hug before Nick could shake his hand.

"Looking good, pretty boy," Gary boomed.

"You're looking pretty good yourself, G." Nick meant it. The big man was, well, bigger, if that was possible, but otherwise, he looked about the same since Nick last saw him at the funeral.

"You know black don't crack," Gary responded reliably.

The leather passenger seat shined, and Nick glided on it like a Slip 'N Slide. It made him think of the times he'd been sent careening across the rear seat while Tony whipped the Brougham around turns. Gary had kept the classic in pristine condition and only pulled it from the garage on special occasions. Nick coming back to the Avenue definitely qualified.

"Don't take 95," Nick said. There are more than a few ways to get to South Philadelphia from the airport. They're all relatively short routes over the Schuylkill River, and the trip can usually be made in about fifteen minutes, traffic permitting. I-95 North is the most direct, and the Broad Street exit merges onto the main thoroughfare, passing alongside Lincoln Financial Field and Citizens Bank Park. Nick preferred Essington Avenue. He liked watching the slow transition from the industrial area, dotted with junkyards, car dealerships, and strip clubs, to the residential neighborhoods of South Philadelphia, once Essington Avenue becomes Passyunk Avenue.

Crossing the Schuylkill River, Center City looms to the north with its skyscrapers, but Passyunk Avenue is the pulsing artery that branches out into the neighborhoods of South Philly. Nick looked out over the city, taking in the old and making notes of the new. Gary tuned the radio to WDAS and turned up the volume on the opening strains of a Harold Melvin and the Blue Notes number. The unassuming, opening keyboard strains were accompanied by a more ominous percussion and soon gave way to the opening guitar chords that presage the R&B atom bomb that is Teddy Pendergrass's voice.

Nick looked over at Gary. His head was nodding rhythmically in time with the beat. Nick gazed out at the scenes of the Avenue as they crossed Broad. The streetlights had just turned on and the sky had a magical glow. People were shuffling about in that transitional time. most on their way home to resigned drudgery, what Thoreau referred to as "lives of quiet desperation." They crossed paths with another group for which the approaching darkness brought only the prospect of opportunity and outrageous fortune. Nick squinted as the Fleetwood ate up the blacktop, starting to feel for the first time in a long time like he was part of the latter group. Most of the stores and shops were unfamiliar to Nick. When he'd left, the Avenue looked like a weathered Botticelli. Now, with the parts all jumbled and out of proportion, it resembled a surreal Picasso. The classically familiar buildings were juxtaposed with a hipster aesthetic.

Teddy began to hum soulfully, a melodic, throaty grunt that conveyed more than any written lyric ever could. Nick felt himself transported in time as soaring strings and horns joined the choir. Gary rapped on the steering wheel twice with his pinky ring along with the hi-hat that pulled the whole composition together as Teddy launched into "Don't Leave Me This Way."

The two of them continued on like that, neither of them interrupting the sonic trance. They passed the restaurants, bars, and stores that bridged the old to the new. Some Nick recognized, but most were foreign to him. An unspoken resolve bound them together. Both men knew they were driving into a tempest. No meaningless words or promises were necessary. Just two heads bobbing in unison, ever so slightly, in time to an old-school beat.

CAFFÉ VECCHIO

Gary pulled the Fleetwood into a spot on the back-street directly behind the Caffé. They walked past a red dumpster with Rose Waste Management emblazoned on the front in a cheerful script with floral graphic that seemed wildly incongruent with the trash business. Gary unlocked a gray steel door and they walked into the kitchen of Caffé Vecchio.

Two Mexican cooks worked the line and spoke to each other in Spanish over horns blaring from a radio. They shouted a greeting to Gary and nodded at Nick. Like most restaurants on the Avenue, Mexicans formed the backbone, and Vecchio was no different. A middle-aged waiter stood watch for an entrée that had yet to materialize. Gary and Nick walked out into the dining room and took seats at the bar. Nick's head was swimming as he looked around the Caffé. He was trying to reassemble all the old pieces and make them fit into a new frame. He broke out in a sweat and rubbed the cold Peroni bottle that had been placed on the bar in front of him against his temple before draining most of it in one swig.

"Feel funky, don't it?" Gary asked.

"You can't imagine," Nick answered as he ran his hand along the old wooden rail.

He could remember sitting on this same stool nineteen years ago, brokenhearted but determined, Gary sitting right where he was now. His foot reached to brace itself against a brass rail that was no longer there, and he stumbled forward just a bit as Gary chuckled at his misstep.

The paintings still hung all around—one over each of the tables that lined the perimeter. At the end of the restaurant, over the waiter's station, a reproduction of Rembrandt's *Christ in the Storm on the Sea of Galilee* formed the focal point. It was the only seascape painted by Rembrandt. The original had been stolen in the Isabella Stewart Gardner Museum heist on March 18, 1990. The collective value of the pieces stolen that night was estimated at over five hundred million, and the standing, no questions asked (allegedly) reward leading to their recovery had been raised to ten million. While many consider Vermeer's *The Concert* to be the heist's crown jewel, Nick had always considered *Christ in the Storm* to be the ultimate prize.

The Gardner Heist was the stuff of folklore, especially in South Philadelphia, where, by all official accounts, at least some of the paintings had at one point found their way. Owing to his father's obsession, Nick had more than a glancing interest, and as a young man, Tony had regaled Nick (along with anyone else who would listen) with his tall tales. As a result, at one time, whether he liked it or not, Nick, if only by osmosis, possessed a kind of encyclopedic knowledge of the theft. Ever since Frank's dubious revelation, Nick had to consider that perhaps they were more than tall tales. And maybe, just maybe, all of Tony's bombast was more than just braggadocio. Perhaps the whole production—the reproductions, the restaurant, the dishes—was a sort of cover, and Tony was hiding everything in plain sight. The other possibility, and Nick couldn't rule it out, was that the whole routine was his father's way of poking someone in the eye, and now that someone was coming around to get what he thought was his.

Freddie the waiter brought out two bowls of *pasta e fagioli* and set them down in front of Gary and Nick. The *pasta e fasul*, as it is also known, was steaming hot and had a distinctive umami character Nick could not place. Gary was smiling at Nick's reaction as Alberto, the bartender, asked, "How's the vazool?" Alberto pronounced the F as a V, which was typical. The bar top *specials* display listed it as Virgil's Vazool, as was consistent with the whimsical nature of Vecchio's menu. The flavor profile of the soup, though, was far more complex than playful. Someone had taken great care constructing this dish, and it showed.

"What's in this?" Nick asked Gary. "Pancetta?"

"Guanciale di vitello," Alberto answered. "Veal cheek. Your father substituted it for the pancetta in the soffrito. It's good, no?"

Nick nodded as he devoured the hearty soup. It was beyond "good." He hadn't realized how hungry he was, and the meal transported him to an era better than any time machine ever could. His mind wandered as they ate and drank in relative silence. Nick was reminded of a dusty copy of Virgil's *Aeneid* that his father kept on the boat, along with *Chapman Piloting & Seamanship*. They sat on a small bulkhead shelf, secured by a bungee cord.

As the night wore on, Gary brought Nick up to speed. The big man told him how some of the Rose's guys had been stopping by, real innocent at first, just grabbing a quick drink or a meal. More recently, the Rose himself was a Thursday night regular, coming in with an entourage and making the Caffé a kind of unofficial hangout. Gary even found a couple of them nosing around the basement and discovered that the second-floor office door had been jimmied, although nothing was missing.

More alarmingly, a slimy FBI agent, Sid Del Ciotto, had been popping up and asking questions. A couple of agents came in with a warrant soon after his last visit, allegedly looking to seize the poker machine (which Gary had wisely disposed of after Del Ciotto's visit) and any other "gambling paraphernalia," of which there was none. Gary suspected the poker machine warrant was a ruse, as the agents went straight for the office. Since that time, Gary had been conducting himself as if the office was bugged, which wasn't hard, because other than some light gambling, there was no illegal business operating out of the Caffé, the Rose's Thursday night ritual notwithstanding.

Gary leaned in close to Nick, in an abundance of caution, as he explained all of this. For the most part, the bar seemed a safe public space, and the music had begun to shift as the night progressed, growing in tempo and volume, transitioning from dinner accompaniment to a more soulful groove. Nick had quietly noted a cohesive thread through the last few songs, which he didn't readily identify. He was listening to Gary while trying to solve a musical puzzle at the same time.

The first song he pegged quickly as "Armed and

Extremely Dangerous" by First Choice, a lovingly produced disco track from the early '70s on the Philly Soul label, he was almost certain. The DJ transitioned nicely into a track by another disco group, Ecstasy, Passion and Pain, called "Ask Me." Nick recalled they also had another decent hit with "Good Things Don't Last Forever." Ecstasy, Passion and Pain weren't signed to any of the Philly labels to the best of Nick's recollection, but they had the distinct and unmistakable "Philly Sound."

Nick was sweetly torturing himself with this trivia and had put himself into a light trance when Gary's booming voice broke the spell.

"Are you listening to all this?"

Nick composed himself. "Absolutely," he responded, but his attention drifted over to the young, good-looking kid behind the laptop in a makeshift DJ platform that had been the waiter's station an hour before. The Apostles scrambled to save the boat, heaving in the waves in the painting over his shoulder. One vomited over the side as a few of the other disciples implored a tranquil Christ to save them.

Oblivious to the storm raging behind him, the kid completed the trilogy with the 12-inch remix version of "Ten Percent" by Double Exposure, on the Salsoul label, and Nick began to detect the cohesive groove connecting the playlist. He was still trying to unwind the riddle and had narrowed it down to the studio musicians that had defected from MFSB to the Salsoul Orchestra. All three songs had a *Philly Sound* feel, but the genealogy was less than overt. Nick frequently found himself engrossed in these internal mysteries, whether musical, literary, or in real life. He could never rest until he made the connection. As a result, he could appear aloof at times, though his mind was probably in overdrive when he seemed most disconnected.

Something clicked, and an image of the cabana scene at the Fontainebleau flashed somewhere in his brain—the twentysomething slightly off to the side of the main group. *Couldn't be*, he thought. He decided to keep it to himself for the time being.

Gary stopped talking and sat up straight in his seat. Nick turned on his stool in time to see Frankie Stone Crab walk through the front door. Frank stopped at the hostess stand, but Nick waved him over. The two men embraced as Gary looked on disapprovingly. His furrowed brow gave him a look so menacing that even Nick felt intimidated.

"I thought we were meeting at the Paradise," Nick said.

"We are, nephew. I just thought I'd stop by here first and grab a quick bite."

Nick pulled out a stool for Frank. "You guys know each other," Nick stated in an effort to break the palpable tension between the men. Gary squeezed Frank's hand just a little longer and a little harder than usual, which was pretty fucking hard to begin with. The tension was primarily on Gary's part. He knew Frank had some connection to the Rose from the old days. It also grated at him something fierce that this Crab called Nick nephew. He took it as a personal affront to his lifetime of friendship with the Di Nobile family and a tacit dig that, because of his skin color, he could never really be blood. Nonetheless, he'd stood sentinel at Anthony Di Nobile's casket and silently taken attendance.

What neither Gary nor Nick knew was that Frank had just minutes before left the Paradise out the back door when he saw the Rose walk in. Frank wasn't ready for that dynamic to occur, not before he played his part, and had no intention of leading Nick into any trap.

Not yet, at least.

Gary left the two men alone, using the excuse that he had to check on the kitchen. Frank was relieved. He was anxious to speak to Nick alone. His eyes were darting around the Caffé, and Nick noticed. Frank ordered a Dewar's and water.

"You a scotch man now?" Nick asked half-jokingly.

"Just taking a break from the vodka," Frank answered while gesturing to his stomach.

"Well, that should help," Nick quipped, and added, "Sorry, it doesn't look like we have any Stoli Elit here. I'll have Gary order a bottle if you plan on being a regular."

Frank just raised his glass in response and clicked Nick's Peroni. "Any luck with that thing?" Frank dove right in while nodding around at the paintings, as if Nick needed any clarification.

"If I did, I'd be long gone," Nick said.

Frank paused mid-sip. "That's not funny."

"Relax, Frankie, I'm only kidding. Besides, I just got here. You didn't think it would just be sitting here in plain sight, did you?"

Frank smiled devilishly. "Actually, I was kinda hoping it was."

"That's assuming this thing even exists, which I still have serious doubts about despite what your *boss* thinks."

Frank let the boss remark slide, even though it stung a little. "What does he have to say?" Frank said, looking toward the kitchen to indicate he was talking about Gary.

"Nothing," Nick lied. "I would leave him out of it if I were you, Frank. Just go through me. Besides, he's not exactly helpless. Feel free to pass that on to whoever you feel needs to hear it." Nick set his beer on a coaster and stepped away to take a leak. "Let's head over to the Paradise when I get back."

Frank ordered a bowl of Virgil's Vazool and another Dewar's, which he planned to nurse. Hopefully, he could stall long enough for the Rose to head to his next stop before they got to the Paradise.

THE PARADISE

PARADISO
CANTO XXI

Already on my Lady's face mine eyes
Again were fastened, and with these my mind,
And from all other purpose was withdrawn;

And she smiled not; but "If I were to smile,"
She unto me began, "thou wouldst become
Like Semele, when she was turned to ashes.

Because my beauty, that along the stairs
Of the eternal palace more enkindles,
As thou hast seen, the farther we ascend,

If it were tempered not, is so resplendent
That all thy mortal power in its effulgence
Would seem a leaflet that the thunder crushes.

The Divine Comedy by Dante Alighieri

Frank walked in first, allowing Nick to hold the door for him. Nick enjoyed feeling the heft of the old wooden door. The antique bronze door handle had a light patina that was worn shiny from years of use. Nick couldn't help but think how much his own touch had contributed to the shine.

The Paradise had been his spot. Nick and his friends held court there nightly in that singularly youthful whirl of music, alcohol, and romance that seems like it will never end—until it does.

Frank's head was on a swivel, scanning the room for any sign of the Rose. Nick's head was swimming for another reason. He hadn't been prepared for how well preserved the place would be. Aside from the endless craft beer taps and flat screens, he could have been walking into the bar in 1998. Two hipster kids were about to leave and graciously offered up their seats at the end of the bar. *We must really look old*, Nick thought. The seats were by the front window and featured a prime view of the crowd, which was substantial. Frank was sticking to the Dewar's, while Nick opted for a Yards Pale Ale.

Nick was starting to get his bearings. His eyes felt like they were adjusting to a dark room after walking in from a sun-drenched day, but nothing could have prepared him for what was about to enter his field of vision. At first, he thought he must have finally cracked and imagined the figure walking toward him from the opposite side of the bar. She was smiling at him as she flipped her hair in that self-conscious way that had always mesmerized him. Her voice penetrated his stupor.

"I heard you were back." Angie's voice sounded like a forgotten song from a heartbreak mixtape. His face must have registered his shock, and he barely mustered a, "Yep."

"I'm so sorry about your dad." Angie rescued him from his momentary paralysis with her sincerity. She squeezed his hand, and he almost leapt from his seat from the electrical charge.

"Frank, this is Angie." Nick introduced her in an effort to gather his composure, as much as out of courtesy.

"I remember," Frank said as he stood and offered his seat. "You're even more beautiful than I recall." The Crab kissed her hand in a grand gesture.

"Easy, Casanova." Nick nudged him, and they all laughed.

"I'm going for a smoke." Frank walked toward the door and winked back at Nick.

"So," Angie said.

"So," Nick contributed back. "How've you been?"

"It's been a long time, Nick. It's good to see you." She sat up on her stool, then reached over to touch his face as she kissed him on the opposite cheek.

Nick remembered how easy it had been to step off a plank into the depths of those eyes. Something, he wasn't sure what, held him back just enough. "It's good to see you too, Angie." Only superhuman restraint kept him from grabbing her with both hands and kissing her deeply.

The years can do miracles to soften the blow of painful memories, and it's easy to forget all the anguish and sleepless nights. He had to remind himself of what pushed him to leave Passyunk Avenue, the City, and Angie for good. Or so he'd thought at the time.

Now, here he was, staring into those eyes again, and the cruel voice welled up inside his consciousness. *Maybe … possibly … what if?*

Luckily, the drinks had filled his bladder and cut his musings short. Nick excused himself to hit the men's room. Frank came back from his smoke break at the same time, and Angie announced she had to get back to running the place.

"Don't leave without saying goodbye," Angie said.

"I won't," Nick said, thinking that nineteen years had passed since the last time he did just that.

She took down his number, and a kissy face emoji popped up on his phone as he waited for the bathroom. Nick didn't save her as a contact, but he didn't delete the text either.

He stepped up to the urinal in the claustrophobic space. The bathroom appeared mostly the same, with the notable exception of an abundance of graffiti, leaning toward the socially conscious and literary. The avenue's gentrification had introduced a progressive group of young people, somewhat unfairly lumped into a monolithic group referred to as hipsters. *The clientele has certainly changed.* He looked closer and realized the wall was a kind of chalkboard and colored chalk sat on a ledge. *I could never have this at the Tiki.* Nick imagined a few of the offensive lines his patrons would happily scribble.

One line in particular line caught his attention.

"Now it was again a green light on a dock. His count of enchanted objects had diminished by one." F. Scott Fitzgerald.

What an odd choice for bathroom graffiti, Nick thought as he washed his hands. Nick considered poor Gatsby, expending his life's energy reaching back for something that wasn't quite what he envisioned, and when it was finally in his grasp …

He looked in the mirror and tried to conjure his father's visage, but all he could manage were his own aging features. He splashed his face with water, grabbed some rough paper towels, and rubbed his eyes until he saw black spots. He was thinking of the kid at the Caffé as he bent over to pick up some towels that had fallen to the floor.

It was then he noticed that old checkered tile. He could still see Jimmy's blood trickling in the grout. He saw Jimmy's face as it appeared all those years ago and felt the whole room shift like the deck of the Galileans' vessel as he blacked out and fell toward the door.

Nick pulled himself up by grasping the sink. Frank must have heard the sound and was at the door with a worried look.

"You okay, Nicky?"

"I'm good, Frankie. Let's get out of here."

"No problem, nephew, where to?"

"The Caffé, Unc. Let's find this thing and be done with it, so you can get paid, and I can be on my way."

The getting paid part wasn't necessary, and Nick could see that it stung the old man. *Too bad*. All that mattered to him at that moment was finding the cursed painting and getting back to Grace.

DEL CIOTTO

By the time they returned to Vecchio, most of the diners had cleared out and only a few locals remained at the bar. The kid had shifted to some party's over, let's wrap it up music, "I Think I'll Tell Her" by Ronnie Dyson. *Wow.* Nick couldn't help but pay the kid a silent complement. It was a lesser-known track, but a local staple of Nick's club days, when it was often featured as the last song of the night before the lights came on.

They went right upstairs to the office. Nick called Gary. He needed his input and hoped to thaw the frost between the big man and the Crab just enough to get the information flowing. Nick hoped there was a reasonable explanation for the crazy fable Frank had convinced himself of. Maybe if he could prove to him (and the forces he answered to) that the painting wasn't in his father's possession this whole fiasco could be resolved without anyone getting hurt or going to prison.

Gary answered his phone. "Come down to the bar. Alone."

Nick didn't question him. He hung up and told Frank he'd be right back.

"No problem, I'll grab a smoke," Frank said.

"Them sticks are gonna kill ya, Unc," Nick stated as he walked down the stairs.

Nick joined Gary at the bar; his back was to the dining room. Gary's right hand was resting on the bar, a toothpick between his thumb and finger. He raised his hand to his mouth, and as he did, he subtly pointed at a table in the rear corner. Nick didn't turn his head. He glanced through the mirror behind the bar while pretending to check a score on the flat screen.

Special Agent J. Sidney Del Ciotto was seated at a corner table beneath a reproduction of Caravaggio's *Judith Beheading Holofernes*. The gory image was no match for the obscene sight of the sleazeball enjoying dinner with a beautiful young woman half his age. Nick silently hoped it was his daughter but knew better. Sid grew up in the neighborhood and was a few years older than Nick. He never quite fit in and led a sort of reclusive existence. No one was really shocked when Sid enrolled in the seminary after high school. When he dropped out of the seminary and resurfaced as an FBI agent on some crusade against guys from the neighborhood, it raised a few eyebrows. But mostly, he was just regarded as an oddball.

As much as Special Agent Del Ciotto pretended to despise some of the guys from the neighborhood, he sure did his best to mimic them sartorially. Even so, his get-up, from the carefully disheveled pocket square to the horse bit loafers, screamed of a guy who was trying too hard. Nick wasn't sure what adolescent trauma had driven him to this vendetta, but his motives were transparent. Nick was sure it would be his undoing. *And now he's focused on me*, Nick thought as the couple approached on their way out the door.

"How ya doin, Nicky?" Del Ciotto chirped as he walked by. Even his speech was a mocking impression of his quarry. Maybe he thought it made him sound tough in front of his date. Nick glanced at her long enough to see she wasn't impressed. Actually, he looked a bit longer than he had intended. She was an exotic creature, who looked even more out of place with Sid now that Nick saw her up close. Del Ciotto paused long enough for Nick to respond.

"I'm good, Special Agent Del Ciotto. I hope you enjoyed your meal." Nick exaggerated the *Special Agent* part. Gary's only comment was pretending to pick at his teeth and making a purposely irritating sucking noise.

"It was fantastic. I had the Rembrandt Rigatoni. I'll come back soon."

Nick began to respond, but Gary spoke over him.

"We'll be here. Tell ya friends."

Del Ciotto buttoned an overcoat from the Damon Runyan collection and made a sarcastic little salute. Nick's gaze was transfixed on the blonde. She locked eyes with Nick for a second as Del Ciotto headed for the door.

"Donna," she introduced herself.

He took her hand. "Nick Di Nobile. Please come again." Nick noticed the pendant she wore on a dainty necklace, three intertwined rings of white, yellow, and rose gold. She turned and followed Del Ciotto, but her eyes remained fixed on Nick.

Gary spit theatrically on the floor after Del Ciotto left.

"You gotta stop doing that, G, unless you want the Health Department to close us down," Nick said jokingly.

Gary pulled up his sagging pants as he stood up to lock the door. "Fuck that motherfucker."

CORRADO

Frank walked in from the kitchen. He had finished his cigarette out back and joined them at the bar. Gary didn't object and walked around the bar to retrieve a bottle of Amaro, pouring a measure for each of them.

"It'll settle your stomach," Gary explained.

"My stomach's not upset," Nick responded.

"I think it's gonna be," Frank added, downing his glass.

Nick stopped arguing and just drank. He brought Frank up to speed on Del Ciotto's visit. Gary shook his head and whispered under his breath as Nick told the story. Frank stared at the bottom of his glass as Nick described the exchange. He looked up when Nick described the woman, though, and seemed especially interested when he mentioned the necklace.

"Did you say she was a blonde?" Frank asked.

Nick laughed. "Yeah, why?"

"Nothing, just curious."

Gary frowned and set three Peronis on the bar. "Y'all done fucking around now?"

Frank and Nick both shrugged like little kids while clinking bottles, not realizing they had been 'fucking around.' Gary began to fill them in on what and *who* had been happening around the Caffé the last few weeks. He told what little he knew about the stories surrounding the paintings. That's all they were as far as he was concerned, some South Philly mythology whispered down the lane over the years and taking on greater stature as time passed. Even so, he didn't tell everything he knew. He wasn't ready to speak that freely in front of Frank, despite Nick's assurances. Nick interrupted him suddenly and looked toward the kitchen.

"Who's back there, G?"

"Just the cooks and the busboy, I think." Gary came out from behind the bar and walked back toward the kitchen. He returned with the kid, his arm draped over the boy's shoulder, causing him to sag a bit from the weight.

"Nick, meet Joey the kid. Kid, this is Nick Di Nobile."

"Nice to meet you, Mr. Di Nobile," Joey said.

Nick smiled despite himself. "Mr. Di Nobile was my dad. You can call me Nick."

Joey shook his hand firmly and looked him straight in the eye, holding his gaze.

The kid definitely has charisma, no doubt about that, Nick thought.

"I was just finishing packing my gear, and Beto was making me some fish tacos," Joey offered by way of explanation.

"Them tacos the bomb," Gary added.

"Sure, kid. Take your time. You earned it." Nick opened a Peroni and handed it to Joey. Joey thanked him and they clicked bottles. As he walked back to the kitchen, Nick hollered after him. "Killer song selection, kid. Where'd you learn that?"

Joey looked back and shrugged his shoulders. "From my mom, I guess," he said as he disappeared back into the kitchen.

"Where were we?" Frank said.

"I believe I was about to end this foolishness once and for all. Tony didn't have no picture worth nothing. Somethin else y'all overlooking. Tony ain't never wanted nothing wasn't his. That's the kind of man he was. Not money, not bricks, not pussy, and sure as hell not nobody's painting. See, that's something that snake can't wrap his thieving brain around. Every painting, shit, damn near everything Tony Di Nobile ever owned, sitting right here." Gary swung his arm out in a circle, taking in the entirety of the Caffé. "So have a look around. Anything you find my man didn't own, you welcome to it." Gary deferred to Nick when he was done. "You cool with that, Nick?"

"Cool," Nick answered.

The three of them began a sort of inventory/walking tour of Vecchio. It was more an exercise designed to give Frank the ability to report back to the Rose and say he did his due diligence. Nick didn't think of it as a genuine search to uncover anything pointing toward the phantom painting's existence.

Nick recalled most of the paintings. Some of them had been put in new frames, but the images were etched upon his memory. Tony would carry on about them, their origins, the subjects, little stories about the artists, their lives often tragic. They ranged from the sacred to the profane, Italian to Dutch, with no discernable pattern or reason. They were just images Tony liked. He never pretended to be a connoisseur. The whole Caffé was always a bit kitschy, but no one seemed to mind. Tony had a genuine personality that couldn't be confused with pretense. There was no more snobbery in his taste in art than there was in his recipes.

"I don't remember this one," Nick said.

It was an image of a young man on a horse in an ancient time. He was wearing a robe of brilliant red. A group of people, mostly older than the rider, were featured to his right.

"He put that up about a year ago. He brought it back from the shore," Gary explained.

"What *shore*?" Nick asked.

"Atlantic City. Some antique store in Ducktown. Been there forever."

Nick could picture the place. He had passed it a thousand times on his way from one watering hole to another, many years ago.

"That place is still there? I didn't even realize it was open for business back *then*. It always looked like it was about to collapse."

Atlantic City was famous for places like that, ancient restaurants, bars, and businesses that survived the town's countless deaths and resurrections. They eked out a hardscrabble existence on the periphery of the supposed glitz of the casinos. Nick knew some *people* who fit that description as well. One in particular stood out.

Nick looked closer at the painting. He could barely make out the signature in the bottom right corner. *V. Corrado.*

NOTHING NEW UNDER THE SUN

What has been is what will be,
and what has been done is what will be done,
and there is nothing new under the sun.

Is there a thing of which it is said,
"See, this is new"?

It has been already
in the ages before us.

There is no remembrance of former things,
nor will there be any remembrance

of later things yet to be
among those who come after.

Ecclesiastes 1:9–11

Nick sat at the kitchen table of the old house that belonged to his grandmother. His head was starting to throb, and he washed down some ibuprofen with tap water from the sink. The search had failed to uncover anything of any value, other than of the sentimental variety. If there was a priceless painting stashed in the Caffé, Nick couldn't find it. He looked at his phone and scrolled through his missed calls and messages.

Ethan had texted that everything was good at the Tiki.

One missed call from Grace.

Nick opened the kissy face emoji text from Angie. *Don't leave without saying goodbye.*

In the daze following his spell in the Paradise's bathroom, Nick had done just that.

He called Grace. She sounded worried. Nick did his best to reassure her everything was fine and he had just drunk a little too much and wanted to get some sleep.

"I love you, Grace. I'll be home soon."

"I'm glad you still know where home is. Don't stay another day, Nick, come home now."

It was rare for Grace to be so forceful, and the certainty in her voice unnerved him. Nick subscribed to the belief all women had psychic powers, but Grace could be downright clairvoyant. Nick's waning faith in organized religion had only managed to bolster his belief in the spiritual realm, and ironically, the existence of a God. Still, Grace nagged him to go back to church.

"I promise I'll be home as soon as I can," was the best he could do and still tell the truth. "Everything is fine here," he added, though that, of course, was a lie.

"Okay, my love. Whatever you say. Just remember who you are and come back to me in one piece."

"Goodnight, Grace. I love you." He ended the call on that note. *Remember who you are*. Nick reflected on that, wondered if that was even knowable anymore. One of the reasons he was drawn to Grace was that she always seemed to see him as the man he aspired to be. *Remember who you are*.

He knew he shouldn't, but he went back to Angie's message. *Don't leave without saying goodbye*. Nick didn't sleep well.

He showered and cleared his head as best he could. He had a meeting with Tony's estate lawyer to sign some financial documents and the listing agreement for Vecchio. He needed to break the news to Gary and felt like shit about it. Tony had provided for a healthy share to go to Gary, and maybe that would soften the blow, but Nick doubted it. But first, he needed to drive to the shore, list the Bertram with the broker, and make a stop in Atlantic City.

Nick made the familiar drive on the Atlantic City Expressway to "The World's Playground." What was once the city's proud tagline was now an ironic punchline. Atlantic City was on the ropes—again.

The sign was weathered and peeling.
A.C. Antiquary
Books, Paintings, Furniture, Memorabilia, Framing
"Nothing New Under The Sun"
Nick pulled up out front. Books were stacked on shelves that formed the front walls of the shop. They were exposed to the elements, and some of the spines were faded. Upon

closer inspection, the shelves themselves were on hinges that closed inward and were padlocked in place when the store was closed.

A bell jangled as he opened the door. It was dark and musty inside. The smell of old books filled the air, and dust particles flittered through a beam of light sneaking through the space where the bookshelf walls folded closed.

A half-eaten hoagie sat on a metal desk. A computer screen was open to what looked like an inventory search page.

"Can I help you?" The voice came from behind the stacks and startled Nick.

"I was hoping you could help me with a painting my father bought here."

The man stepped out from the row of books and wiped his face with a napkin. He looked intently at Nick through thick glasses.

"I'm Nick Di Nobile. My father—"

"Yes, of course. I'll be right back." He spun on his heels quite deftly for a man of his girth and disappeared back into the stacks. Nick heard a door creak toward the rear of the shop and saw a light flick on in a connected room.

The bookstore was the front portion of a labyrinth of rooms and connected buildings that housed a collection of antiques, lamps, oriental rugs, and paintings. A.C. Antiquary was also a repository of Atlantic City memorabilia, highlighting its golden age, along with all its subsequent permutations. In its present version, the shop survived primarily as a book curation service, the bulk of which transacted online. It also operated as a custom frame shop.

The man shuffled back sideways down the center aisle carrying what appeared to be a painting wrapped in brown paper.

"What's this?" Nick asked, somewhat sheepishly.

The man rested it down for a moment. He looked a bit disappointed, perhaps fearing he wouldn't be paid. "Your father's painting. Isn't that what you're here for?"

This can't be that easy, Nick thought.

"He gave me a deposit months ago. I was afraid he had forgotten it."

"Yes, of course. What do I owe you?"

"Three hundred for the frame," the man replied. "My name is Max. I looked at you when you walked in and saw your father's eyes before you said your name."

"Pleased to meet you." Nick shook his hand.

"How's Florida?" Max asked, catching Nick off guard. He must have noticed Nick's reaction because he quickly clarified, "Your father told me all about you. Besides, that tan gives it away."

"Can I see it?" Nick asked.

"But of course." There wasn't much room in the shop, but Max rested one side of the frame on the metal desk, next to his sandwich, and held up the other side while Nick peeled back the brown paper a bit at a time.

Beneath the paper, an oil painting revealed itself. A man in a blowsy cloak, sword at his side, sat with a giant upraised glass of what appeared to be beer. A woman sat upon his lap. He was looking back over his shoulder, his left arm around the woman, his right arm raising a toast. A huge smile was on his face, and an ornate feathered cap sat upon his head. The setting seemed to be 17th century, but the man's face was in the unmistakable likeness of Anthony Di Nobile.

"I don't understand." That was all Nick could manage.

"You don't like the frame?" Max frowned.

"No, the frame is fine. This painting. Where did it come from?"

"Your father had it done by that crazy painter. The one who talks to himself and paints in the park. He's a minor celebrity. He's a little nuts." Max made a twirling gesture with his finger at his temple. "But what great artist isn't?"

"What's his name?"

Max continued to peel down the brown paper, revealing the artist's signature. *V. Corrado*.

"Virgil Corrado," Max said.

"Did you say Virgil?"

"Yes, like the Roman poet. I have a beautiful copy of the *Aeneid* from 1877 if you're interested."

But all Nick could think of was the *pasta e fagioli*. "No, thank you, maybe some other time. What park?"

"Excuse me?"

"You said he painted in the park. What park?"

"Yes, I'm sorry. Rittenhouse Square in Philadelphia."

"Is there anything else you can tell me?" Nick asked.

Max laughed good-naturedly. "Sure. It's a reproduction of a Rembrandt painting, *The Prodigal Son in the Tavern*, sometimes referred to as *The Prodigal Son in the Brothel*."

"Anything else?"

"Yes," Max answered. "You owe me three hundred bucks."

Nick paid the man with three bills. There wasn't a register in sight. Max wrote out a handwritten receipt on carbon paper and placed the bills under a desktop calendar covered with unintelligible scribble and coffee cup rings.

"Tell your father I said hello," Max hollered after him as Nick walked out to the car.

Not wanting to deal with the man's inevitable reaction to the news of his father's death, and worse, his own tortured feelings, Nick just waved back weakly and softly said, "I will."

Still dazed, he maneuvered the painting into the trunk, carefully covering his father's face as if he was pulling a sheet over a corpse and then closing the lid like a casket.

Nick drove south on Fairmount Avenue toward Ventnor, the next town over, and home to Old Port Marina. A black Mercedes S 600 pulled out a few moments later and fell in line two cars back. Nick was too distracted to notice.

OLD PORT MARINA

TONY ROME, the old Bertram's transom announced in gold leaf lettering. She was up on blocks in the yard of Old Point Marina. Her bottom was clean and appeared to have been recently soda blasted. Two bronze propellers shone like jewels. Nick had expected to find her shrink-wrapped, but a ladder sat opened to her starboard side. Someone had been working on her.

The Bertram 31 is a coveted sport fishing boat that was made by Bertram Yachts from 1967 to 1983. Less than two thousand were produced. It is a classic in every respect, and its lines are iconic. The hull was designed by naval architect Ray Hunt. Known as the Hunt Deep V, her seakeeping abilities are legendary. As a result, the hulls are favorites for restoration. Finding a Bertram 31 in a boatyard is the equivalent of stumbling upon a Shelby Cobra in a junkyard.

Nick climbed the ladder and swung his leg over the gunwale and onto the deck. He stood and looked out over the transom. It was an odd sensation, standing in the cockpit of a boat on land, especially when Nick had spent so many days in that very spot looking out at an endless ocean. He looked up at the flybridge, half expecting to see his father at the wheel, but his eyes were met only by a gray, unforgiving sky.

Nick stepped down into the cabin.

The cabin is the last place a seasick person should go, yet it's inevitably the first place they retreat to. Nick always thought it was because of some denial instinct. *Maybe if I don't look at the waves, they will cease to exist.* In reality, the inner ear takes over, the eyes are no longer synched with the brain, and misery ensues.

Nick had been taught at a young age to keep his eyes unwaveringly on the horizon. *No matter how much the deck shifts beneath your feet, the horizon never moves*, he could still hear his father say. Even so, in that enclosed cabin, on dry land, for the first time in his life, Nick began to feel nauseous. Nick looked out at the boatyard through the windshield and regained his composure.

He heard footsteps approaching and focused his attention on a hatch below the settee, wondering if Tony's trusted .38 was still in there. He dispensed of that thought and walked back out to the cockpit, where he saw George, the owner of Old Port Marina, approaching.

"Permission to come aboard?" George smiled cheerfully. He recognized Nick right away and seemed genuinely happy to see him. George and Tony had gotten to know each other over the course of many years at the marina. Tony regarded him as a man of integrity, and the two had become good friends. Nick spent his childhood summers exploring the marina and had last seen George at Tony's funeral. The two of them sat there in the cockpit for a while, catching up on things, mostly George's children and grandkids and the marina business. Eventually, the conversation turned to the *Tony Rome*.

"What's all this about?" Nick was referring to the work that appeared to be ongoing.

"I'm restoring her. Whaddya think?" George was obviously proud of his workmanship.

"I think we should talk," Nick responded. "Who's paying for all this?"

"Well, your dad paid for most of the parts. She already has two fresh diesels in her. We were splitting the labor between us. He had another guy helping him too, doing the fiberglass work."

"Big black guy?" Nick doubted it as soon as he said it. Gary hated the water and would probably get seasick even if the boat was on blocks.

"No, this guy was white, heavyset, with a white beard," George said.

That didn't match up with anyone Nick could think of. "And then what?" Nick asked.

"Well, fully restored, she could fetch close to $150,000. Your father and I had a handshake agreement; he was cutting me in for a third." A worried looked momentarily appeared on George's face, and Nick felt a pang of guilt.

"My father's handshake is good enough for me, George. Can't wait to see how she turns out. Thanks for everything you did for us over the years."

George took off his hat and stared out at the boatyard that was his life's work. "He was so proud of you, Nicky."

This was the part where Nick would usually interrupt. He didn't want to hear these things from people who didn't really know or understand their complicated relationship. But this time… Maybe he respected George too much. Perhaps it was because George was out of the whole South Philly circle. Maybe he was just weary, but he let the man speak.

"He thought you did the right thing, leaving and all."

That caused Nick to perk up.

"Your father said to me on this very boat, '*He's the smart one, George. If I had any sense, I would sell the Caffé and move down there with him.*'"

"My father actually talked about selling the Caffé?"

"He did. At least that once. He was glad you made a life away from the city, Nick, but he still worried."

"About what, George?"

George raised his voice just a little, if only to signify his incredulity, and tapped Nick lightly on the skull. "About you, you brick head. You think it didn't hurt him that things were strained between you two?"

"No, you're right. I knew that, but the years pass and it just gets harder to reconcile. I'm not trashing my father, George, but there are things you don't know."

"I'm sure you're right, Nicky. But you should think of something as well. Your father was once a son himself, and I'm sure there are things he went through that were a lot harder than you can imagine. After all, every good father was once a prodigal son himself.'"

"What did you say?" Nick was starting to feel nauseous again.

"I didn't say it, your father did. It was one of his sayings. He would kind of half sing it in Italian, but I didn't understand, so he translated for me. I never forgot it."

"Take a walk with me," Nicky said.

The two of them climbed down the ladder and walked over behind Nick's car. Nick opened the trunk and peeled back the torn paper.

"Does this mean anything to you?"

George looked like he was going to faint. "Jesus Christ, it's your dad."

"I know that. I mean the painting itself. Do you know what it represents?"

"I'm just a broken-down boat mechanic, Nicky, this is above my pay grade."

Nick closed the trunk, shook hands with George, and got in the car.

"Let me know if you need anything, George."

"We're good, Nicky. I'll keep you posted. One of these days, I'm gonna come down to your Tiki bar, and maybe I'll never come back."

"A lot of people do just that. I'm gonna hold you to it, George."

George stood at the door of Nick's car, but was looking to the rear. "They with you?" he asked.

Nick looked through his rearview mirror just in time to see the Mercedes' brake lights before it pulled away.

"Maybe they're looking for a Bertram."

"We're not that lucky, Nicky," George remarked, then tapped the roof of Nick's car just like he'd tapped Nick's head earlier.

No, we're not, Nick thought as he drove away. He made a sharp right, opting to take the long way back to the city, staring through his rearview mirror as he crossed over the Margate Bridge. Nick drove slowly across the barren causeway connecting Margate to the mainland. No car followed as he crossed over Dock Thoroughfare and Risley's Channel. A lifetime ago, Nick had navigated these back-bay waterways in his skiff on endless summer afternoons. It was low tide, and Nick could see that the channels had shifted over the years. They hardly seemed navigable now.

The rickety billboards on either side touted competing real estate brokerage teams. Nick half expected to encounter the eyes of Doctor T.J. Eckleburg looking down upon him, but they were nowhere to be found.

Instead, a Rolex billboard beckoned from across the sod banks.

THE TRUST

Nick drove the expressway back to the city. He decided to bypass South Philly and took the Ben Franklin Bridge into Center City instead. He pulled into the underground garage of the Wanamaker building and took the elevator to the lobby. He presented himself at the security desk and received a sticker after the guard called up to verify his appointment.

Leonidas Manos, Esquire, specialized in estate and probate law. His father owned a few diners back in the day, along with a waste disposal business. Leo had become the go-to lawyer for wills and trusts for quite a few wealthy South Philly Italian families. Nick had a theory it was because Italians didn't want other Italians knowing their financial business, but it was just a theory. Tony was good friends with Leo's dad anyway, and the old man was a fixture at Vecchio before he was convicted of fraud and died in prison.

Leo greeted Nick like a long-lost brother. They had crossed paths years ago on the nightlife circuit, and Leo was a regular in the clubs back in the '80s. They would occasionally share a drink and a quick story. Nick recalled him traveling with a crew of Albanian guys. There was never any friction between the two of them. Their relationship was more of the "hi and goodbye" variety. Maybe that's why Nick was caught off guard by the overfamiliar bear hug.

"Good to see you, Nicky. How long has it been?"

"I'm not sure, twenty-five years maybe?"

"They don't have clubs like that anymore. I miss those days." Leo clapped his hands and bit down on his lower lip while churning his clenched fists. "I had all the moves back then."

"Looks like you still do. You go by Manos or Manero these days?"

And with that reference, Leo pointed to the sky in his best impression of the iconic *Saturday Night Fever* pose. "Haha! I still got it. Come on back, Nicky, have a seat."

Nick took a seat across from the Greek's desk.

Leo's tone turned solemn, like he suddenly recalled the sad occasion for Nick's visit. "I'm so sorry for your loss, Nick. I should have said that first, but seeing you triggered such good memories."

"That's quite alright, Leo. Thank you. I feel the same way." Nick lied just a little. "And my condolences on *your* father's passing."

Leo stared down at his hands, folded together on his desk, and was silent for a moment. He may have been praying. "God rest both their souls." The smile returned to his face quickly, and Leo promptly segued to the business at hand. "So, I have the agreements of sale for the house and the Caffé."

Nick signed the first agreement, for his grandmother's house, reluctantly and only after some tortured hesitation. His pen also hovered over the signature line of the agreement for the Caffé.

"Something wrong?" Leo asked.

"Nothing's wrong; I just want to hold off on the Caffé for now."

"That's fine, Nicky. After all, you're the trustee. But I have to tell you, there's been a lot of interest and the appraisal is as high as ever. Booms don't last forever, and some people believe the bubble is about to burst."

"Maybe, Leo. I'm not saying no, I'm just saying not right now. There's a few things I still need to iron out."

Leo seemed disappointed, but maybe it was just that he saw some billable hours slipping away. "No problem, Nicky, just let me know when you're ready. I'll stall the broker for a little while. What about the boat?"

"Apparently, it's being restored, so hold off on that too." Nick was having serious reservations about selling the Bertram. It was chock-full of memories, and despite their differences, Nick could honestly say it was where they shared their best times. He wished he was back there now, out on the ocean trolling the depths, his dad at the wheel. If he had it all to do over, maybe things would have been different between them. The ocean was the one place where they never disagreed. Back on land… well, you can't have more than one captain. At that moment, Nick settled it in his mind. He would pay George whatever he wanted and keep the *Tony Rome*.

"Let me ask you something, Leo. Did my father ever discuss a painting with you."

"A painting? Only the paintings in the Caffé. They're mentioned in the trust. They fall under furnishings of the Caffé, I presume. Why do you ask?"

"Just curious. You know my father; he was quite a character."

"That he was. There's not many left like them, our fathers, that is."

Leo swung his chair around and reached into a zebra-wood humidor, withdrawing a stick. He offered it to Nick. "Fuente Shark. They're almost impossible to get. Enjoy it in the best of health, my friend."

Nick took the cigar. He realized he still hadn't smoked the Opus X he had with him at the Fontainebleau. That day seemed like a lifetime ago. He thanked Leo and placed the Shark carefully in the breast pocket of his coat. When Leo had turned to the humidor, Nick noticed a cardboard file box sitting under the credenza. It read *Estate of Anthony Di Nobile* in thick black sharpie print. He didn't think much of it, but it was one of those odd reminders his father was gone forever. Other than the Caffé and the remnants of his ashes swirling somewhere in the Atlantic, that box represented the last physical evidence the man had ever existed. *That's what we're all reduced to, in the end*, Nick thought. He knew Gary would think differently. Nick could practically hear the big man's voice in his head. *Bullshit, Nicky. He still lives on in you.*

Leo walked Nick to the door and hugged him again. This time not quite as crushing as the hug he had greeted him with. "Take care of yourself, Nicky. Give me a call when you make up your mind. No hurry."

"Thanks again, Leo. Keep working on those dance moves."

Leo waved to Nick as he walked toward the elevators. Nick looked back in time to see the Greek bite down on his lower lip and bust a hasty, awkward moonwalk back into his office.

Nick rode the elevator down to the lobby and took another elevator to his car. He weaved through the ancient labyrinth of the underground parking lot and emerged back into the light at street level.

Leo practically ran back into his office and plopped down in his high-back desk chair. He spun in the chair and slid the file box out from under the credenza, lifting it up to his desk. He took off the lid and pulled out a manila envelope, placing it next to the box. The file read *Do Not Open Until My Death*.

He pulled out his cell phone and sent a text. *He just left. Didn't sign.*

Leo's phone vibrated, indicating a text in response. *Good, be right there.*

The text was from a contact Leo had saved as *Big G.*

THE GOAT IN RITTENHOUSE SQUARE

Nick was headed south on 12th Street back toward the Caffé. He caught the light on Walnut, and when it turned green, he made a right on a whim. Nick hadn't been in Center City in a long time and thought he'd cruise around a bit.

Rittenhouse Square is something of a small urban oasis in the middle of a vibrant restaurant and shopping district. The surrounding area is decidedly upscale. High-end apartment buildings line its perimeter, and the clientele skews toward a ritzy demographic. Being a stone's throw from South Philly, downtown guys frequently planted a flag in one of the neighboring bars and lounges, establishing Sunday afternoon outposts.

Nick circled twice. The park itself was beautiful in all seasons, but he found himself thinking of a particular lazy spring day spent drinking Negronis in a café overlooking the square.

The world seemed full of endless possibilities back then, and if he had any doubts, all he had to do was look across the table at Angie's beautiful face. If he closed his eyes, he could still picture her gazing at him lovingly, framed by the cherry blossom trees that seemed to shed their petals in approval. The blossoms had been raining down in the gentle breeze and piled at their feet. It wasn't long after that Nick found Jimmy in the Paradise. The cherry blossoms lived out their painfully brief bloom, and Angie stopped looking at him that way. Every season has a singularly identifiable moment when it peaks. And every relationship has that golden moment when the universe seems like a truly magical place and you possess the wand. It's that moment that causes the cherry blossoms to return, keeps the junkie craving the needle, and dares foolish lovers to reach back for the past.

Nick was so caught up in these thoughts he almost rear-ended the rideshare car that stopped short in front of him to let out a passenger. As he was stopped, Nick caught his breath and shook himself out of his daydream. He couldn't even remember circling the park the second time, having found himself in that peculiar mental auto-pilot. Nick looked over to the park on his left and saw a tall man painting on a canvas set upon an easel. Nick continued to watch him as he circled and miraculously found a metered spot on Locust Street, right off the square. Nick found he couldn't parallel park quite as expertly as he once could but managed to get in the spot okay.

As he crossed 18th, Nick could see that the painter was packing up his things, and he hurried his pace. The man had a crazy shock of gray hair that looked like it had been combed with a firecracker. He was inexplicably wearing a blue surgical mask. *This has to be the guy*, Nick thought. He slowed so he didn't give the impression he was running up on the painter.

The man was standing before a statue of a small bronze goat, which appeared to be the subject of his painting. From what Nick could see of it, it looked pretty damn good.

"Nice goat," Nick said while looking at the painting and instantly felt foolish for the banal statement.

The painter simply looked up at Nick from his stooped position, then turned away as he continued to collect his tools, which he placed in a paint-splattered canvas tote.

Nick regretted his blatant approach and was trying to think of something clever to say when he heard the painter mumble something over his shoulder. Nick couldn't make it out through the muffling of the mask and said, "Excuse me?"

The painter stood up, turned, and wiped his hands on his overalls. He pointed toward the sculpture. "I said, this one is a replica. The original is gone."

Nick could remember the little bronze goat sitting in the park since he was just a kid—Nick, that is. This guy was definitely living up to his billing.

"What happened to the original?"

"They moved him over to the library. This one was made from a cast."

"Why?" Nick asked.

The painter had gathered all his things and placed the canvas in a protective case, which he slung over his shoulder. "All those little brats touching him and rubbing him for a hundred years. They wore the metal thin."

Nick thought about it. He was one of those brats, of course. Tony had taken him to the park many times. The goat's horns always had the same shiny patina as the door handle at the Paradise.

"They rubbed his horns to a sharp point. That's the danger of loving something too much. Eventually, you turn it into a weapon. But I believe you know that already," the painter said as he began to walk away.

Nick caught up and began to walk with him. Even lugging his bags, the man was hard to keep up with.

"Who said that, Sun Tzu?" Nick asked as he walked alongside.

"No," the painter snapped back. "I did."

"I'm Nick." He would have offered his hand, but the painter's hands were full, and he was still moving at a furious pace as they weaved between the pedestrians on Walnut Street.

"I know who you are. You're Anthony's son."

Nick was impressed. "Is it my eyes?"

This stopped the man dead in his tracks. He turned and looked at Nick like *he* was the crazy one. "No, don't be ridiculous. Max called and said you would be looking for me." The man walked to a storefront and opened the door to Holt's cigar shop. Nick grabbed the door behind him, holding it so Virgil could turn sideways with his bags and shuffle in. Nick followed close behind.

"Where are we going?" Nick asked innocently enough. He was familiar, of course, with the storied cigar aficionado's mecca, but Virgil was quirky, to say the least.

"You're going to buy me a box of Opus X," Virgil responded confidently.

Nick laughed. "I am? What makes you so sure?"

"Two things." Virgil held up two fingers as they walked into the humidified environment of the showroom. "First, you're your father's son, so that makes you a gentleman." Virgil signaled to a well-dressed salesman, who retreated dutifully to retrieve the box, which had obviously been set aside for the painter.

"What's the second thing?" Nick asked, walking right into it.

Virgil pulled down his mask for the first time, revealing a broad, if crooked, smile. "The best reason in the world." Virgil deftly cut one of the sticks and paused to leave Nick hanging as he preheated the foot of the Opus and then began puffing on it furiously. The cigar combusted in a joyous cloud of white smoke. "You want something from me."

The salesman was behind the counter ringing up the box of Opus X. He had been courteously pretending not to overhear the conversation.

"Andy, what stick do you recommend for my new friend?"

Andy reached into the glass case beneath the counter and produced a Fuente Hemingway, handing it to Nick. "It's called the *Short Story*," Andy explained.

"Excellent," Virgil exclaimed approvingly.

Nick handed over his Amex sheepishly and stashed the Short Story in his pocket for later. *That makes three*, including the other two sticks he hadn't gotten around to smoking.

They parted ways at the door. "I'll stop by the Caffé around seven," Virgil said. "That should give Beto enough time to make a fresh pot of *Pasta Vazool.*"

Virgil charged off down Walnut Street. Nick walked toward his car on Locust, wondering what the hell just happened. He texted Gary, asking him to have Beto whip up Virgil's special.

Gary was hustling out of the Wanamaker Building when he got Nick's text. He paused before the revolving door. Breathing heavily, he texted back a hasty thumbs-up emoji. Gary continued through the door, his bulk barely fitting between the panels. He was carrying an accordion file folder under his arm containing two items. One was a manila folder with Tony's handwriting on the front. The other was a FedEx envelope containing a copy of the manila folder's contents. The label was made out to an LLC with an address on Camino Real in Boca Raton. He placed it in a FedEx drop box on Chestnut Street, lumbered down the stairs to the Broad Street Subway, and jumped on a southbound train. He sat with his legs spread wide, taking up two seats, clutching the file between his arm and chest.

ROSA WASTE MANAGEMENT

Frank flicked away a half-smoked Marlboro, wondering whether it would be his last. He exhaled as slowly as he could and walked up the concrete stairs alongside a loading dock. Frank knocked on an unmarked metal door and looked up into a security camera. He heard a buzz as the lock clicked and pulled on the handle with his good arm. The Rose's office at Rosa Waste Management was devoid of any visible phone, file cabinets, computer, or any other indicia of normal office operations. It consisted of a desk and chairs, a leather sofa, a 60-inch plasma television, and a wooden bar built into one corner.

Frank recognized the property as the old Athens Carting and Hauling property. They sponsored a softball team in the early eighties. Frank couldn't play, but he went to all the games. They were the stuff of legend. Not so much for the games themselves, but for the amounts wagered on them. Frank recalled a particular game with bets in excess of fifty thousand, and this was in the eighties. Athens had blue and white jerseys with a figure of Zeus. That graphic appeared on blue trucks and dumpsters that stretched from the Navy Yard to Germantown. Then, one day in the late '90s, the Manos brothers got hit with a racketeering indictment, and seemingly overnight, the trucks and dumpsters turned a bright red and sprouted roses.

"Have a seat, Frankie." Bobby De Rosa gestured to one of the chairs in front of his desk. The Rose placed two glasses on the desk and poured from a bottle of Seagram's V.O.

They exchanged a *salute* and drank.

"So, how goes it?"

Frank knew the Rose was inquiring about the search for the painting. "Not so good, Bobby. We tore through the Caffé, and believe me, there's nothing—"

The Rose held up his hand, signaling Frank to save his breath. Frank's better judgment caused him to cut his story short.

"Did you know that little bastard was in Atlantic City this morning and walked out of some shithole with a fugazi painting under his arm? No, of course you didn't. You know why? Because you were too busy drinking and playing grab-ass with him and that washed up, Barry White looking motherfucker."

"Bobby, listen, the kid doesn't know where it is. If he did, I think he'd turn it over—"

"No, you listen. I think you're forgetting who's paying you. Nick Di Nobile is just like his father. He wants everybody to think he's all innocent, but he's every bit as crafty as his old man. It's either that, or maybe you're thinking of cutting your own deal."

"What?" Frank got out of his chair in protest. He was straining with every fiber of his being not to check over his shoulder. "That's bullshit. You can have your money back, and I'll be back in Florida tonight."

"You ain't goin nowhere Crab," the Rose barked as he reached under the desk.

Frank thought of his kids, thought of Marie. He even thought of the half-smoked cigarette he had flicked away moments ago.

The Rose came up not with a gun, but with a duffel bag. He tossed it across the desk to Frank. "Except the parade."

Frank unzipped the bag and saw two Mummers comic suits inside. He felt the heft of a heavier item sagging in the middle of the bag under the costumes, but thought better of reaching in to check it out in his present surroundings.

"That Caffé belongs to me, along with everything in it. That prick Tony thought he was too good for us, like he was some Passyunk royalty or something, and the kid is even worse. Strutting around the Avenue like George fucking Hamilton or something. You just do the fucking job I paid you for and leave the rest to me."

Frank turned and walked out, the duffel bag over his shoulder. The door slammed closed behind him. The cold air in his lungs made it feel like he had been holding his breath the whole time inside Rosa. He lit a Marlboro and took a deep, satisfying drag, feeling like he had cheated death for at least one more day.

Frank threw the duffel bag in the trunk of the rental car Ralph had reserved for him at Newark Airport. Upon his arrival, he had driven to an Italian deli in Staten Island, where the owner took him into a back room for further instructions.

He hadn't flown into Atlantic City, and he sure hadn't stayed at Resorts.

Frank pulled onto Packer Avenue and drove toward the Caffé. A black Mercedes S 600 pulled out of Gabriel's Wholesale Seafood parking lot and followed a few cars behind.

FLESH AND BLOOD

Nick took a seat at Vecchio's bar. He had been fighting the temptation to wallow in the old familiar hurts. After the events of the past couple of days, his resolve had worn thin and those painful memories beckoned like the only loyal friends he had.

Nick opened a bottle of Amarone, not bothering with a glass. He walked over to the vintage jukebox, reached behind, and pressed the power button. The machine lit up. Nick scanned the selections he once knew by heart and could call out by letter and number. It was the musical equivalent of drunk dialing, and Nick was totally in. He figured he'd start slow with a Kim Weston number, "Helpless."

Yeah, that hurts real good, he thought, taking a long pull from the bottle.

Beto peeked out through the kitchen door window, saw Nick at the jukebox with the bottle in his hand, and decided to stay in the kitchen.

Nick was wading into the deep end of the pool, and the heartbreak reunion was in full swing. All the old crew were invited; Teddy, Marvin, Levi, and David RSVP'd. Then the Delfonics crashed the party.

Grace doesn't know this side of me. She doesn't know who I was. Let's face it, who I still am. If she did, she'd be gone in a second. She thinks I'm some fucking saint. If she only knew I'm the motherfucking devil.

Teddy started singing "Love T.K.O.," and as if on cue, Angie Romano came walking through the front door. Nick was leaning against the jukebox with both arms. He shook his head ever so slightly. It was at moments like this Nick thought maybe there was a God. *And he has an exquisitely cruel sense of humor.*

There are women who would take one look at a guy like Nick in this situation and pour him a cup of black coffee. And then there are those who would grab a glass and join him. Angie was decidedly one of the latter.

Angie placed two wine glasses on the bar and took a seat like she had an appointment.

"You want to take a seat and have a civilized drink with me like a human being?" Angie, unlike Grace, had seen this side of him before. Nick sat down and poured two glasses, draining the bottle. They sat there and drank and listened to the jukebox like two veterans of a long-forgotten war. All that remained were the scars.

David Ruffin's "My Whole World Ended" continued the mood for Nick.

"What happened last night?" Angie inquired.

"Nothing. I wasn't feeling good. I'm sorry I left without saying goodbye."

"Which time?" she jabbed.

"I deserve that," Nick acknowledged. "But you weren't exactly innocent yourself."

"Relax, Nick, I didn't come here to fight about the past,

as much as I might love the soundtrack. That was always the problem with you; you saw yourself as some prince on a white horse."

"Still do." Nick's tone was a little mocking as he raised his glass.

"That's hysterical, Nick, but did you ever stop to think for even one second? What does that make me, some evil queen?"

Nick was about to make a crack about *if the shoe fits* but decided silence was the safer option.

"Yep, that's your problem. You always thought of yourself as some heroic figure, like in one of your books. And the rest of us as what, supporting characters? Take a good look around this Caffé Nick. See all these paintings? Maybe you're not as different from your father as you always thought, just because you traded Passyunk Avenue for Ocean Drive or whatever the fuck they call that road. Life went on here after you left, in case you were wondering. And all these people in these paintings? The one thing they all have in common is they're all dead. And people like me and Gary and Joey? We're flesh and blood."

Nick looked Angie up and down. Her words hit pretty hard and true, but he wasn't ready to give her that satisfaction just yet.

"Some of us are even more flesh than I remember."

Angie's eyes flashed death rays, and she would have punched Nick in the face if he didn't smile that infuriating smile and put up his hands in surrender as she balled her fist. She settled for a tap on the shoulder.

"I look fucking *good,* and you know it." Angie smiled as she said it. "And I suppose you think all that salt and

pepper hair makes you look distinguished, old man?"
She brushed his hair with her fingers as she said it. She
withdrew just as quickly and turned serious again. "Look,
don't think I don't still have feelings for you. God help
me, I wish I didn't, but we don't have time for all that
right now. I came here to tell you something important.
You're in danger."

"No shit."

"I'm serious, Nick. I hear things at the Paradise."

"Really? Did you ever hear who killed Jimmy?"

Angie looked genuinely hurt by the remark. She finished her drink and gathered her handbag.

"I'm sorry, Angie. That wasn't fair. Don't leave."

"You're damn right it's not fair. He was my friend too."
She settled back onto the stool but folded her arms in front
of her. "You need to worry about yourself, Nicky, and the
people who are still here. Jimmy had his own demons, and
none of us—not me, not you, not Tina—could save him."

"What's Tina up to these days anyway?"

"Struggling, just like the rest of us. Just like you."

"I'm not struggling," Nick protested.

"Really? Be careful, Nick, your pride is showing." She
was right, and Nick knew it. "Mostly, just be careful. And
stay far away from that snake Bobby De Rosa."

"You mean Tina's old sugar daddy—that Bobby De
Rosa?"

"There you go judging again. Tina was my best girlfriend. We had no secrets back then, and believe me,
the closest that old creep ever got to Tina was three feet
across the bar."

Something Angie said earlier was coming back to

Nick now.

"Who's Joey?"

"What?" Angie looked confused.

"You said people like you, Gary, and Joey are flesh and blood."

"Yeah? Aren't we?"

"Joey who?"

Angie looked at him like he was an alien. "Joey. Your DJ. Tina's son?"

Nick's head was spinning. He was starting to feel like he'd felt the other night in the men's room of the Paradise.

"Are you okay?" Angie was holding on to him now. Without preamble, she kissed him hard on the lips. Somehow, that snapped him out of his spell. In the past, it had always had the opposite effect. "I'm sorry, I shouldn't have done that."

"Yeah," Nick muttered. "Don't ever do that again."

That made Angie giggle, and for a moment, Nick heard that girl from so many years ago and pictured the cherry blossoms falling around her face.

"The kid is Tina's son?"

"I just assumed you knew. I mean, after all, he does work here, and he was always around your dad."

"Who's his father?" Nick asked.

Now it was Angie who looked like she was going to pass out. "Jesus Christ, Nick, you really are a piece of work. This is exactly what I was talking about."

"I don't understand. Why are you getting mad at me?"

"Why? Because for as smart as you supposedly are, with all your alleged sophistication and culture and your books and your music, sometimes you're just as oblivious as the rest of these barbarians on the Avenue. Think, Nick. You seriously mean to tell me you never noticed? His smile, his walk, his mannerisms."

"But how?"

"How the fuck you think? Do the math."

"I should never have come back." Nick looked deflated.

"What's the matter, a bit too much reality for you? So all this other stuff—your father dying, people wanting you dead, Del Ciotto up your ass, and I'm not too modest to say it, seeing me after all these years—and this is the thing that sets you off? That your best friend left a son behind? Maybe you *should* leave, Nick. Just run away. That's what you do best anyway, right?"

"Who's not being fair now, Angie?" Nick was hurt by her little diatribe, but he knew she was right. Angie always had a way of cutting through the bullshit.

She saw the hurt on his face, had mercy on him, and put her hand over his on the bar. No apologies. No explanations. Just her touch. That's all it ever took.

"I Wish It Would Rain" started up on the jukebox. Angie walked behind the bar and opened two Peronis. She extended the neck of her bottle for Nick to clink.

"To Jimmy," she said.

Nick clinked back. "To Jimmy."

She walked back around the bar, sat close to Nick, and buried her face in his shoulder. They stayed there like that until the song ended.

YOU CAN'T SMOKE IN HERE

Nick was a little late getting back to the Caffé. He had stood under the showerhead for a long, long time trying to process the crushing avalanche of information that had enveloped him. The warm water helped him achieve a state where he could begin to assemble the facts, people, and theories that had blanketed him since his return. He strained to synthesize the old knowledge with the new revelations, just like he struggled to reconcile the old avenue with the changing landscape. He understood why some people constantly seek refuge in the comfort of the classics, people like Anthony Di Nobile. *There's nothing new under the sun*, Nick thought. He recalled seeing that phrase somewhere recently but couldn't remember where.

When Nick's fingers had begun to prune up and the water turned cold, he'd wrapped himself in a scratchy towel, dressed quickly, and hustled back to the Caffé to meet the Mad Painter of Rittenhouse Square.

"You can't smoke in here." Nick could hear Alberto's voice booming from the bar before he even walked out of the kitchen. Nick shook his head, knowing full well he what he was about to encounter.

Sure enough, Virgil was perched at the bar puffing away on an Opus X, his surgical mask tucked under his chin. His hairstyle (if you could call it that) would have filled Don King with envy. He couldn't have appeared crazier had he lopped off his ear and handed it to the hostess. Nick gave Alberto a reassuring look as he weaved his way through the room, indicating that he would handle it.

"Hey, Picasso, care to join me outside for a word?" Nick had already opened the door and gestured with a sweep of his arm, as if he were inviting Virgil to join him in the library for cognacs. To Nick's pleasant surprise, Virgil complied without protest.

"You're late," the painter declared as they stepped outside.

"I'm sorry," Nick replied. "But did you have to light that before I arrived? The dining room is still half full." Nick said a silent prayer of thanks that Gary had run out to the liquor store and hadn't witnessed the transgression. "What are you drinking?"

Virgil seemed to think for a long time before answering. "A mojito."

Nick opened the door and hollered in. "Alberto. A mojito, please." He closed the door, looked over at Virgil smiling like a loon, and opened the door again. "Alberto, make it two, please."

"What about my pasta vazool?"

Nick was starting to wonder how much of this was real, how much was an act, and how the hell his father was friends with this lunatic.

"Virgil, you can have a fifty-five-gallon drum of *pasta e fagioli*, a bucket of mojitos, and Christ, I already bought you a box of Opus X. Just please chill the fuck out."

"I'm sorry, Nick." To Nick's surprise, Virgil actually seemed contrite. He put the cigar out in the planter after peeling off the band and pulled the mask back up over his nose and mouth.

"Thank you, Virgil," Nick said somewhat ceremoniously. "Can I ask you a personal question?" Virgil shrugged like he didn't mind. "What's up with the mask? Are you sick or something? I mean, maybe you shouldn't be smoking all these cigars. Pardon me if I'm being too nosy."

"I'm not sick. Not yet. But soon, everyone will be."

Nick immediately regretted asking the question. *Maybe it wasn't an act.* "I'm not sure I get you, Virgil."

Virgil looked at him with a serious expression. "A plague is coming, Nick."

"I don't doubt it." *What else can I say to that,* thought Nick.

"I know everyone thinks I'm crazy. I hear what they all say about me in the park. But you know who didn't think so? Your dad. He treated me with respect, and he listened to me."

Nick felt bad for Virgil and hoped he hadn't gone too far. "I don't think you're crazy, Virgil. Thank you for being a friend to my father." *Who am I to judge anyway? This man was probably closer to my father the past nineteen years than I was.*

Alberto came out with two mojitos on a tray.

Thank God, Nick thought. He thanked Alberto and asked him to hold Virgil's seat at the bar and put in for two vazools. *Fuck it, I might as well join him.*

Virgil pulled down his mask and raised his glass. "To Murillo."

Nick knew better than to ask questions. "To Murillo."

They drank. The mint was fresh and gave off a pleasant aroma.

"I know what you're thinking," Virgil said.

"I didn't say anything," Nick protested.

"He was a Spanish painter in the 1600s. He didn't come to prominence until the plague ravaged Spain, and he was one of the only painters left in Seville. The others had either fled to Madrid or perished. So you see, it is possible to flourish even when surrounded by pestilence and death."

"That's a beautiful story, Virgil. Would I know any of his paintings?"

"No, you definitely would not," Virgil stated abruptly and definitively.

"How can you be so sure?" Nick asked.

Virgil didn't answer. He just raised a lanky arm and pointed a bony, arthritic finger at Vecchio's front window, toward the painting of a young man on a horse.

THE EYES OF SAINT LUCY

As Virgil devoured two bowls of his eponymous soup, Nick went to meet Gary up in the office. He told him about his visit to the Antiquary, the painting in his trunk, and the Mercedes. Gary didn't appear surprised by any of it, but then, not much surprised the big man these days. Nick warned him that Virgil was in the house.

"He don't bother me none," Gary said. "Lots of motherfuckers round here wearing masks. At least I can see his."

"Let me ask you something, G. Was he always like this?"

"He has good days and bad days, I suppose, just like you and me. All I know, your old man had a soft spot for him. Said he was some kinda modern-day Master or something. When he talks about art, he sounds like a professor or something. Other times, he act just like a little kid."

Nick was drifting off. He was thinking of Angie and their conversation.

"By the way, where's the kid tonight?"

"He off tonight. Probably with that fine girl of his. I know that's where I would be, I was him."

That certainly sounds like Jimmy, Nick thought, but didn't mention anything to Gary. He couldn't handle that discussion and Virgil in the same night.

Suddenly, there were hurried footsteps on the staircase, and Beto burst into the room. He was rambling on about something. He could make out "Virgil" and "Del Ciotto" and what sounded like "Santa Lucia." Gary was off his chair, through the door and halfway down the stairs before Nick could react. He followed him down the darkened staircase and into the light of the dining room.

Sid Del Ciotto was in Virgil's face and had him pinned up against the bar. Virgil's blue surgical mask was crumpled up in a ball on the floor. Gary separated the men with his bulk as the dining patrons watched with rapt attention. They didn't seem at all offended. Quite a few were smiling and whispering in the ears of their tablemates. For some, this is what they had come in hopes of witnessing. Gary had his hands up in front of Del Ciotto's face, his palms spread open in a gesture meant to be overtly peaceful yet subtly menacing. Few could pull that combination off so well. Gary took a few short, shuffling steps forward, and Del Ciotto had no choice but to take a seat back at his table.

Sid picked up a small side plate, and for a second, Nick feared (for Del Ciotto, that is) he was about to hurl it across the room. Instead, he was holding it with one hand and pointing at it with the other.

"You see what this vagrant put on *my* table?"

Gary spoke softly but unmistakably. "First of all, it's *my* table and you're a guest. Second, all I see is two olives."

"It's not just that, it's what he said." Del Ciotto explained that Virgil had taken two blue cheese stuffed olives from the bar and arranged them next to each other before placing the plate in front of Del Ciotto.

"Okay, so? What did he say?" Gary asked.

Before Del Ciotto could respond, Virgil spoke up behind him.

"I said, the eyes of Saint Lucy are upon you. They shine their light upon your transgressions."

Del Ciotto started pointing again. "Yes, that's what he said, the crazy fuck! Why do you let people like that in here anyway?"

Gary looked at Virgil, and after a few seconds, he turned back to Del Ciotto. "You know what? That's exactly what people say to me about you. And I'm starting to believe they're right. So why don't you do yourself a favor? How 'bout you give the Caffé a break and go sample some of the other fine cuisine this Avenue has to offer—before I forget that you're an FBI agent and I'm a felon."

Del Ciotto stood up in a huff, made a big production of tossing his linen on top of the plate, and threw a crumpled ten-dollar bill on the table. He sidestepped past Gary, who had his giant mitts on his hips. Beto went back to the kitchen, and Freddie, the waiter, cleared the table. Everyone else went back to their meals. Gary uncrumpled the ten and handed it to the hostess. "Cheap motherfucker," he mumbled under his breath.

Gary walked over to the bar, Nick right behind, and they sat on either side of Virgil. He was smoothing out the surgical mask on the bar, his head hanging down. He looked like a little kid expecting to be reprimanded. Nick thought the man was about to burst into tears.

"I'm sorry, Gary," he whispered softly.

"You good, my man." Gary rubbed him on the back, and Alberto set a fresh mojito in front of him. "Just don't be fucking with my olives; them jawns expensive as shit."

Nick busted out laughing, and even Virgil shook with a little chuckle.

ART HISTORY 101

The Parable of the Lost Son

Jesus continued: "There was a man who had two sons. The younger one said to his father, 'Father, give me my share of the estate.' So he divided his property between them.

"Not long after that, the younger son got together all he had, set off for a distant country and there squandered his wealth in wild living. After he had spent everything, there was a severe famine in that whole country, and he began to be in need. So he went and hired himself out to a citizen of that country, who sent him to his fields to feed pigs. He longed to fill his stomach with the pods that the pigs were eating, but no one gave him anything.

"When he came to his senses, he said, 'How many of my father's hired servants have food to spare, and here I am starving to death! I will set out and go back to my father and say to him: Father, I have sinned against heaven and against you. I am no longer worthy to be called your son; make me like one of your hired servants.' So he got up and went to his father.

"But while he was still a long way off, his father saw him and was filled with compassion for him; he ran to his son, threw his arms around him and kissed him.

Luke 15:11

By 10:30, the place had pretty well cleared out. One couple remained in the corner. They seemed engaged in some pretty heavy negotiations, and from the looks of it, the guy was on the losing side. Freddie gave them their privacy, and no one was eager to rush them along. That's what was great about the Caffé. If you were a guest from out of town, you weren't treated like an intruder, and if you were a local, you felt like it was an extension of your living room but with better food.

Virgil had recovered from his little episode and had launched into a lightning round of art history a la Vecchio. He identified the Caffé paintings, the original artists, themes, methods, and controversies swirling around each of them. Each painting seemed to have its own scandalous history, questionable attribution, or outright tragedy attached to it. He paused at the painting of the young man on a horse that bore his signature.

"I painted this for your father last Christmas. It's a copy from a series by Bartolomé Esteban Murillo, the Spaniard I told you about earlier."

"It's stunning, Virgil. I especially like the way the red cape on the rider draws your eye."

"Good for you, Nick," Virgil responded. "You're on the right track."

"Does it have a name?" Gary asked.

"Departure of the Prodigal," Virgil said. "It is one of six paintings in a series based on the biblical story of the prodigal son."

"I thought Rembrandt painted the Prodigal Son," Nick said.

"He did. Multiple times throughout his career, as did Murillo and countless others."

Virgil spoke of Rembrandt's tumultuous life and financial struggles, how he sold virtually everything to avoid his creditors. His personal life was also filled with sorrow, Virgil explained.

"Rembrandt revisited the theme of the prodigal throughout his life. His suffering changed the way he treated the subject over his career. His last work is thought to be *The Return of the Prodigal Son* in 1669, the same year as his death. His son, Titus, had already died the year before. The version hanging in the Hermitage is a huge work, over eight by six feet. It was likely finished by the pupils at his school. That wasn't uncommon. Don't forget, Nick, this was a business first and foremost. The painting you are looking for, if it exists, is the first, original prototype of *The Return of the Prodigal*, except on a smaller scale and created solely by Rembrandt."

Nick had brought in the painting he picked up at the Antiquary. He unwrapped it, and Virgil looked at it like a long-lost friend.

"This one is my interpretation of Rembrandt's *Prodigal in the Tavern*. Rembrandt painted himself as the Prodigal, and I decided to insert your father in Rembrandt's place as a tribute."

No one said anything. They all stood around the painting, which was lying flat on a table, in silence. Finally, Gary walked away toward the kitchen.

"Where are you going?" Nick called after him.

"To get a hammer and nails. That should be hanging somewhere special."

Gary returned with a small kit containing hooks, nails, and a hammer. It was decided that it should hang above the jukebox so people could look at Tony raising a glass as they picked out their songs.

They all took a step back to admire Virgil's work. Gary played "The Thrill is Gone" on the jukebox and closed his eyes as he did a little air guitar tribute, pounding his palm with the back of his hand between riffs. Virgil rocked side to side, shifting his weight from one foot to another. It was the closest he could get to dancing.

By then, the lone couple had made their exit. The two of them had that unmistakable look people give off at the end of a love affair. That fitful, wrenching stage of parting when one is trying to hold on desperately as the other pulls away. Nick thought back to the fateful day when he packed his bags nineteen years ago. His only plan had been to go somewhere far enough away to make the pain stop. Nineteen years later, all he had to do was close his eyes and think of those days and the pain was fresh as a newly dug grave.

When the song was over, they walked over to the bar and settled in for a long night of drinking, reminiscing, and, most importantly, plotting.

IL SEGRETO

Walking into Il Segreto had been like stepping into a reliable, cushy time machine. The décor was classic but somehow never tired, just like the food. Segreto used good ingredients, consistent recipes, and had an atmosphere that made tourists and out of towners feel like they'd discovered some private club. They just couldn't wait to bring back their friends to show them how cool they were. For locals, it provided reliability and, above all, discretion.

Their meal was in a semi-private room, made fully private for their visit. Any wanderers who might make a wrong turn out of the men's room were met with an icy stare. Reggiano Parmigiano was sliced extra thin and placed out at the beginning of the meal. The thin slices practically exploded on your tongue in tiny crystals of umami flavor meant to prep the taste buds for the symphony yet to come. A bottle of Pio Cesare Barolo was uncorked, and the Rose tasted it. After nodding his approval, he stacked the slices of cheese into one mound, effectively defeating all that careful paper-thin slicing, and crammed the whole glob in his mouth. He gulped the glass of Barolo before he finished chewing.

Frank did his best to hide his disgust. He honestly couldn't tell whether it was some test to gauge his response, or if the man was genuinely oblivious. The Rose was known for playing these little loyalty tests, and they generally revolved around food, drink, and women. Frank wasn't taking the bait. He ordered the Lobster Francaise, excused himself, and walked to the men's room. As he stood at the urinal, he heard the door open. The kid moved to the sink and began to wash his hands.

"I can't fucking stand when he does that." Joey was saying it into the mirror, but it was clearly intended for Frank.

Frank played it like just another nuanced layer of the Rose's loyalty games.

"I'm not sure what you mean," Frank responded blandly. He stood next to the kid for a second as he washed his hands also. He hurriedly dried his hands with a paper towel and maneuvered past him on his way back out to the table.

"Hey, Frank." The kid looked at him through the mirror, and Frank locked eyes with him that way for a few seconds. "If you want to find out who controls you, ask yourself who can't you criticize."

"Thanks, Joey, I'll remember that." Frank let that sink in as he walked back to the table. It was an odd thing for a young guy to say. Frank had to admit though, it was pretty fucking true.

The Rose had his own ideas about where Tony had hid the painting. He was adamant it was in the Caffé and seemed to speak with a certainty that suggested he had some inside information he wasn't sharing. Frank resolved himself to have one last heart-to-heart with Nicky to encourage him to just hand the cursed thing over and go back to Lauderdale on the next available flight. If Nicky was holding out, he was doing a great job. On top of all that, Nick's head seemed like it was in the clouds the last few times they spoke, like he was lost in the past. If it was an act, it was Oscar-worthy.

They finished their meal, and the kid grabbed the check before anyone else could reach for it. Frank took it as a classy act for a young guy. *He might be broker than me, if that's possible*, Frank thought. His only visible source of income was the few days DJ'ing at Vecchio. Then again, he might have money coming in from another source.

The Rose looked down at his phone in disgust. "Fucking goomah. They're worse than wives." The Rose walked to the bar, presumably to respond to the goomah's text. The thought of any woman playing that role for the gruesomely ugly Bobby De Rosa was more than a little disgusting. Frank tried to erase the mental picture the thought conjured.

Frank shook Joey's hand and thanked him for dinner. Joey surprised him by asking him straight out, "You ready?"

Frank answered like every other down-and-out old-head did when asked that question by a cocksure youngster. "Since before you were born, my young friend."

Joey got a kick out of that and gave Frank a wink.

Good-looking little bastard. Frank laughed and rubbed the kid on the shoulder.

"Hey, Frank," Joey called after him just as he was about to walk down the steps. Joey walked close to him and spoke in a hushed tone. "Ever notice how he jumps every time the goomah calls?"

Frank took a good measure of the kid before he responded. What he was insinuating was pretty extreme. Maybe it was another loyalty trap set by the Rose.

Frank *had* noticed, and had filed it away with lots of other things about the Rose that didn't make sense. So when he finally answered the kid, he said the only thing he could under the circumstances.

"You know what, Joey, I never did notice." And he winked at the kid before he walked down the stairs.

The Rose was at the bar having an after-dinner drink. He held his phone at waist level and read a text on an encrypted app. *Meet me at 12:00. I'm sleepy.*

The Rose knew that meant to meet at the rest stop on I-95 in Newark, Delaware, at 11:00. It was about a forty-five-minute drive, so he finished his limoncello and walked with Joey to the parking lot. Both cars were kept up by the valet booth, so the valet simply handed them their keys.

The Rose palmed the valet a ten.

Joey tipped him a fifty.

The valet thanked them both, made a mental note, and passed a silent judgment. That was the real underground currency of the neighborhood, and it fluctuated more than the stock market.

One stock rises, another falls.

At the age of eighteen, Joey was learning the most important lesson of any market—diversification.

The Rose drove off first, after responding to the text.

Joey let him get about a block away and allowed two cars to pass before he followed. He fell back to a greater distance once both cars got on I-95 south.

THE INDIAN IN THE SIDEWALK

Frank left the meeting and stepped out into the cold. The Rose had offered him a ride back with the kid, but Frank politely declined, using the excuse that he was stopping by an old friend's house in the neighborhood. The truth was, Frank had a lot to think about. New Year's Day was fast approaching, and he had preparations to make. He figured a long walk back along the Avenue was just the right thing to get his head straight. It didn't hurt that he would be walking right by a particular house, and he couldn't resist the temptation to observe from a distance.

Frank walked south on Seventh Street until it intersected Passyunk Avenue and continued his walk back toward the Caffé. He passed the brightly lit cheesesteak palaces, thinking, when was the last time he had a genuine "wiz wit."

He continued closer to the heart of the Avenue and paused near the Acme supermarket. He diverted down Tenth Street past Annunciation Church, where he intended to turn back toward Passyunk. But first, there was something he needed to see. It was a two-story row-home, much like the others on the block. Christmas lights still illuminated the brick front and railing, and a nativity scene was carefully assembled in a bay window. The boxes outside told a tale of Christmas magic for the children who lived inside. A cardboard box that had contained a 65-inch Samsung flat-screen rested against the front wall, waiting for trash pickup. The lights were on, and Frank thought he could make out some figures inside through the drapes. He wondered what they were doing in there, Frank Jr., his wife, and the grandkids. *Probably eating butter cookies and pizzelles.*

It had been years since Frank had a homemade pizzelle. He bought the boxed ones in Publix, but they were horrible. He thought back to his mother's baked specialties. She always went out of her way to make cookies and biscotti for the neighborhood, until Frank's father burned her arm with a pizzelle iron. He tried to make like it was an accident, but Frank knew better, even though his mother played along in the cover-up. She never baked again.

Frank kept moving before someone came to the door and discovered him lurking around. He took two of his fingers and kissed them before gesturing toward the house. It was all he could think to do. He walked fast, back to Passyunk, deciding to hit the Paradise before making his way to Vecchio. As he did, he walked over one of the many decorative medallions set into the sidewalks of Passyunk Avenue. They were the size of manhole covers and depicted a Native American in a headdress with the neighborhood community organization's name around the perimeter. It was meant to acknowledge the indigenous people who inhabited the area centuries ago, but turned out to be a controversial issue as the headdress was more accurately worn by the Indians of the Western Plains. There was a movement to have them removed and replaced with something more politically correct.

He wasn't sure exactly why, but Frank felt like he had a lot in common with the figure in the medallion. Maybe it was because he had faced plenty of discrimination and stereotyping himself as an Italian growing up when he did. More likely, it was because since his return he felt like a useless relic, unsure of what he even stood for anymore.

THE REST STOP

Joey was able to follow the Rose pretty easily once they were both on the highway. Traffic was light, but there was enough volume for Joey to tuck behind a car or two without being detected. Even if he was, it wasn't exactly unusual to be driving on 95. Once the Rose moved to an exit, Joey would have to make a quick decision whether to follow. That would depend on several factors, most importantly, where the Rose eventually decided to get off the highway.

They passed Lincoln Financial Field, and soon the airport came and went. The Rose was cruising in the left lane with no sign of slowing up. Joey checked his gas gauge. He had a quarter tank and cursed himself for not filling up earlier. Then again, he had no idea he would be driving to Delaware.

South Philly guys mostly drive to the shore, New York, Delco, and occasionally, the Poconos. Delaware is not a popular destination. Joey could remember attending a wedding at the DuPont Hotel in Wilmington and taking a ride with a guy to buy cartons of cigarettes, but that was it.

They kept going past Wilmington. Joey was going to run out of gas soon. He saw signs for a travel plaza and decided to give up the recon mission and pull in to gas up and take a leak. Two cars ahead, the Rose put on his turn signal and moved into the entrance lane for the rest stop. One of the cars between them fortuitously exited as well. Joey slid in behind.

The Rose pulled into a spot at the plaza. Joey drove in the opposite direction. There was no way he could explain this as a coincidence if he was spotted, so he was careful to find a spot a safe distance away with multiple lanes of parked cars between them. The Rose would not pass anywhere near him when he got back on 95. Joey was facing away and did his best to observe through his rearview mirror, which he adjusted for a better angle.

He could make out part of a vehicle pulling up alongside the Rose's BMW. The two cars were pointed in opposite directions, driver's sides facing each other like two cop cars in a parking lot. He couldn't make out the person in the other car, which looked like a late model black Mercedes. He couldn't be sure, but it looked like the guy in the Mercedes passed something over to the Rose. Joey was starting to regret drinking all those beers at Segreto and was looking around the car for something to piss in when both cars began to pull out.

Joey hunched down until he thought it was safe, then jogged into the rest stop to relieve himself. The best explanation for what he witnessed, he figured, was the Rose was picking up a cash drop, though the whole scenario seemed a bit extreme for that. There were one hundred easier ways to do that, and none of them required a trip to a Delaware rest stop. Picking up money, or laundry for that matter, was something the Rose usually asked Joey to do.

Joey returned to his car and drove past the plaza to the adjacent Sunoco station. He was about to pull up to an available pump when he noticed he wasn't the only one running low on fuel. A black Mercedes was also stopped, and a man was standing next to it pumping gas.

Joey made a quick left and drove to the air pump instead. He wasn't one hundred percent certain it was the same Mercedes, but it sure looked like it. Joey parked next to the air pump and again used the rearview mirror to watch the Mercedes. When the man finished filling his tank, he turned to return the nozzle. Joey recognized him right away. He had been in the Caffé a few times when Joey was DJing. Joey thought the man was trying too hard, right down to his wardrobe, which seemed overdone and contrived, like a sheep playing at being a wolf. It had stuck in his brain.

The DJ booth is excellent for that. Everyone thinks you're like some anonymous robot up there. They do things in front of you as if you're invisible, like some appliance. But Joey watched everything and everybody, and he learned. Silently, he absorbed it all, took notes, and learned the game. The one everyone played but no one talked about. He soaked it up like a tiramisu soaked up espresso and vowed to master the dance; that sinister *tarantella* where everyone held hands and smiled at each other while hiding a dagger until just the right moment. It was like that song Gary always requested, "Smiling Faces" by the Undisputed Truth. *What a great name for a band*, Joey had thought when Gary first turned him on to it.

The lyrics blew him away. *I'm not going out like that*, Joey had resolved, *not like my father*. Joey knew his father hadn't killed himself, and he was pretty sure he knew who had.

So when he recognized Special Agent Del Ciotto as the driver of the Mercedes and the man who had handed over a package to the Rose, he knew he'd struck gold.

SAL MONTE

Virgil was speaking at a manic pace. Nick tried to keep up, but the mad painter of Rittenhouse Square had lapsed into another persona. Despite his mania, or maybe because of it, Nick was convinced the secret to locating the missing Prodigal, if it existed, was hidden somewhere in his ramblings. He had some wild theories, but there was no denying the man possessed an encyclopedic knowledge of lost paintings and newly discovered, alleged masterpieces.

Virgil was especially fixated on something he called the *Isleworth Mona Lisa*. The theory went that da Vinci had painted this earlier portrait of a young Lisa del Giocondo. The more extreme position was that the painting hanging in the Louvre wasn't painted by Leonardo da Vinci at all, and the "Earlier Mona Lisa," as it was also referred to, was in fact the one and only. It had been in storage since 1975 in a Swiss vault, Virgil explained and had come to prominence more recently due to a dispute over its ownership.

"Have you ever heard of the *Salvator Mundi*?" Virgil asked.

Much to Nick's surprise, Gary spoke up.

"Yeah, I know that cat." He looked at Nick for confirmation. "He from Twelfth and Wolf back in the day."

"That's Sal Monte, you crazy motherfucker." Nick laughed and shook his head, wondering who was crazier, Virgil or Gary.

"The *Salvator Mundi*, or 'Savior of the World.'" Virgil went on to describe Leonardo's painting of the face of Christ. "For years it was thought to be a fake. Critics scoffed at it. It was purchased for about $1,000 at an estate sale in 2005."

"Where is it now?" Nick asked.

"It was restored and displayed in London. It was sold and flipped a few times until a Russian billionaire purchased it for 127 million."

"Jesus Christ," Nick gasped.

Gary just whistled.

"That's not even the best part. In 2017 the Russian listed it for auction at Christie's. It sold for 450 million to a Saudi Prince."

"That's insane," Nick exclaimed.

"No," Virgil responded. "What's truly insane is that your missing Prodigal would sell for much, much more. The only paintings that could possibly be valued higher are *The Concert* by Vermeer and *Christ in the Storm*, Rembrandt's only known seascape." Virgil gestured to the copy of the *Storm* at the rear of the Caffé. "And both of those went missing in the Gardner Heist in 1990, as you well know."

Virgil told the history of the Murillo Prodigal as well.

"Murillo, too, painted the Return of the Prodigal multiple times. It was originally commissioned by the La Santa Caridad, a charitable brotherhood. It was displayed at the Hospital de la Caridad in Seville, Spain, as part of a series. Now, only two of the six remain. The other four are copies."

"So where is the original Murillo Prodigal? Hidden in some vault?" Nick asked.

"Not at all," Virgil answered. "It's proudly displayed in the National Gallery of Art in Washington, DC. The provenance states simply that it was 'removed by government decree' or some such nonsense. Meanwhile, back at the Caridad, they are referred to as stolen."

"So, what's the upshot of all this?" Nick asked. "I mean, it's all very informative, but what does it mean for us?"

"It means that truth is stranger than fiction and perception is reality in the art world. So maybe it's not so far-fetched Rembrandt painted an earlier, smaller version of the Prodigal, and the version hanging in the Hermitage was finished after his death."

"That's not the part I find far-fetched," Nick responded. "What I find hard to believe is that my father, Anthony Di Nobile, king of the bullshitters, possessed this priceless painting all these years and it's somewhere in here."

"Priceless paintings have been discovered in far less likely places. Klimt's *Portrait of a Lady* was recently discovered in Italy. It was found by a gardener, covered by a trash bag inside a wall covered by ivy. It was presumed stolen decades ago when the empty frame was found near a skylight. All these years, and it had never left the grounds of the gallery," Virgil remarked.

Gary nodded his head in agreement, like he knew that to be true.

Nick and Gary were doing their best to process Virgil's oral dissertation when the Stone Crab appeared at the door, and Virgil clammed up.

Nick unlocked the door to let Frank in.

"Hello, nephew." Frank gave Nick a kiss on the cheek and had a seat at the bar.

"Peroni?" Nick asked.

"Why not?" Frank answered. He was still reeling a little from Joey's comments and his little detour to the land of *Christmas Past*. "I'll have a Dewar's too, if you don't mind."

"I'd like a Dewar's," Virgil chirped.

Gary poured shots all around.

"Ever since y'all been back, this turned into a social club. Somebody best put some money up on this motherfucker," Gary said with feigned outrage.

Virgil reached in his pocket and placed a five on the bar with a worried look. Nick laughed and shook his head gently while handing the bill back to Virgil.

Frank took the lead this time. "Disaster to the wench who did wrong by our Nicky."

Gary, Frank, and Virgil raised their shot glasses and downed their scotch.

"Who's the wench?" Virgil asked Nick in all seriousness.

Nick looked down at his phone like he was getting a call and raised it to his ear, even muttering a fake "Hello" as he walked away from the bar. He couldn't join in that toast, even in jest, after seeing Angie the other day. He walked back to the men's room with the phone against his ear, thinking of the cherry blossoms. His reverie was interrupted by the rude vibration of the phone against his ear. It was a text from Angie. *Can you meet me at Paradise?* Nick didn't hesitate. *I'll be there in 30,* he texted back.

Nick returned to the bar, where he formally introduced Frank to Virgil. The clock was ticking, and Nick had no time for any more feeling-out period.

"Cards on the table time, boys. That goes for you too, big man." Nick grasped Gary on the back reassuringly as he said it but could barely get his hands around his traps. "We either get to the bottom of this thing now, or I'm headed back to Florida after New Year's Day. Let the chips fall where they may. Unc, I know you're under a lot of pressure, but I can't hand over something I ain't got."

"I don't see why you gotta hand over shit anyhow," Gary said.

"See," Nick answered. "That's exactly what I'm talking about. We're never gonna figure this thing out unless we're all pulling in the same direction. Unc, tell them what you told me at the Fontainebleau—everything."

Frank recounted everything he had told Nick at the Bleau Bar, but left out a few incidentals and omitted some names, which was to be expected. It didn't take away from the point of the story. In 1990, Frank drove a smelly fish truck loaded with at least a half-billion dollars of paintings from Boston to South Philly. That part was accepted as fact. Frank was given a cheap copy of a picture for his trouble and had sold it to Tony. *We'll have to take the Crab on his word about that,* thought Nick, but it seemed entirely plausible.

"The Rose thinks he's entitled to the painting for some reason, if not the whole Caffé," Nick said.

"Over my dead body." Gary stood and spread his arms, like he was inviting the world to take a shot at the champ.

"That's exactly what we're trying to avoid," Nick said, but the big man had had enough.

"Tell that rat cocksucker to come see me," Gary said to no one in particular. "I ain't shy about letting that hot shit fly. We'll see what's what." Gary stormed off into the kitchen.

Virgil was visibly upset and started twitching uncontrollably. He reached for two olives but stopped when Nick wagged his finger at him like he was a naughty schoolboy.

Frank picked up his Marlboros and lighter and walked to the door. He lit up and took a deep drag as he surveyed the lights and storefronts of the Avenue. It was plenty different from the old days, but some things still looked familiar. He looked for the brick fronts, the telephone poles, the cornices on the roofline, anything to help him get his bearings. Something Gary said had made his ears perk up. He didn't just call Bobby De Rosa a cocksucker. Frank had heard a hundred people call him that, and worse, himself included. Gary had called him a *rat* cocksucker. Of all the things he had heard the Rose called over the years, rat wasn't one of them. Frank reflected on this and dropped his barely smoked cigarette on the pavement. He put it out with the bottom of his shoe, right on top of the Indian in the sidewalk. Frank walked back in.

Nick had managed to calm Gary down enough to get him back out from the kitchen.

"Look, it's late. It's been a long day for all of us. Let's call it a night, get some rest, and reconvene tomorrow," Nick said.

Frank nodded in agreement.

Gary said, "Fine by me."

Virgil saluted Nick.

"You got a ride home?" Nick asked Virgil. Virgil shrugged. "I'll call you an Uber," Nick said and took out his phone to do just that. He opened a text from Grace first. *You okay? I haven't heard from you all day.* Nick responded with a quick reply. *I'm fine, sorry, been a little busy. I'll call you when I get home.* Nick realized he had referred to his grandmother's house as "home." He hadn't precisely meant it like that, like *home*, and he hoped Grace understood too.

"Frank, do me a favor. Make sure Virgil gets in his Uber safely," Nick said. Frank assured him he would.

Nick hugged Gary. "You good, G?"

"Fuck yeah," Gary answered.

"Cool. I'll see you tomorrow." Nick knew nothing more was going to get accomplished that night. They all needed some time to let their collective knowledge marinate and come up with a better plan. He'd have been lying to himself, though, if he didn't admit he had rushed to wrap things up so he could get over to the Paradise.

Nick allowed his mind to wander on the walk over. Maybe he was reading too much into her text, but he couldn't help thinking of old times and what could have been—what should have been. The last few days, the combination of seeing Angie again, being around the Caffé, listening to those songs was intoxicating. Well, that and the fact he was actually intoxicated. Whatever it was, whatever she wanted, wherever it went, Nick didn't care. He was ready to go along with it all.

Nick texted Angie when he was outside, and she unlocked the door to let him in. She greeted him with a kiss on the cheek and locked the door behind them. It was 3:00 a.m., way past closing time, and the place was empty. The chairs were on the tables, and Nick could smell that sickening scent of disinfectant in the air. He followed as Angie led him to the back of the bar. Her eyes cut to a small dining room that was partitioned off from the main room.

"Nick, there's someone here who would like to talk to you." Angie looked down at the bar, pretending to wipe the spotless surface with a dirty rag.

He felt sick to his stomach. He glanced over at the dreaded men's room, turned to check the front door, and for a moment, thought about bolting for it but remembered Angie had locked it when they came in.

Maybe it was the alcohol, maybe it was the memory of Jimmy, but Nick was fed up with everything: The Caffé, the Rose, the painting, his whole fucking life. *Fuck this*, he thought as he charged into the dining room, ready to accept whatever fate awaited him there; a baseball bat to the ribs, a knife in the back, a bullet in the head.

But it was his disappointment in Angie more than anything else, her seeming betrayal, that drove him into that room.

MIGHTY MICK

Nick could make out a lone figure sitting at a table with his back to the corner of the dining room. The figure seemed familiar to Nick, familiar but changed somehow. Just like the Avenue. Just like every other rotten thing Nick encountered since he returned.

"Tommy? Tommy McKenna? Is that you?"

"Have I gotten that fucking fat?" the red-faced, white-bearded man asked.

"Not at all," Nick answered as he ran over to the man and jumped in his lap. "But is it too late to tell you what I want for Christmas?" Nick gave him a big loud smooch on the face as Kris Kringle pushed him off in violent protest.

"Get off me, you crazy guinea," Tommy yelled.

Nick was so happy to see his grade school best friend (and not be stabbed or shot), he could hardly contain himself.

"I missed you, harp."

"Hey, watch it with the ethnic slurs."

"You fucking started it."

Angie interrupted the reunion with two Rolling Rocks. "I see you two boys are getting along."

"Just like old times," Nick said as he raised his bottle.

Tommy raised his bottle in return. "Just like old times," he said, but a bit subdued.

Angie left the two childhood friends to catch up and placed the keys on the table.

"Lock up when you're done and throw the keys back in through the mail slot. I'll pick them up in the morning. And clean up after yourselves."

"Okay, Mom." Tommy cracked, and Nick laughed. Just like they were back in St. Nicholas of Tolentine. Tommy must have been reading his mind because he raised his bottle again. "To the good old days."

Nick drank. "Yeah, but they weren't always so good."

"I guess you're right," Tommy said. "By the way, I miss your pop. Now that's what we should be drinking to." Tommy got up and went to the cooler to fetch two fresh Rocks.

Nick had overcome his initial shock, as pleasant as it was. When Tommy sat back down, he asked the inevitable question. "So, Tommy, I gotta ask to what do I owe this honor… at this ungodly hour?" *Suddenly I'm a pretty popular guy*, Nick thought as he said this.

"You know, Nick, when my mom died when we were in fifth grade, I came over your house every morning when my old man left for work, and your father made me breakfast. Do you remember?"

"Sure. Runny eggs, sunny side up, and black coffee. Said it would make men out of us."

"That's why I eat them scrambled to this day." Tommy laughed. "True story."

"Well, your old man worked the graveyard shift if I recall correctly."

"My old man was an abusive drunk, and trust me, I recall correctly."

"They were different times, Tommy, these kids today are spoiled."

"They weren't that different. A prick was a prick, even back then."

"I suppose you're right."

"Fucking-*A* I am. Anyway, I never forgot those breakfasts and the way your father spoke to me. Not like an annoying kid, like my father did, but like a person. Like I mattered. Like I wasn't worthless. You know, it was your father who convinced me to enter the police academy."

"And look at you now. Detective Thomas McKenna. *Homicide* Detective McKenna. I bet you made a hundred fifty thousand in overtime this year."

"That's none of your fucking business, wop. And by the way, it's retired Homicide Detective McKenna."

"No shit," Nick said. "Congratulations."

"Thanks, Nicky. I meant what I said about your dad, though. That's why I'm here."

"I should have known," Nick said.

"That's not what I mean. Just listen for a minute. You might learn something, you stubborn dago."

"Here we go with the slurs again."

Tommy stood up and walked around the table. "Let's go sit at the bar. I've got something important to talk to you about."

Nick followed him to the bar and took a seat as Tommy walked behind the bar. Tommy reached into the cooler like he owned the place, like he knew just where to reach.

He came out with two more ice-cold Rocks, which he placed on grimy coasters.

"Do you remember when your dad took us to see *Rocky* at the Colonial?"

Nick answered without hesitation. "Which of the five times?"

"The first time. You asked me what my favorite part was. I said when Rocky put Apollo on the canvas or broke his ribs or something. Do you remember that, Nick?"

"I think so. I mean, that was a long time ago."

"And then I asked you the same question, what was your favorite part? Do you remember what you said?"

Actually, Nick did remember. It was still his favorite part, but he wanted to see if Tommy knew or if this was just another elaborate charade.

"No. Why don't you refresh my recollection."

"You said it was the part where Mickey comes to Rocky's house. You know, after the shitty way he treated him at the gym, and now Rocky has a shot at the title. Rocky forgives him and gives him another chance. That was your answer, Nicky. When Rocky forgives Mickey."

Tommy was right.

"I've asked a lot of people that question since, and no one's ever given me that precise answer except one other person."

"Oh yeah, who was that?" He had a feeling he knew the answer.

"Your father."

Nick sat there and let it sink in. It burned in his chest like a fireball of regret.

"You were what? Ten years old? And you came up with that answer? You had lost your mother the year before I did." Nick still recoiled at the memory that triggered. "That made us members of a sad brotherhood, Nicky, the kids who made little silk flowers for the grave when all the other kids were making crafts for Mother's Day. I think that's what made us so close. You were always different, Nick, and so was your dad, God rest his soul."

"I appreciate all that, Tommy, truly I do, and it's great to see you, but I'm sure you didn't summon me here to talk about *Rocky*."

"That I didn't, Nicky ... that I didn't." Tommy hung his head solemnly. He paused for a long moment before reaching beneath the bar. Nick watched his hand as it came back up. Tommy was holding a manila folder, and he plopped it down on the bar with a thud. "This is why I brought you here."

Nick just looked at it. Took a long sip of his beer. He had no idea what was in that envelope, but Tommy McKenna was not a man given to theatrics. If it was that important— important enough to drag Nick here in the middle of the night after nineteen years and scare him half to death—it clearly contained a bombshell. Tommy slid it across the bar, closer to Nick. *This is a Pandora's Box*, Nick thought. *Once I open it, there's no turning back.*

Nick opened the envelope and slid the contents out onto the bar.

PA-2273

Papers. That's all that was in the envelope—a stack of stapled memos in a binder clip. Nick looked a little closer. There were names and abbreviations Nick didn't recognize. Large portions had been redacted throughout. The reports started in the eighties and continued to the present, but there appeared to be a conspicuous gap in the nineties. The whole thing was written in officious cop talk.

"Police reports?" Nick asked.

"No, FBI reports," Tommy answered. He was gripping the bar with two hands and leaning close to Nick. "You're in danger, Nicky. More than you can imagine."

"I'm starting to believe that. This whole business with the—" He almost slipped.

"The painting? Is that what you were going to say?"

"How do you know?"

"There is no painting. The whole thing is an elaborate ruse set up by that conniving rat to save his own ass. He's not after any painting, Nick, he's after this." Tommy tapped hard on the stack of papers three times.

"Wait, I don't get it. Why do you have them? If what's in here puts Bobby De Rosa in jail, why not just turn them over to whoever?"

"Oh, they don't put him in jail, Nicky. He's never going to jail, and that's kinda the point."

"I don't understand."

"Read," Tommy answered.

And by the light of the neon Paradise sign, that's exactly what Nick did.

Nick recognized some of the names and places, events he had only read about in the papers or seen on the news—robberies, shootings, murders. The memos told a sordid tale in a drab governmental language that only a bureaucracy can produce. Three items were repeated consistently: the abbreviation T.E., the name J. Sidney Del Ciotto, and the code PA-2273.

"Get it yet?" Tommy asked after Nick had scanned over most of it.

"What's T.E.," Nick asked.

"That's the right question," Tommy said. "One of them anyhow. T.E. stands for top echelon. It's an informant program used by the FBI for elite, highly placed sources."

"So what is PA-2273?"

"And that's the other question. Congratulations. Except it's not what, it's who. Let me ask you something. Ever notice how after all these years, this scumbag was never indicted? Other than that bullshit State pinch in '92, which incidentally is why he was closed out for ten years or so until Del Fucko revived him. Meanwhile, all around him, people go to prison while he just gets richer. The Greeks from Athens Hauling, remember them? How do you think he started Rosa Waste? The fucking FBI delivered it to him on a silver platter after he set them up. He was ranting and raving all these years calling everybody a rat, and he was the king rat. PA-2273 was the number assigned to him in 1982. PA-2273 is Bobby De Rosa, T.E. informant for the FBI."

"I can't believe he got away with it for all these years." Nick said.

"Yeah, I knew that would be your first reaction. It was your father's first reaction too."

"What? You told this to my father? Why?"

"I knew the Rose was squeezing your father for the Caffé. I couldn't just sit back and watch that happen. So I gave him a copy of this as insurance."

"What did he do with it?"

"He told me he gave it to his lawyer for safekeeping."

"And then what?"

"And then the next time the Rose came around, I heard your father said something to him in Italian, something about 'in plain sight' or something and spit in his face."

"Whoa. I never heard that story. Gary would have told me."

"Gary's been protecting you from a lot of things."

"So, the painting?"

"Like I said, it's a ruse. He even has Del Ciotto fooled. Sid is completely off the reservation. He stopped filing memos on the Rose a year ago. He's in it for the money now. He thinks Bobby De Rosa is gonna split the proceeds with him, and they're gonna retire to some island like Winthorpe and fucking Valentine and blow each other on a pile of Krugerrands or some shit."

"Nice *Trading Places* reference." Nick and Tommy both took a break and clicked bottles.

Something else was nagging at Nick. He should have been worried about the Rose and what he was willing to do to recover the memos. But what was really troubling him was a sort of melancholy realization that after all the crazy events of the past few days, it turned out the painting wasn't real. As much as he had always doubted its existence, deep down, a secret part of him wanted to believe it, to believe in his father. Now, it turned out to be just another one of Tony Di Nobile's bullshit stories.

"So what do I do now?" Nick asked.

"That part I can't help you with, Nicky. This is as far as I go. Which is already way further than I should have gone."

"Of course, Tommy. I appreciate the risk you took for my dad. I'm sure he did too."

"You know, when I first made Homicide, I knew that bad men were going to get away with murder. That's the nature of the beast. It's a numbers game, and you can't overcome probability. What I wasn't okay with, is that those same numbers and probabilities also demand that a certain number of people, much smaller, but not insignificant, were going to get convicted and go to jail for things they didn't do. I wasn't alright with that, Nicky. No one should be. I did my best to make sure that didn't occur on my watch. I didn't want to get that cancer, the one that settles in your bones and tells you that even if a bad man didn't do that particular crime, he has done and will continue to do plenty others. So what does it really matter? Once you start making those justifications, Nicky? You're lost. That's why I really retired."

"I just figured you flunked a physical exam."

"Fuck you, Di Nobile."

"I'm just breaking your balls. You're a good man, Tommy, always were," Nick said.

"Not really, Nick. I'm no hero. I'm a fat fucking drunk, and I made my share of mistakes. But I'm trying to make that right."

"You're fat, Tommy. I don't know about the rest."

"I know this must all seem strange coming from a hard-assed Irish cop, but I'm trying to find my way back. You know, like Mickey."

"That's not strange, Tommy. We're all searching for something, that one thing we would do over or fix if we could just go back. Life doesn't work that way though. I'm learning that the hard way."

"That brings me to the hard part."

Nick almost spit up the last warm sip of his Rolling Rock. "Are you fucking serious? So the part about the Rose being Whitey fucking Bulger and wanting me dead and that there is no painting, that was the easy part?"

Tommy thought about it for a second. "Basically. Yeah."

"I am so over this fucking city." Nick shook his head in exhaustion. He needed to get home and get some sleep.

"It's about Jimmy."

"Motherfucker. I was hoping you weren't going to say that."

"It was the Rose."

He should have been surprised, but deep down, Nick always knew. He had been pushing that thought out of his mind for a long time. It gave rise to implications he didn't want to think about, so he had convinced himself otherwise in some subconscious act of self-preservation.

"I suppose Del Ciotto helped sweep that conveniently under the rug."

"Bingo. It's all in there." Tommy pointed to the papers on the bar. "Any one of those memos standing alone reveals nothing, but read together, they are pieces of a puzzle that form a clear and inescapable picture, and they bury the Rose. What you do with it is up to you."

"How did you get these anyway? Philly PD doesn't have access to this stuff."

"Let's just say not everyone in the FBI is thrilled with Del Ciotto's unholy alliance. They're just not ready to blow their own career by becoming a whistleblower."

It all made sense. It was a whole lot easier to believe than the alternative; the preposterous notion a priceless, previously undiscovered masterpiece was hidden in Caffé Vecchio by the renowned art collector Tony Di Nobile. Still, Nick felt like a little kid when he finally discovered that Santa Claus wasn't real.

"There's one other thing," Tommy said.

"Oh, just fucking shoot me," Nick responded.

"Look at me, Nick. This is important, and I want you to hear it from me." Nick obliged his old friend and looked up.

"You've been gone a long time. Hell, no one thought you'd ever be back, the way you left and all. Anyway, what I'm trying to say is, Angie and me—"

Nick stepped in to save him. "It's okay, Tommy. I know."

"You do? How?"

Nick paused as if he was trying to remember something. "How do you think? Nothing's a secret for long in this neighborhood. I'm happy for you. Happy for both of you."

"So you're not mad?"

Nick got up off his stool and walked around the bar. He hugged his grade school friend as best he could in the narrow space.

"Just do me a favor."

"Anything, Nick." Tommy sounded relieved.

"Lose some weight for Chrissakes."

"It's on my to-do list. I'll have plenty of free time to exercise in the sunshine."

"Sunshine?" Nick said, like it was some foreign force that never penetrated the clouds hanging over the Avenue.

"St. Pete. Angie and me. We're going to watch the Phils in Clearwater for spring training, and well, if she likes it, I'm pulling up the stakes and we're moving down there. You know, pull a Nick Di Nobile."

Nick was floored. "A what?"

"That's what we call it around here when someone just picks up and leaves—a Nick Di Nobile."

Now I've truly heard it all, Nick thought.

"Yeah, that's a good one. Good luck, Tommy. God bless. Come and see me if you ever come over to the east coast, you know, the *real* Florida." He punched Tommy playfully on the arm.

"Too rich for my blood, but you never know." Tommy turned serious for a moment. "Promise me you'll be careful, Nicky. Nothing's more dangerous than a cornered rat. Why don't you just go back home, buddy."

Nick thought about that, especially the *home* part. "Not just yet, Tommy. Not just yet."

"I figured you'd say that too." Tommy reached beneath the bar again and, this time, came up with a .38. Nick stared at the gun in Tommy's hand for what seemed like a long time.

"You're gonna need this then." He placed the gun, which was in an ankle holster, on the top of the bar. "Be careful. It's loaded."

"I would certainly hope so." Against his better judgment, Nick took it and began strapping the Velcro holster to his ankle.

"You made two mistakes already," Tommy barked.

Nick looked up at him. "I did?"

"Yeah. One, you didn't check to see if it was loaded."

"You just told me it was."

"Exactly, that was the first mistake. Don't trust anyone, Nick, not even me."

Nick pulled it out, flipped open the cylinder, and saw it was loaded. He gave it a spin before flipping it back into place. He bent back down and began strapping the holster around his ankle again.

"That's the second mistake." Tommy was pointing down with a disapproving finger. "You're putting it on the wrong ankle."

Nick took his advice and strapped it around his left ankle. Nick placed the manila envelope in a plastic bag under a six-pack of Rolling Rock, and Tommy let him out the front door.

"I'll lock up," he said. "Be careful out there."

"I will," Nick hollered back as he walked down Tasker Street toward home.

"Hey, Nick," Tommy hollered after him.

For fuck's sake. What now? Nick thought as he turned around.

"Just remember one thing."

"Yeah, what's that?" Nick had his arms spread wide.

Tommy looked at Nick for what seemed like a long time before answering. He screamed it down the street. "Mickey loves you."

Nick smiled and waved as he turned.

From the back of a trash truck sitting at a light at the corner, a black guy in an Eagles hat shouted, "I love you too!" and bust out laughing.

Nick had lied. He had no idea Tommy and Angie were a couple, but he figured he'd let his old friend off the hook. It was the least he could do in return. After all, he had no claim to her. Not anymore. That was all a long time ago, and it was Nick who had left. Still, out of all the revelations of the night, that was the one that landed the hardest. He would have preferred a bat to the rib cage.

He walked east on Tasker. The weight of the pistol on his ankle was unfamiliar and made him feel off-kilter. His head was spinning from all the alcohol he'd consumed. He couldn't stop thinking about the other day when Angie came to the Caffé and they sat there drinking and listening to the jukebox, like the world wasn't on fire all around them.

The streetlights created strange shadows from the bare branches and cast them upon the sidewalk. Nick looked up at the old trees as he walked. A cold wind shook their branches. There wasn't a cherry blossom in sight.

NEW YEAR'S EVE

When I was a child, I spoke as a child, I understood as a child, I thought as a child; but when I became a man, I put away childish things.

1 Corinthians 13:11

Nick felt like shit. He still wasn't used to waking up in the strange bed. Except, it wasn't really so strange, was it? Nick had gone to live with his grandmother after his mother died. He slept in this room, in this very bed, until he was nineteen and started flopping over at Jimmy Musante's apartment on Mifflin Street. Even so, he still needed a few seconds to get his bearings each morning, to realize he wasn't in Lauderdale and Grace wasn't next to him. *Shit. Grace. I never called her back yesterday.* Nick had been sucked up by the whirlwind of events and revelations the day had produced and forgot to call her. The drinking didn't help any either. In his defense, what could he truthfully report? *"Hey, Grace, how's it going? Me? Oh, I'm fine. Let's see, a psychopathic arch-criminal who's really an informant is trying to kill me. The priceless painting I've been chasing in circles doesn't really exist. My dead best friend who killed himself was actually murdered by said psychopath and had a son I never knew about. Also, my other grade school friend is going out with the girl I used to love and probably still do. How was your day?"*

Nick walked down to the kitchen. He was going to miss this old house when it sold. His time spent living with his grandmother was perhaps the happiest of his life. Sure, he missed his mother desperately, but his grandmother was like a rock. She provided for all his needs and encouraged him every step of the way. His father was around, in his way, coming over every morning to make him breakfast and see him off to school, and Nick spent every afternoon in the Caffé. He loved the Caffé back in those days. It felt like a magical place, and he felt so important sitting at the bar, drinking his soda, and watching all the wild characters pass through while his father held court. At some point, when he was twenty or so—when most young men start to believe they are smarter than their fathers—the Caffé began to lose its magic. The music started to sound corny. His father's epic stories became tired and silly after count-less retelling. (Nick noticed, too, how little details would change or suddenly appear). And all those wild charac-ters? Well, it turns out they were just old, broken-down drunks. So Nick did what every headstrong young man does in that position. He rejected all those things that once made him smile, moved a thousand miles away, only to recreate his own version of Caffé Vecchio. And all the palm trees, pina coladas, and suntan lotion in the world couldn't disguise the single overarching theme of his life. He had become just like his father.

Nick dressed for the day. He had quite a few things to accomplish before the clock struck midnight and the ball dropped, at least he hoped to. Thank God Grace was handling everything at the Tiki. His crew had done the whole New Year's Eve thing so many times it was really no more than just another busy night, with decorations. He started to have the craziest thoughts as he sat at the old kitchen table, sipping his coffee where he had plotted so many moves in his youth. The old percolator couldn't compete with his De Longhi machine at home, but he had to admit, it made a pretty good cup of coffee. It got him to thinking. *Maybe things didn't have to be so complicated. Maybe he should just follow the path of least resistance.* He considered what a life would be like back here in Philly. He could sell the Tiki and run Vecchio with Gary. *How many people*, Nick thought, *run away by coming back home?* Of course, in his case, it would be like fleeing paradise. He would be leaving Grace. She would never move to the City, and he would never ask her to. He would be trading the Tiki for the Caffé; the circle would be closed. It made him think of old cons who were so institutionalized they couldn't survive outside the walls. So, subconsciously, they willed their inevitable return. They called it throwing rocks at the penitentiary.

Nick grabbed his keys and phone, downed the last of his coffee, and threw on his coat. He stared at the holstered pistol on the table next to a statue of the Blessed Mother. He finally caved in and strapped it to his left ankle, thinking of Tommy. He hustled out the front door on his way to the Caffé, his pockets full of rocks.

TASKER MORRIS VENTURES, LLC

Boca Raton, Florida

Ralph found a spot off Federal Highway, also known as US Route 1. He didn't like parking in the Dunkin' Donuts parking lot. Inevitably, some spoiled rich kid would ding his door in the tight spaces. In Boca, it seemed like most people treated yellow lines like a polite suggestion, which they believed they had the prerogative to simply ignore.

The guys assembled outside Dunkin' every morning. Somehow, all these guys from different cities on the east coast (Chicago guys went to Tampa) moved to South Florida and landed at the same coffee shop on Federal Highway. Ralph hated it. He hated Dunkin' Donuts in Philly, and it was no better here. After checking in with the *Brain Trust*, Ralph would usually scoot over to a local cafe for a proper espresso. In Lauderdale, he favored Dolci on Oakland Park Boulevard, which was conveniently located next to a cigar bar. *Maybe I'll take a ride down the beach*, he thought as he walked over to the crew.

They were mostly Italian guys, though not all, average age around seventy, making Ralph Cappello a young head.

Most of the men were what would qualify as wealthy. Not inherited money, but first-generation, started from the streets type of wealth. The kind of journey kids today rapped about but could never imagine. Some had started out in unions: carpenters, electricians, ironworkers. Old man Abe spent his childhood in the Bielsko ghetto and the forced labor camp known as Gross-Rosen. Ralph's own carpentry apprenticeship, not to mention a promising boxing debut, had been cut short by a trip to Ray Brook Federal Correctional Institute, where he took up a different trade.

Ralph was certainly no angel as a young man growing up in South Philly, racking up more than his share of scrapes. Oddly enough, he was sentenced for crimes outlined in an indictment alleging he was part of a conspiracy he had no knowledge of. Ralph didn't even know ninety percent of his co-defendants, who were just as perplexed by his presence among them. Still, he was never bitter about it, and it never occurred to him to rat on anyone, not that he knew anything. Not that that ever stopped anyone. He accepted his fate, did his time, and hit the ground running upon his release. He rarely thought about those early years. Ralph had given up wondering how it had all come to pass—how he had found himself imprisoned, at the age of twenty-two, for a conspiracy he neither knew about nor profited from. Today, at the age of sixty, that was all about to change.

The men were all shareholders in Tasker Morris Ventures, LLC, a Delaware corporation with its headquarters in a nondescript office in a dull, boxy building on Camino Real in Boca Raton. The "office" was little more than a cubicle. The "work" was primarily transacted at the Dunkin' Donuts. Tasker Morris was Ralph's creation. It was basically a pool of money, invested in hard money lending, real estate acquisition, and anything else that was profitable. Ralph thought the name Tasker Morris gave the company a kind of colonial, aristocratic air, and everyone liked it. In reality, it was the name of the Broad Street subway stop in Ralph's South Philly neighborhood.

Subway stop or not, it made an obscene amount of money.

Vincent was the token hang-around, running errands, driving them to lunch or doctors' appointments, basically serving as a personal assistant to the group. He lived "off the fat of the land," as they used to say, depending on the crew's largesse for his sustenance. For a nineteen-year-old kid with nothing else going on, Vinny lived pretty damn good. Presently, he was sitting in a chair outside the Dunkin' Donuts, eyes closed behind Bvlgari sunglasses. A foil tanning reflector was propped up under his chin. Ralph walked over and kicked his outstretched feet, startling him into reality.

"Where do you think you are? Outside a fucking pork store?"

Vincent bolted upright. "Sorry, Mr. C."

"You've been watching too many movies, kid." Ralph barked. "Maybe we should all start wearing matching T-shirts, maybe some jackets."

Abe must have really liked that because he started shaking and tapped his cane on the sidewalk furiously.

"And now you're upsetting Abe."

"He's not upset," Vinny protested.

Ralph winked at Abe and tapped Vinny on the face.

"Did you pick up the mail?" Ralph asked.

"Absolutely." Vinny folded the reflector and jogged to the car to get the mail.

Ralph caught up with the crew and made the usual small talk, mostly about football, the weather, everyone's ailments, who got laid—the typical board meeting agenda. There was no new business to discuss, other than New Year's Eve plans, so Ralph brought the meeting to a close as soon as Vinny returned with the mail. It wasn't much—the usual bills, junk mail, and a FedEx envelope. Ralph was eager to take a ride down the beach for an espresso, and maybe he would treat himself to a croissant. Dolci had great pastries. Ralph rubbed his growing midsection and had second thoughts. *Fuck it, you only live once.*

Ralph said his goodbyes and Happy New Years, and Vinny walked him to the car. Ralph peeled off five hundred-dollar bills and stuffed them in Vinny's pocket. Vinny put up his hands in faux protest out of respect.

"Happy New Year, kid. Be *good*," Ralph said. *Good* was a heavily weighted word the way Ralph used it in this context, containing all kinds of nuance and implications Vinny understood implicitly. Ralph tousled his hair and kissed him on the cheek. He got into his car and threw the mail, including the FedEx envelope, on the passenger's seat.

The ride along the beach was spectacular. *Maybe that Stone Crab is on to something*, Ralph thought as he cruised along A1A, taking in the sun and sights that were the main reasons people moved down here in the first place. For Ralph, it had been a long, circuitous and, at times, painful journey to get there.

Ralph took a shortcut and turned into the Walgreens right before Oakland Park Boulevard. He weaved through the parking lot and parked in front of Dolci. Inside, he ordered a double espresso and eyed the pastry case. He knew he shouldn't, but the ricotta cannoli were lined up in a creamy, dutiful row that beckoned him. *Fuck it*, Ralph reasoned, *tomorrow is the New Year and I'll start my diet then.* Ralph knew he had a better shot at playing shortstop for the Phillies than starting a diet, but this was how he rationalized the indulgence.

In his early twenties, before his extended vacation, he roamed the streets of South Philly at 155 pounds of rock-hard muscle and sinew. At sixty, Ralph Cappello tipped the scales at 250 plus. He sat down with his espresso and cannoli, and like every proud but delusional man his age, was comforted by the certainty that the lean, dangerous young man still lurked inside him. And if not, he still had a left hook that could land like a freight train. That part was not a delusion.

La Flor Sportivo Cigar Bar was just opening for the day. It was still a little early for a full-bodied stick that Ralph usually favored, so he picked out an Ashton Churchill.

"Make it a box," Ralph added. He thought of the Tasker Morris Brain Trust Boys and wanted to have plenty to hand out on New Year's Day. A full-bodied Padron would put old man Abe in a coma, so the Ashton was a safe choice. He used the bar top cutter to make a V cut and lit the stick with a torch lighter as he threw the Tasker Morris mail onto the bar. He skipped over the junk mail and went right to the FedEx envelope with a Philadelphia return address. He peeled back the tab and placed the contents on the bar.

At first, he couldn't quite figure out what it was. But as he continued to read, a distinct picture began to emerge. From within the grimy chronology laid out in the reports, one name emerged as conspicuous by its absence. Ralph knew the people and events laid out in the reports. Some he had witnessed firsthand, which is how he noticed that although they were essentially true, some of the facts had been altered. But why? One particular memo concerned the Greeks from Athens Hauling. Ralph pitched for their softball team a lifetime ago and did some time with Al Manos before he died of a heart attack. Ralph had saved the Greek's ass on the yard more than once. They came to every game at Southwark schoolyard on 8th and Mifflin, wagering Super Bowl size sums on the contests. They were straight, stand-up guys, and Ralph had always wondered how they got jammed up. Ralph continued reading about a back-in-the-day scam that he knew for a fact someone else had orchestrated. Again, *that* guy wasn't named in any of the reports.

Then he read his own name. Ralph 'The Rifle' Cappello. It was in a report dated July 20, 1980. It had never been disclosed or turned over in discovery in his case. It appeared right after the paragraph that stated, PA-2273 relates as follows.

"You motherfucker." Ralph spat the words out through clenched teeth.

The bartender looked up, but went right back to cutting limes after one glance at Ralph's face.

Ralph stormed out, bought a prepaid phone in Walgreens, and headed toward I-95. He caught the open bridge over the Intracoastal and used the delay to activate the phone. He drove west and picked up 95 south, headed for Miami.

OH, DEM GOLDEN SLIPPERS

Some time later God tested Abraham. He said to him, "Abraham!"

"Here I am," he replied.

Then God said, "Take your son, your only son, whom you love—Isaac—and go to the region of Moriah. Sacrifice him there as a burnt offering on a mountain I will show you."

Early the next morning Abraham got up and loaded his donkey. He took with him two of his servants and his son Isaac. When he had cut enough wood for the burnt offering, he set out for the place God had told him about. On the third day Abraham looked up and saw the place in the distance. He said to his servants, "Stay here with the donkey while I and the boy go over there. We will worship and then we will come back to you."

Abraham took the wood for the burnt offering and placed it on his son Isaac, and he himself carried the fire and the knife. As the two of them went on together, Isaac spoke up and said to his father Abraham, "Father?"

"Yes, my son?" Abraham replied.

The fire and wood are here," Isaac said, "but where is the lamb for the burnt offering?"

Abraham answered, "God himself will provide the lamb for the burnt offering, my son." And the two of them went on together.

Genesis 22

Frank walked to the front window of the second-story, one-bedroom apartment overlooking the Avenue. The apartment was about a half-block from the Caffé and on the opposite side of the street. Frank had a good view of the front door and who came and went.

Frank remembered when the building housed a boxing gym. All the neighborhood kids would sneak up to hit the bag or jump rope, until they made too much noise and Shorty would kick them out. Shorty was a renowned trainer and cut man. He had once trained a promising young Italian middleweight from the neighborhood whose career was cut short by a stint in federal prison. The kid went by the name "The Rifle." Shorty mixed a crazy concoction of rubber cement glue and tea leaves that was guaranteed to stop any bleeding. It was also highly illegal and got Shorty banned from boxing. Now, the first floor housed a juice bar/yoga studio.

The Rose had put Frank up in the vacant apartment while he was in town, and it was pretty bare. He slept on a lumpy old mattress that made him homesick for the sofa in the cabana. Frank went through the duffel bag in preparation for his New Year's assignment. It was all there—the two comic wench costumes, gloves, greasepaint, the satchels, and the hardware.

Frank opened the cylinder and dumped the bullets onto the table. He inspected each one and methodically wiped them down, along with the entire gun. The two costumes were from the two largest Wench Brigades on the street: The Shunk Street Strutters and The Grays Ferry Yankee Clippers. The *wench* costume was the oldest and most traditional costume in the Mummers Parade.

It was a cheap costume, easy to make, and favored by the lowly comic brigades, whose only rehearsal was drinking a case of Miller Lite and a fifth of Crown Royal. They had a history of getting disqualified before they reached City Hall.

Frank would walk out the door dressed in a red and gold satin outfit, identical to at least 350 other guys set to march. He would switch suits at the first checkpoint, complete his assignment, then switch back to the first costume at checkpoint two. Any store security cameras or Ring doorbells that picked him up from the apartment would show a red and gold Strutter wench. Any video near the scene would show a Clipper dressed in black and white, just like 350 other guys on the street. He would switch back to red and gold for any possible video that picked him up after the job. Not that it really mattered. Over the course of the morning, Frank would alternately look identical to and indistinguishable from over 700 other wench comics.

It wasn't foolproof, nothing was, but it was as close as you could get. You could only pull it off one day out of the year (not counting Halloween, which is an entirely different story). The cops were already strained to the max from the previous night's mayhem and would have their hands full managing the crowds at the parade. Another fucked-up tradition was shooting guns in the air on New Year's Eve and Day. The earliest Mummers were known as Shooters, derived from this reckless stupidity that had killed more than one person over the years.

Consequently, police weren't unaccustomed to random gunfire and fireworks, and it barely raised an eyebrow, even among the neighbors. It would be the equivalent of calling 911 to report a dog shitting on your pavement. Frank had concocted the plan a long time ago and hoped he never had to use it.

The Crab took a pair of old work boots from a plastic bag and placed them out on the fire escape. He had schlepped them all the way from Florida for this very purpose. The Mummers tradition dictated that the marchers wear "golden slippers." He was surprised he could still find a can of gold spray paint left on the shelf at Home Depot. In fact, there were only three left. He shook the can and sprayed the boots with a glorious coat of metallic gold.

When he was done spraying the boots, Frank walked down to the juice bar to see if he could find an espresso. The place was full of women carrying yoga mats on their backs and sipping green smoothies. Frank made his way to the counter and asked a girl with a tattoo sleeve if she could make him a double espresso. She looked at him like he had leprosy.

"We ain't got none of that here," said a voice from the back room.

Frank could make out the form of a man sitting on an ancient recliner in the shadows. The man strained and managed to stand up after what seemed like a great effort. He walked to the counter slowly, rocking from side to side. An oxygen tube in his nose was trailing behind him like an umbilical cord.

"Shorty?" Frank asked.

"Guilty. I was born this way." The old man told the same joke he'd recited on a loop fifty years ago. "And I recognize you too. Used to come in here with a young kid hit like a trick mule, went by the name of the Rifle. What ever happened to him?"

"He moved to Florida," Frank said.

It has often been repeated that only in Philadelphia could you come across two bums fighting in an alley and both of them would be hooking off the jab. But the Rifle was no bum. He was something special.

"How's the arm?" Shorty asked.

Frank was shocked that the old man remembered. He had to be eighty-five years old. When Frank first brought Ralph in to train, Shorty had noticed Frank's arm and asked him to stay after when Ralph was done. Shorty moved around the ring with Frank, showed him how to circle, how to slip punches, how to counter. He taught him how to cover up in a crouch when he needed to, weight on his back foot, arms crossed in front of him in the crab style that had come to be known as the "Philly Shell."

Frank could still recall Shorty's instruction. *"You a dangerous man cause they never see you coming. You like one of them crabs with one big killer claw, then you pop out your shell—whomp!"* Shorty had demonstrated on that day, long ago.

And *that* is how Frank the Crab first got his name. It had morphed into *Stone Crab* when he moved to Florida.

"We don't have no espresso, but Badger here make a mean wheatgrass shot."

Badger grabbed a bunch of wheatgrass and made Frank a shot, which she placed on the counter in front of him.

"Best give him a pineapple chaser," Shorty said, and Badger nodded in agreement.

"This still your place?" Frank asked.

"Yeah, why? You ain't never seen no black man own a yoga studio?"

"Actually, no, but I didn't mean it that way, Shorty. Just happy to see you're still doing well."

"Didn't I teach you a long time ago? It ain't how you hit, it's how you pivot."

Frank thought about it for a second. It was about the wisest thing he heard since he'd been back. Then he downed the wheatgrass shot and thought he was going to die.

"Drink the chaser." Shorty was either wheezing or laughing, it was hard to tell. Maybe a little of both.

Frank drank the pineapple juice shot, which helped a little. He pulled out some money, but Shorty refused.

"No charge for my old student Frankie Crab. And remember …" The old man assumed a fighting stance, bobbed his head, weaved to one side, and then threw a surprisingly crisp straight right. "It ain't how you hit, it's how you pivot."

"I'll remember that, Shorty. Thanks for the shot. I think."

"And say hello to the Rifle for me," Shorty said.

"I will," Frank replied. "He goes by Ralph these days."

THE RIFLE OF 9TH AND MORRIS

July 5, 1976

Nicky bolted out the door and sprinted across the street to unlock the garage that housed his uncle's fruit and vegetables in a homemade walk-in box. All the men in Nicky's family were either bricklayers or "hucksters." They drove their trucks through the city streets, their sing-song inventory blared over a loudspeaker, luring housewives curbside. Uncle Frank's mantra would precede his arrival by a block or two. "Hey, come on now, sweet as honey." Their fathers before them sold produce from horse-drawn wagons, the garages actually built upon converted city stables. Nicky had heard countless tales of their exploits.

In addition to selling produce, Uncle Frank was also a number writer, taking bets along his route for the daily three-digit "street" number. This was right after the Commonwealth of Pennsylvania got in on the action. Nicky always marveled at the prodigious wad of money that exploded from his uncle's pockets when he peeled off a buck or two for his nephew. Nicky could count on at least a dollar from Uncle Frank for unloading the truck and loved the feel of the cool, dark walk-in box on a hot summer day.

That summer, Uncle Frank had hired a part-time helper named Mario. Mario was fresh from "the other side," as Italian immigrants were commonly referred to in the seventies. Uncle Frank would hire them off the docks of the market. Mario spoke broken English and smelled of overpowering body odor.

Mario walked ahead of the truck and stepped into the garage as Nicky was sliding open the door to the walk-in box. Nicky was preparing to pre-bag the loose grapes into brown paper bags for sale to unsuspecting housewives. It was no more dishonest than fluffing strawberry pints that had been packed tight. A good fluffing netted an extra pint per flat.

"Nicola." Nicky spun around, startled.

The hum of the compressor had muffled Mario's approach, but his stench already filled the small box. Mario smacked Nicky's ear with a doughy hand, a little too hard to be playful. "Put uppa you hand, I give a you a lesson."

Nicky was silent. He hated being called that name. Born on December 6th, his parents named him after San Nicola of Bari. Only two people called him Nicola—his grandfather and Mario. He thought it sounded like a little girl's name. He put his hands up and held them like Jimmy had shown him. He tucked his chin and tried to sidestep Mario's slaps but was sorely overmatched. The slaps were scoring on his head, and they became closed-hand blows when Mario began to hit him in the body. Nicky's eyes and nose began to water. He was stuck in the corner of the garage, his bony legs straddled a drain. Mario taunted him between punches; no more slaps now.

"You gonna cry, lilla girl?" He mocked him in a broken English crybaby cadence.

Nicky could do nothing now but cover up. He heard Jimmy's voice in his head. *"Everybody has a plan. Until they get hit."* At that moment, he knew exactly what Jimmy meant. Mario laughed, wheezing from a combination of his workout and the Marlboro reds rolled in his shirtsleeve. Nicky balled his tiny fist and threw a blind, desperate uppercut that improbably connected directly on Mario's chin. He never saw it land but heard the clicking of Mario's teeth and felt the electric jolt travel up his arm. Mario took a step back. Blood dripped from his mouth. Enraged by the punch, his eyes bulged, and he began to remove his belt to administer a thrashing.

A few older boys had been playing half-ball, and one of them walked over to investigate the commotion. Raphael "The Rifle" stepped from the shadows. Nicky couldn't tell how long he had been there. Mario didn't see him until the Rifle snapped, "Hey, greaseball." Mario turned, the belt slipping from his sweaty hand, the blood draining from his face. "How bout we take this out in the street?" Mario put up his hands in protest and began to stammer a weak explanation through a quivering smile. Before a syllable slipped from his bloody lips, a trip-hammer jab snapped his head back.

Raphael was not in the habit of throwing single punches. The jab was merely exploratory, designed to find his range and test Mario's reach. More importantly, the Rifle had no intention of restricting the beating to the confines of the garage. The neighborhood needed to witness this.

Mario reluctantly put up his hands. Raphael noted the southpaw stance and instinctively began to circle to the left. He heard Shorty's gravelly bark echo in his head. "*Throw straight rights.*" Raphael waited patiently to land his money punch, a sledgehammer left hook. Mario actually managed to muster a few lazy jabs that Raphael swatted away as he continued to circle, driving Mario toward the open door and into the daylight.

Fighting a southpaw (for a right-hander) is like looking at a mirror image. Consequently, both fighters' lead foot is often in the same place, causing frequent tripping. Raphael was mindful of this as Mario became square with the door. Suddenly, Raphael stopped circling left, planted his right foot, and uncoiled a straight right hand, snapping his wrist square at just the right moment. Mario's nose exploded as Raphael felt the crack of the septum against his knuckles. His fist quickly recoiled back into position, even before the blood and snot erupted from Mario's nose. Mario tumbled backward out the door and onto Mountain Street.

By now, Uncle Frank had parked his truck. He was delivering a watermelon to Nicky's grandmother, Filomena, directly across the street from the garage. Frank spun at the sound of Raphael's blow, which could have been a firecracker left over from the 4th or even a .22. Filomena fumbled the handoff in the commotion, and the watermelon hit the sidewalk. It was a hot summer day, and the street was filled with kids playing half-ball and deadbox.

The younger kids swarmed to the broken melon like ants to a picnic. A fight and a watermelon feast. *What a day!*

Raphael circled methodically, purposefully. The Rifle was careful not to be overconfident. Mario was still a grown man and was fighting for pride. Losing to a teenager in front of the whole neighborhood would sting for a long time. Mario telegraphed a looping haymaker that would have caused damage had it landed. Raphael deftly slipped it. The punch was so ill executed, the Rifle initially registered it as a feint. The overswing caused Mario to spin wildly, and the Rifle made him pay with a crushing hook to the kidney. Mario arched his back as his unshaven face registered wincing pain.

Still, Raphael circled, only now to the right. He faked a jab, which brought Mario's hands up to cover his face. Raphael dipped, twisted his hips, and chopped at Mario's puffy beer belly with a hybrid hook/uppercut. The breath left Mario's lungs in an audible whoosh.

Mario could not endure another body blow. He reached out to a small sidewalk pole for support. It had been painted red, white, and blue for the Bicentennial. The Rifle wiggled his right hand like a swaying cobra. Mario froze, fixated on Raphael's right hand. Raphael dipped and weaved to the left. Mario's hands dropped to protect his torso from another punishing body blow, and the Rifle saw his opening. The outer edge of his Puma Clyde sneaker dug into the asphalt like an anchor. A left hook followed an unforgiving orbit. It met a slack jawbone at its apex. Like all objects in motion, it remained in motion until its energy was absorbed by Mario's now shattered mandible.

He didn't topple over so much as drop straight down, as if some force greater than gravity accelerated his descent. Like an imploded building, his joints simply folded simultaneously as he crumbled within his own space like a beach chair. His cheap shoes jutted out unnaturally, making them appear even more ridiculous, the worn sole bottoms exposing his dirty socks. The children of Mountain Street erupted. Filomena took her first breath since dropping the watermelon. A ten-year-old boy fired up a Marlboro sent scurrying from Mario's sleeve.

Uncle Frank walked over from where he had been watching the fight. He leaned over and barked at his groaning worker. "You're fired! Capisce?"

Uncle Frank put his arm around Nicky as they walked to the corner store, and he reached into his bulging pocket. "Here, this is for you," he said as he slipped what felt like a rock into his tiny hand. Nicky glimpsed at the object in his palm. It *was* a rock. *What the fuck is this?* he thought, but a meek, "Thanks," was all he could muster.

"It's kryptonite. I found it on the route. Keep it in your pocket for protection when I'm not around." Nicky knew this was his uncle's way of saying, "I'm sorry I let that piece of shit torture you for the past three months." *Bullshit*, he thought, but he appreciated the gesture. He knew Uncle Frank loved him because he was always saying he would throw himself in front of a bus for him—whatever the hell that meant. Then, Uncle Frank pulled out a folding knife and pressed it into Nicky's palm.

"What should I do with it?" Nick nervously managed.

"Keep it in your pocket," Frank said. "Just in case the kryptonite don't work."

That line became a running gag between the two of them for decades.

LINCOLN ROAD

South Beach, Miami

South Beach, Miami is only thirty-five miles or so from Oakland Park Boulevard in Fort Lauderdale. In ideal traffic conditions, Ralph could make the run in forty minutes or less. But it was New Year's Eve in South Florida, and the conditions were decidedly not ideal. Ralph had also made a quick stop at a Staples on Commercial Boulevard to make a copy of the file.

Frank wasn't answering the burner Ralph had given him for this very purpose. The combination of bumper-to-bumper traffic and the espresso, cannoli, cigar combo was doing a number on Ralph's stomach. Things eased up a bit when he veered into the Sun Pass Express lanes. By the time he got to the Lincoln Road Mall, Dmitry had finished his lunch. Lincoln Road is an outdoor pedestrian mall of shops and restaurants that stretched from Washington Avenue to Alton Road in South Beach, Miami.

Dmitry was seated with two younger Russian guys who looked like UFC fighters in suits that appeared two sizes too small for their physiques. Ralph had noticed the trend among younger guys at the club. That, and suit pants hemmed two inches too high, set off by sockless dress shoes. Ralph sized up the two. He figured he could maybe drop one before the two of them got him on the ground. None of that was even a remote possibility, but Ralph was always making these calculations anyway. Old habits die hard.

A beautiful blonde sat in a chair to Dmitry's left. She was dressed in a business suit that would easily transition from boardroom to nightclub. At least that's how it appeared to Ralph. Then again, maybe it wasn't the suit so much as it was the woman wearing it. She appeared to have stepped out of the cover of *Vogue* and pulled up a chair.

Dmitry waived for Ralph to have a seat and raised a finger over his shoulder that conjured a waiter out of thin air better than any Vegas magician could. The waiter materialized at Dmitry's side, and he simply nodded in Ralph's direction. The waiter came over to Ralph. He ordered a mimosa for no discernible reason other than he saw them all over the surrounding tables. Dmitry was engaged in a three-way conversation with the woman. She was speaking to Dmitry in Russian. Dmitry responded to her in English but lapsed into Russian when he became a little heated. She, in turn, related Dmitry's comments to the individual on the other side of the phone in what sounded like Dutch. From Dmitry's remarks in English, it sounded like a dispute over a boat, but Ralph couldn't be sure. Dmitry smiled over at Ralph as if to convey his apology for not greeting him more graciously. Dmitry was probably one of the three most dangerous men in Miami, but he was nothing if not gracious.

The waiter returned surprisingly fast, not with a mimosa, but a carafe of freshly squeezed orange juice and a bottle of Dom Perignon. It seemed like an abomination to mix it with orange juice, so Ralph asked the waiter to pour it straight. He also asked the waiter to come back with glasses for everyone at the table. Ralph wasn't about to sit at Dmitry Ivanov's table drinking champagne by himself like some *gavone*. Dmitry may have appeared engrossed in a high-stakes negotiation, still, he noticed Ralph's gesture and nodded to himself like he had made the right choice about something.

Dmitry wrapped up his call around the same time the waiter had returned and poured a glass of Dom for everyone. Everyone looked to Dmitry as he raised his glass.

"*Za nashu druzjbu.*"

Ralph had been around plenty of Russians and had been out drinking with Dmitry on quite a few occasions, but he had never heard this particular toast. It seemed to carry some weight with the rest of the group, and it was directed to Ralph. The woman echoed the toast in English for Ralph's benefit.

"To our friendship," she translated.

Ralph drank as Dmitry began to explain.

"These Dutch shipyards. They pride themselves on being the world's greatest but then cry at every request."

Ralph wasn't sure what the request was, but more than once during the conversation he heard Dmitry mention a submarine.

"Good luck on the build." Ralph raised his glass. He had been a guest on Dmitry's mega-yacht for last year's Super Bowl, and it was unreal. Dmitry had mentioned at the time he was commissioning an even larger vessel. "How big is this one going to be?"

"One hundred forty-two," Dmitry answered.

Ralph whistled. "That's almost half a football field."

The woman corrected him gently. "One hundred for-ty-two *meters*."

One of the men chuckled, drawing a sharp look from Dmitry, who said something to him in Russian. The man excused himself from the table and walked away sheepishly.

"So, my friend, I am pleased to have you at my table on this day." Dmitry rose and walked over to Ralph. "I see you brought something for me," he said while looking at the papers Ralph had rolled up in his fist. Ralph had disposed of the FedEx envelope in a dumpster behind Dolci and gripped the documents like a night stick. "Let us go for a smoke."

The two men started toward a cigar shop on Lincoln. The remaining man rose to follow, but Dmitry motioned for him to remain. At the shop, Dmitry picked out a box of Padron 1964 Anniversary Series, along with a Le Grand S.T. DuPont lighter. Dmitry opened the box and took out two cigars. He cut both cigars and offered Ralph a light first. A serious-looking salesman stood at attention. Dmitry asked him for two bags. In one bag, he placed the box of Padrons and the lighter, which he handed to Ralph. He then opened the other bag and gestured to Ralph. Ralph loosened his grip on the paperwork and placed it in the bag, which Dmitry tucked under his arm. Ralph noticed that Dmitry didn't pay and figured he had a house account.

As they exited, Ralph felt it necessary to emphasize the importance of the documents.

"You need to read that soon," Ralph said. "It can't wait."

Dmitry smiled at Ralph. "I already know what it says. It is being attended to as we speak, but thank you, my loyal friend." He placed his hand on Ralph's shoulder as he said it.

Ralph didn't doubt it for a second, and knew better than to ask how. They hugged and wished one another Happy New Year.

"Did you make a copy?" Dmitry asked.

Ralph didn't even consider lying.

"Good," Dmitry said. "Read it until it is engraved on your brain and then burn it."

Ralph thought of something as they parted ways. "Dmitry, your lighter."

"The lighter is for you," Dmitry answered.

Ralph turned the lighter over in his hand and it glistened brilliantly in the sunlight. *Za nashu druzjbu* was engraved on its side.

JUST FRIENDS

By the time Nick walked into the Caffé, Gary and Frank were going at it. He could hear their raised voices before he even opened the door. Frank was talking with his hands like only a South Philly Italian can, and Gary was standing there with two mahogany tree trunks folded across his chest. They paused for a moment when Nick walked in. The jukebox was pumping out a snazzy jazz number with some great work on the Hammond organ.

"What's this?" Nick asked, tilting his head toward the jukebox.

Gary pointed to Frank, who answered. "Pat Martino, 'Just Friends,' one of your dad's favorites."

"Nice keyboard," Nick remarked.

"That's Trudy Pitts on the Hammond. They're both from Philly. It's from the album *El Hombre*," Frank said, just as a jazz guitar solo kicked in. "*That's* Pat Martino," Frank clarified.

"This guy can really cook," Nick said, marveling at the masterful guitar licks.

"That's what I've been trying to tell B.B. here."

Gary piped up. "This cat ain't shit next to B.B."

"His comping behind the organ solo is where he really shines. He was just twenty-two years old when this was recorded," Frank said to Nick.

Nick liked what he heard, even if he didn't have a jazz connoisseur's ear. There was an economy and restraint to the notes, like the musicians held back just enough for the listener to fill the spaces between with their own imagination. He could totally understand why it was one of his dad's favorites.

"Is that what you guys are arguing about? I thought we had bigger fish to fry."

Frank pulled him aside. "Didn't your father ever tell you the story of Pat Martino?"

Nick shrugged. "Not that I recall."

"Pat Martino is a world-renowned guitar prodigy, a freak of nature. He's easily one of the top five jazz guitarists of all time, and he grew up Pat Azzara right here in the neighborhood."

"Okay," Nick said. "What happened to him?"

"He used to suffer these seizures. They thought he was crazy, locked him up in mental wards, gave him electroshock treatments. Years later, turns out he had a giant tumor in his brain all that time. They did the surgery at Pennsylvania Hospital, removed the tumor. I guess it saved his life, but it had some side effects."

The Crab could really tell a story. Nick took a seat. "And?"

"And he woke up with total amnesia. Didn't even know who he was, and worse, had no idea how to play the guitar."

"You've gotta be kidding me. This can't be a true story."

"The fuck it ain't. Your father taught me all about him.

Martino's old man decided to start playing all his old records for him, and slowly, he taught himself the guitar all over again. Can you imagine that? He came to consider the tumor a blessing because, not having any memories, he was forced to live in the present instead of being stuck in the past. And that my friend," he said loud enough for Gary to hear, "is why Pat Martino is the greatest guitarist of all time."

Gary was watching television and just gave Frank the finger over his shoulder.

Nick reflected on the part about living in the past. He considered that maybe a little amnesia would serve him well right about then. *Grace would love this story*, Nick thought. He wished he was back at the Tiki, playing Pat Martino on the jukebox and telling her all about it.

Nick looked around the Caffé and noticed all the paintings had been removed from the walls. "What the fuck?"

"Relax, they're all in the basement," Gary explained. "We were waiting for you to start taking them apart. You know, like in case there's one painting hiding another one underneath, or there's some secret code or some shit, like Virgil was saying."

Nick was finally convinced they had all lost their minds.

"Where is Virgil?" Nick said.

"He's down in the basement. Said your father stored his kayak down there or something." Nick had to laugh at the idea of the mad painter paddling down the Schuylkill.

"Virgil owns a kayak?"

"Apparently," Gary answered. "I told him ain't no kayak down there, but he insisted on looking for himself. Says your dad kept it in storage for him during the winter."

Nick grabbed two six-packs of Peroni from the box, and they all went down to the basement to take apart the frames and assist Virgil with the case of the missing kayak.

They carefully stripped the paintings down from within their frames and inspected behind each one. They didn't discover any clues leading to the location of the Prodigal of Passyunk, as Virgil had started referring to it. They had no better luck with Virgil's kayak, and Nick was starting to doubt that either existed. They returned to the dining room, and Gary put a bottle of *1942* on the bar. Virgil began to rubbing his hands together like a fat kid on Thanksgiving. Gary poured three shots but hesitated before pouring one for Virgil.

"What's wrong?" Virgil asked. His hair looked even more wild than the day Nick found him in Rittenhouse Square. He couldn't have looked crazier if he was wearing a straitjacket.

"Nothing wrong, Doc, just don't want you crashing the DeLorean."

Virgil looked confused while they all had a harmless laugh at his expense.

"Pour him a shot," Nick said to Gary. He tipped an invisible hat to Gary, adding, "Nicely done."

Frank raised his shot glass first. "To Virgil."

The painter seemed genuinely honored and raised his glass, striking a dignified pose.

Gary added to the toast. "Back to the future!"

They all drank, and this time, Virgil laughed too.

JIMMY'S VINYL

Joey carried the milk crate up from the basement. Tina was starting a roast for New Year's Day. She would be working at the Paradise, but she wanted to make sure Joey had a roast pork sandwich to take with him for lunch.

"You marching in the parade this year?" Tina asked him, even though she knew Joey detested the parade. She did a little Mummers' strut around the kitchen to make sure she was fully on his nerves.

Joey rolled his eyes in embarrassment. "You're such a dork, Mom," he said, but couldn't help laughing a little. "I'm working at the Caffé."

Now it was Tina who rolled her eyes. "You and that Caffé. Aren't you a little young to be hanging around those old drunks?" Tina wanted him to be around kids his own age. *He's growing up so fast*, she thought. In truth, she much preferred him working at the Caffé than hanging around that snake in the grass Bobby De Rosa. She'd nearly had a fit when he went to Miami with him. "You're supposed to be going to EDM festivals or rap concerts or whatever kids are into these days, not drinking sambuca and playing gin with a bunch of old hoods." She looked at him as he was flipping through the albums in the milk crate. He had become so mature in the past year, so tall, so serious — just like his father.

She was about to holler at him for putting the dusty old crate on her kitchen table, but walked behind him and draped her arms around her son instead, causing him to squirm as she showered him with loud, annoying kisses. He made a halfhearted effort to escape from her grasp, but truth be told, it felt good—safe and familiar as a security blanket. Joey allowed himself that momentary indulgence but quickly shook himself back to adulthood and turned to look at his mother.

"What was he really like, Mom?"

Tina's hazel eyes turned sad at that moment and they searched her son's face, looking for some way to ease his pain, answer his questions, fill the void.

"He was tall. He was handsome—"

Joey interrupted. "That's not what I mean, Mom. I've seen the pictures. I mean, what was he *really* like?"

Tina understood completely. Mothers always do. She didn't answer right away. She sat down and started flipping through the crate. The albums were the only things of Jimmy's she possessed. Joey sat down beside her.

"He was smart, Joey, sharp as a tack. And he was, what's the word … tenacious. When he got a hold of something, an idea, a plan—me." She smiled at that. "He never let go."

Joey nodded like he understood. His eyes were focused on the albums as Tina continued to flip them, occasionally taking one out and turning it over.

"Mostly," Tina continued, "he was fiercely loyal, just like you, honey."

Joey wiped at his face like he had dust in his eye from

the old albums, but Tina knew better. Her heart was breaking.

"Loyal to what?" Joey asked.

"Loyal to what mattered most." Tina picked out an album and walked over to one of Joey's turntables that were set up in the living room where he practiced. She pulled a record from its sleeve and blew on the vinyl, placing the needle carefully on a track. "Loyal to me. Loyal to his friends. Loyal to Nick Di Nobile," she had to add begrudgingly.

She reached out to Joey with outstretched arms, beckoning him to join her in a dance.

Joey sat at the table, shaking his head and laughing. This time he didn't try to hide the tear he wiped from his face.

"Come on," Tina chided him, "dance with your old mother."

Joey stood obediently and walked over. "You're not old, Mom."

Tina wiped the tears from his cheek in gratitude. "Goddamn right, I ain't."

They held hands and started to dance in the clumsy way of mothers and sons. They stumbled around the living room laughing wildly as Tina tried to teach her son the tango hustle to Tavares's "More than a Woman."

Joey would think back to this moment many times throughout his life. It was one of those magical days he would occasionally conjure up; the smell of the roast, the melody of the song, his mother's laughing face as he spun her around the living room. A brief shining moment where nothing else existed, and everything was right in the world.

The glorious spaces between.

THE NIGHT WATCH

The three of them killed the bottle of 1942, minus a couple of shots for Beto and Carlos, the busboy (before Gary cut them off). Virgil was pretty pickled and was rambling on about Rembrandt's *The Night Watch*. He told of how the painting had been removed from the Rijksmuseum in Amsterdam during World War II to hide it from the Nazis. Virgil described how Hitler had seized countless art treasures during the various occupations and stored many of them in the salt mines that served as repositories for their loot. Most were recovered by the Monuments Men, but thousands of others were feared lost or destroyed. Virgil believed the Prodigal they were seeking was one of the stolen Nazi paintings, stashed away, then stolen and bartered from one criminal organization to another over the years.

"I think you've had enough, Doc," Gary said when he finished.

If Virgil wasn't fond of his new nickname, he wasn't letting on. "Do you know why it's called *The Night Watch*?" Virgil asked.

"No," Gary answered, "but I have a feeling you're gonna tell us."

"For years, the scene in the painting was thought to be nocturnal. It wasn't until it was restored and cleaned in 1942 that the layers of varnish were removed and the light was revealed, showing it to be a daytime scene."

"So what are you saying?" Nick chimed in.

"I'm saying…" Virgil paused like he was really savoring this "If you want to find *The Prodigal of Passyunk*, maybe you need to remove some of the varnish from your own eyes."

The Prodigal of Passyunk. Funny how as soon as you give something a name it suddenly takes on a life of its own. Nick thought about it. Virgil definitely made sense at times if you could weed your way through all his other wackiness. He was thinking more about what Tommy McKenna had shown him, though, and the varnish that had been stripped from the Rose. Tommy's words rung true in his head. *There is no painting. He's not after any painting, Nick, he's after this.*

People were starting to filter into the Caffé. The small dining room was fully booked, and Gary was doing a *prix fixe* seating with a wine pairing at nine. The bar would be packed all night with the regulars, as well as a few unattached New Year's Eve stragglers with no other plans. Hardcore bachelor types confident the woman of their dreams would come traipsing in at the stroke of twelve looking for true love. Hope can be a nasty thing like that, especially when you pretend it doesn't exist. It had the same outcome as ignoring cancer.

It was going to be a long night. Nick was headed home to rest up and shower. Gary put Virgil in an Uber, and

Frank offered Nick a ride home. They walked to Frank's rental.

"You okay to drive, Frankie?" He didn't look it.

"I'm okay for city driving, Nicky." They drove in silence for a couple blocks, and then Frank went first. "This has been one crazy trip, Nicky."

"I don't disagree, Unc," Nick replied. "Can't say it hasn't been fun, though."

"Just like old times, huh, nephew?"

"Yeah, something like that. If your idea of old times is disappointment and heartache."

Frank lit a Marlboro and blew the smoke out the driver's window. "Story of my life, Nicky. Story of my life." They pulled up in front of Nick's grandmother's house. "You know, Nicky, all kidding aside, if this is all just a diversion and you know where this fucking thing is, well, now would be as good a time as any to turn it over."

Nick seethed.

"First of all, Unc, the joke's on you, or rather, your boss. The painting doesn't exist. It never did. Whatever you may have sold to my father back then was just a worthless piece of shit, and he was right to toss it in the trash. I'm starting to think this was my father's final "fuck you" to the Rose and just another in a long line of messes he left for me to clean up. Secondly, and I want you to listen carefully in case you have to repeat this to somebody, in the unlikely event it *did* exist and I *did* know where my father hid it, I would burn the motherfucker before I turned it over to that rat fuck."

Frank was caught off guard a little by Nick's anger, but it wasn't unwarranted, and he knew Nick wasn't out of line. He was actually proud of him in a twisted way.

"*First of all,* Nicky, he's not my boss. *Secondly,* I may not be an art expert like that crazy fucking Virgil, but I know what I gave your father. More importantly, I remember the look on his face. You've been away a long time, we both have. This thing is bigger than you or me, and somebody's gonna get hurt."

"You fucking threatening me, Unc?" Nick's eyes flashed with a violence he hadn't felt in a long time. Frank recognized it and retreated a little. Nick was expecting Frank to snap back, maybe worse, and was surprised to see a look of genuine hurt on the old man's face.

"I would never hurt you, Nicky. I'm your uncle ... and I love you."

"Yeah, I love you too, Unc, but that never seemed to stop anyone before."

Frank couldn't argue with that, so he just reached over and pinched Nick on the cheek, the same way he did when his nephew was just a boy.

It took Nick a few seconds to calm down. In his anger, he'd let the *rat* comment slip. He wasn't quite ready to entrust Frankie with what he'd learned from Tommy. Nick got out of the car and turned to Frank before he shut the door.

"See you tonight, Unc?"

Frank stared straight ahead and blew some smoke out the driver's window before answering. "I don't think so, nephew."

"Whaddya have a big date or something?"

"Something like that."

"Okay then, see you in the morning?"

Frank didn't answer the question. Instead, he just said, "Happy New Year, kid."

"Happy New Year, Unc." Nick waved as Frank drove away.

Frank drove back to the apartment. The whole time, he kept playing Nick's words over in his head. *See you in the morning.*

PLAN B

Frank circled the block three times before finally caving in and parking in the bus zone on 12th Street. *Who the fuck is taking a bus on New Year's Eve anyway?* he reasoned. *Besides, it's a rental.* Frank was about to unlock the front door that led to the second-floor apartment he'd called home for the last few days when he heard a woman's voice.

"Got a light?"

He turned to see a figure step out of the shadows, and what a figure it was. *It can't be.* She stepped under the streetlight. Her hair was blonde now, but there was no mistaking that face. The yellow, white, and rose gold medallion settled in her cleavage like the Christmas star and erased any doubt.

"Donna? What the fuck?" It was a weird thing to say, but the shock of seeing this vision sprouting out of the sidewalk like a desert rose left him dumbfounded.

She must have sensed his distress and walked over to him, took his arm like they were old friends, and gave him a kiss on the cheek.

"Let's go get us a drink, Frankie."

Too stunned to protest, Frank just went along with

the program, and the two of them walked to the corner and had a seat at the bar of Smokey Joe's Tap Room. Frankie had hung out at Smokey's decades ago, except it wasn't called Smokey's back then. He had a complicated history with the place, and he prayed the bricks didn't have memories.

"Just like the club, Frankie, don't you think? I may order a pina colada, how 'bout you?"

"This ain't a frozen drink type of joint," Frank answered her like she was serious—maybe she was.

She put her handbag on the bar and ordered two shots of Maker's Mark.

"Hold the umbrella," Frank mumbled.

"See? That's funny, Frank. I knew I liked you when we first met. Do you remember what you asked me?"

Frank thought about it. "If I recall correctly, I said something like 'what are you doing here?'"

"Good memory. And then I said, 'You mean, what's a nice girl like me doing in a place like this?' Do you remember what else I said?"

"You said, 'Maybe I'm not such a nice girl.'"

"*That's* the one, Frankie. And I most certainly am not—a nice girl that is."

They drank their shots. *I'm starting to believe you*, Frank thought.

"We have a mutual friend in Miami."

Frank knew exactly who she meant but maintained the charade. "I have lots of friends in Miami. Which one are you referring to?"

"This one has really long arms. They can reach all the way from Miami to Moscow and back to Philadelphia."

Frank signaled for two more Maker's. "Does my dear friend perhaps have a message for me?"

"That he does, Frankie."

They clicked glasses and knocked back the whiskeys. Donna leaned in and wrapped both arms around Frank's neck. She was so close that her necklace rested against his shoulder and her pouty lips brushed against his ear as she whispered the message in two moist syllables that made the hair stand up on his neck.

"Plan B."

SUN TZU

All warfare is based on deception. Hence, when able to attack, we must seem unable; when using our forces, we must seem inactive; when we are near, we must make the enemy believe we are far away; when far away, we must make him believe we are near. Hold out baits to entice the enemy. Feign disorder, and crush him.

– Sun Tzu, *The Art of War*

Nick got back to Vecchio around ten. The party was in full swing. The nine o'clock diners were finishing their entrees, and Joey had shifted into an up-tempo selection with Eddie Kendrick's "Date with the Rain." Alberto was shaking up a martini in dramatic fashion. Gary was helping Carlos clear a table, and they were laughing about something Gary had said.

Nick watched all this from the sidewalk through the gold leaf lettering that spelled out Caffé Vecchio on the plate glass windows. Joey's songs leaked out each time someone opened the door and hurried out for a smoke. From Nick's vantage point on the sidewalk, it all seemed so cheery and carefree. A souvenir snow globe from back home—*Greetings From Passyunk Avenue!*

Nick was hesitant to walk in, as if his entry would disrupt the natural habitat. He tapped on the window as Gary walked by and pointed toward the back of the restaurant. Nick walked around the corner and turned up the alley leading to the back door. They met in the kitchen.

"What's up, slick? You got a delivery or something?" The big man was smiling at Nick like they didn't have a care in the world. Nick being back was an accepted fact now, and it was starting to feel like he never left. And that's exactly what Nick was afraid of. Well, that and the lengths the Rose was willing to go to in order to recover the file he held in his hand.

"Let's go upstairs, G. There's something I need to show you."

Gary looked down at the envelope Nick held in his hand and smiled. "Can it wait? It's kinda busy out there, in case you hadn't noticed."

"It's important. Sorry about the timing."

Gary turned and walked up the stairs to the office, and Nick followed behind. Gary took a seat behind the desk and took out a bottle of Knob Creek. He poured a measure in two glasses and placed them on the desk.

"So," Gary said, "what's so important that it can't wait till the new year?"

Nick just blurted it out. "There is no painting. That's not what the Rose wants." Nick took the memos out of the envelope, turned them to face Gary, and placed them on the desk. "He's after these."

Gary took a pair of readers out of the desk and started to skim through the pages, too quickly to actually read them. He grunted as he shuffled through them and nodded his head. He placed them back in the envelope and slid them back across the desk.

"Where did you get these?" Gary asked.

Nick hadn't been prepared for that reaction. "What does it matter, G? Do you know what it says? Did you even read it?"

Gary folded his hands in front of him like the steeple on a church. "You know, Nick, you're a smart guy. Smarter than me, that's for damn sure. But I once knew a guy even smarter. This guy sat back and looked at all the pieces on the board, took it all in while the other players scrambled and fretted. Like he wasn't even playing the game. You ever heard of Sun Tzu?"

Nick smiled, knowing where the big man was going. "No, Gary, why don't you tell me."

"Sun Tzu was this Chinese cat, smart motherfucker lived thousands of years ago. Wrote about strategy and such, how to act when your enemy is stronger than you, shit like that."

"It's starting to sound familiar." Nick played along.

"Anyway, Sun Tzu had this particular saying that my man was fond of repeatin', you know, while he was hawkin' the board in the game he wasn't playing? It goes something like this: 'Let your plans be dark and impenetrable as night, and when you move, fall like a thunderbolt.' That's the way it was told to me anyhow. And I never forgot it."

Gary took a set of keys from his pocket, unlocked a desk drawer, and pulled it open. He took out a file and placed it on the desk.

"Your old man knew this day would come. And he knew just what you'd do." Gary was smiling now, like he was enjoying an inside joke at Nick's expense. "That's why he made me promise to do my best to keep you out of it. And that's exactly what I'm gonna do."

"So you knew the Rose was a rat all this time?"

Gary nodded.

"And that Del Ciotto is knee-deep in all of it?"

Gary kept right on nodding. "That too."

"So what are we gonna do?"

Gary stood up. "*We* ain't doing shit. *You* gonna handle the business what brought you here in the first place, go back to your tiki hut and that fine chica, and shit here gonna be what it gonna be."

"How about Frank?" Nick asked.

"Frank's a big boy. He can make his own decisions."

Gary's phone vibrated with a text. Nick could see his alarm as he looked at it. Gary jumped up from his seat and hustled to the door.

"You wait here," he said firmly as he pointed at Nick.

Nick got up and followed two seconds after Gary left. Nick could see right away what the commotion was about. The Rose and one of his guys were seated at the end of the bar. Nick took a second to take in the scene and process the situation. He watched through a small window in the kitchen door as Gary approached them. It occurred to Nick this was the first time he'd actually seen the man who was causing them all this aggravation, other than that distant glimpse at the Fontainebleau. That seemed like years ago.

"We done seatin' for the night," Gary said as he walked up to the men.

"We're just having a New Year's drink, that's all," the Rose snarled.

"Good, why don't you finish up then? This a private party from here on out." He looked over to Alberto, signaling for the check. "I got this."

Rose's man must have taken offense to being spoken to like that. He rose off his stool and pointed at Gary. "Listen, you fucking nig—"

He never got the word out of his mouth. Gary hit him with a flat-footed straight right that didn't look like it had much on it but sat the man right back on his stool.

"Next one, I set my feet, and you can ring in the new year from Methodist," Gary said, referring to the closest hospital.

By this time, Nick had come rushing from the kitchen. Joey came out from behind his DJ station. The Rose laughed and put his hand on the man's chest to signal for him to stay seated. Nick stood next to Gary.

"Well, if it isn't the heir apparent," the Rose quipped. He turned his attention to Joey. "Have a drink with us, Joey."

"I can't, Bobby, I'm working," Joey answered sheepishly, pointing at his station.

"That's right," the Rose answered. "Working. That's what I thought you were doing here." Joey just stared at the ground.

"Leave the kid out of it," Nick said.

"You giving orders now?"

"On this side of that door, yeah, I guess I am." The pressure of the last few days was building inside Nick, and he saw no reason to hold back any longer.

Gary must have sensed Nick's growing courage because he shot him a look that seemed to suggest *not now*. Nick thought of something his father had always told him. *Discretion is the better part of valor.* If he didn't understand it then, he understood it now.

Gary stepped in. "I'm in charge tonight. The kid works for me."

"Is that right?" De Rosa seemed amused by the statement.

Nick was watching the Rose's man. He had draped his jacket back just enough to reveal the handle of a pistol in his waistband. The Rose saw it too. He had made his point and couldn't afford a shooting in the middle of a restaurant on New Year's Eve. Even his cozy arrangement with Del Ciotto couldn't get him a pass for that. He stood up and buttoned his jacket. "Let's go, Richie."

The Rose turned to Joey as he was about to walk out the door. "See you tomorrow, kid." Then he turned to Nick. "You too, Di Nobile," he said through a menacing smile.

Nick wasn't sure what prompted him to do what he did next, but he walked over to the cheese cart, pulled back the cloth, and grabbed a chunk of Reggiano as he hollered toward the Rose, just as he was about to walk out. "Hey, De Rosa."

The Rose turned.

"Happy New Year," Nick said as he tossed the Reggiano toward him.

The cheese seemed to hang in the air for a long time. Gary was staring at it like he was watching a buzzer-beating three-pointer in mid arc. The Rose didn't expect it either, so he did what most people would reflexively do in that situation—he caught it.

For that brief moment, Bobby "The Rose" De Rosa stood in front of a packed house in Caffé Vecchio on New Year's Eve holding a piece of cheese.

The Rose recovered from his initial shock, then the "King of Rats" hurled the "King of Cheeses" across the room before storming out.

Joey and Nick shared a long look.

THE JEWEL OF PASSYUNK AVENUE

The room soon returned to normal. The Caffé had seen far worse, and a few of the patrons got their first Vecchio story. A little piece of folklore to coddle, nurture and shuttle back to the suburbs. That was the magic sauce Tony was huckstering all those years; an experience. A story you could retell long after you savored the wine and digested the food. A sense of being part of something. That was what people like the Rose didn't get, would never get. Tony was a storyteller first, a restaurateur second. The Caffé was the medium, but Tony was the message. And the paintings? They were the most indispensable tool in the old sorcerer's bag of tricks; the diversion. While everyone was focused on the pictures on the walls, Tony was performing his sleight of hand somewhere else.

A few minutes before midnight, the bar was packed. The dinner guests who had stuck around were ready to hoot and holler at the stroke of midnight. Gary and Nick were huddled together near the hostess station, drinking Peronis and keeping a careful watch for any late arrivals lurking out on the Avenue. At 11:55, one showed up.

Nick had been busting Gary's balls. "I thought you hit harder than that, big boy. What happened to you?"

"Shit. That was just a little love tap put that boy on his ass. He softer than Q-tip cotton. Besides, you know how much that plate glass window would cost?"

Nick was laughing at Gary's remarks when he spotted the unexpected visitor approaching quickly from across Passyunk Avenue.

Angie Romano looked flustered. Radiant, but flustered. Nick pushed open the door for her, and as she brushed past him, her perfume hit him with a jab that rivaled Gary's love tap. Gary made some room at the bar and rustled up a stool for her. Nick took her coat and handed it to the hostess before joining her at the bar.

"I figured you'd be at the Paradise," Nick said. "I mean, I'm glad you're here, but … is everything okay?"

"It's Tommy," she said.

For a moment, Nick had a horrible thought and an even worse image. "What do you mean?" he asked urgently. "Is he okay?"

"Oh, he's okay, alright. More than okay. He broke up with me. Said he's been seeing someone else. They're in love, blah-blah-blah. Bottom line, he's going to Clearwater with her."

Nick actually burst out laughing until he was bent over, trying to catch his breath.

"Get the fuck out of here." He was looking outside, fully expecting to see his old friend burst in dressed like Baby New Year or something, blowing a horn, banging a pot, and they would all have a laugh on poor old Nick Di Nobile. But Tommy McKenna was nowhere to be found. "This is a fucking joke, right?"

She was sipping a Ketel and club while she shook her head. "No joke."

"Okay, so my fat fucking Santa Claus looking friend, against all odds, lands Angie Romano, the jewel of Passyunk Avenue, the face that launched a thousand Coupe DeVilles, then he decided to rip up the winning Powerball ticket?" Nick shook his head. "I don't believe it."

"Believe it." Angie put her drink down on the bar a little hard to punctuate her seriousness. "And I liked the part about the Cadillacs, Nick, but are you sure it was my face that got all those engines revving?" She got up, gave him a tender kiss on the cheek, and whispered in his ear. "I liked the part about the jewel too, Nicky. You always had a way with words."

The crowd was starting the countdown.

"TEN... NINE ..."

Nick signaled to Alberto, who poured Nick a hurried shot of Ketel since that's what he happened to have in his hand.

"FIVE... FOUR..."

Nick and Gary clicked glasses. Joey was at his station, a knockout at his side. Beto came out from the kitchen and joined them at the bar.

"TWO... ONE."

Angie and Nick locked eyes.

"HAPPY NEW YEAR!"

The crowd went wild. Outside, fireworks, M-80s and gunfire erupted out on the streets of South Philly. A few old-timers banged on pots and pans. Virgil had snuck in at some point. He must have got some love out on the Avenue because his mask had an enormous set of red lipstick lips dead center, making him look like the Joker. Gary took one look at him and bust out laughing.

Angie jumped into Nick's arms. He felt her tears on his face and knew she was telling the truth about Tommy. She pulled back for a moment to look into his eyes. "Happy New Year, Nick," she said, then she kissed him long and hard. This time, not on the cheek.

Nick's head was spinning. He felt like his skull was a giant snow globe and the hands of fate were shaking it, except instead of snow, cherry blossoms swirled around inside.

"Excuse me, Angie." He needed a minute to compose himself because he was in danger of diving headlong into the deep end of her eyes, where he had almost drowned all those years ago.

Nick walked to the kitchen, went out by the dumpster for some fresh air and quiet and called Grace.

It was pretty loud at the Tiki, so Grace walked away from the bar and onto the beach when the phone rang. She was crying when she answered. "I'm looking out at the ocean and thinking of you, but you're so far away, like the lights of the little boat I see."

"I'm not that far, Grace. I'll be back with you soon, I promise."

"Don't make a promise you can't keep, Nick. You're a better man than that. I swear, if I thought you were on that boat, I would swim out to you in the dark."

Nick thought about it. "You know what, Grace, I believe you would. But this is my swim to make."

"Okay, Nicky, just come back to me, my love. This is where you belong."

Nick knew she was right. And in that moment, everything became clear to him. He knew what he needed to do.

"I know, Grace. I love you. Happy New Year."

"It will be happy when you're here with me, not a minute before."

Grace hung up.

Nick was about to go back inside when he heard a crash from behind the dumpster. He froze for a second until he saw a rat scurry along the wall. The filthy vermin had made all that racket.

SAKURA

Nick walked back in and wished the guys in the kitchen Happy New Year. He gave Beto five hundred for himself and three hundred to split between the cooks and the busboy. Beto gave Nick a big hug and fished a Corona out of a five-gallon bucket. "Feliz Año Nuevo," Beto toasted, and they drank to the new year.

Out in the dining room, the crowd had thinned out. The last two tables were wrapping up, and a few people were waiting for their Ubers and Lyfts. Joey and the knockout were canoodling at a corner table. Virgil and Gary were sitting together at the bar. Angie sat at the other end of the bar, nestled with her back to the wall. An empty stool was in front of her, clearly reserved for Nick.

Nick walked over to Angie and rested his forearm on the bar. He swung a leg over the stool but didn't fully take a seat, preferring to hover for the moment.

"Angie, I'm not trying to put you through anything, but indulge me for a minute. What exactly did Tommy say?"

"That's the funny thing. There was no big blowup, not even a disagreement. He just announced it, like he was canceling a dinner reservation."

"It doesn't make sense." Nick stared at his Corona like the answer was in there. "Are you sure you didn't maybe… do something, and Tommy found out?"

She looked at Nick for a second, first like she was a little hurt, but in a flash, like a demon. "Fuck you, Nick."

"Whoa, hold on. It's a legitimate question. I mean, think about it. Which scenario makes more sense—Tommy leaves you for God knows who, or maybe he misunderstood something and decided to break things off preemptively, you know, to save face?"

"You mean like you, Nick?"

Fuck, Nick thought. *I walked right into that one.*

"We both know it wasn't like that, Angie. But for the record, since we're airing things out, I apologize for anything I did to hurt you. I was hurt myself, but I take full responsibility."

"Thanks, Nick. Believe it or not, even after all the years, I still needed to hear that. I apologize too. I wasn't blameless. But it was a long time ago, and we're both different people now, I suppose."

Nick drained the rest of his Corona. "I suppose we are." Nick sat down and faced her. "Can I ask you something though?" He didn't wait for her answer. "Did I imagine it all? I mean, were we really that special, or was that just me being young and stupid? Sometimes I think I just idealized it because it looks so perfect at a distance. Then I think, what if we'd stuck it out? Would it have just turned ugly, like everybody else?"

Angie smiled. She finished her drink, picked up her coat, and stood. "I don't have all those answers, Nick. I'm just a silly South Philly girl, remember? I'll tell you something I do know, though. Every year since you left, when the days start to grow longer, I go to Rittenhouse Square by myself and I have a drink for us. And those cherry blossom trees? They remind me of you. Isn't that silly?"

Nick gazed into her eyes, knowing it might be the last time he saw her for a long time — maybe ever. "Positively ridiculous," he answered with a smile.

She touched his face, then walked out into the cold New Year's night.

WHEN THE SAINTS GO
MARCHING IN

Frank put on his makeup, coating his face with white greasepaint. After his little run-in with Donna, he'd called it an early night, knowing he had a long day ahead of him. Ralph called as he was getting ready.

"Where you been, Frankie? I called you all day."

"Sorry. I left the phone home. What's up?"

"That thing we talked about? In Miami? Turns out it's true."

Frank was thinking of his conversation with Donna, if you could call it that.

"Yeah, I kinda figured that."

Ralph laughed. "Donna get to you?"

"You know her?" Frank asked, but the picture was coming together.

"Okay," Ralph said, "so you know what to do." It was more an order than a question.

"Yeah, Ralph, I know what to do." Frank started to say Happy New Year, but Ralph had already hung up. Frank threw the greasepaint smeared phone into his sack.

He pulled on his long johns, dressed in layers, and pulled on a black and white Clippers costume. He then slipped the red and gold Strutters wench suit over it so that it was completely covered. Frank topped it off with a red and gold hat that covered his ears and walked out onto the fire escape. Frank looked at the old pair of boots he had spray painted the night before, just like he had in his youth. He sat at the top of the steps and donned his golden slippers. The gold paint formed a residual outline on the fire escape landing. It sparkled like the remnants of a stellar corona.

Frank carried a satin bag that matched the Strutters suit. That bag contained a similar bag within that matched the Shooters suit, along with a folded-up Shooters hat, dark sunglasses, gloves, and a Smith & Wesson snub-nose .38 loaded with hollow-point bullets. Frank walked out into the crisp morning air, took a deep breath, and exhaled. His breath was visible and hung there for a second. It felt like old times.

He walked quickly and with purpose. He had a long circuitous route mapped out in his head, and he had to cover a lot of ground quickly. Frank walked at a brisk pace but swerved just enough to appear drunk, or hungover. He kept his head down, hat pulled tight, sunglasses on.

Any other day of the year, he would have looked like a maniac, but on this morning, he was just one of thousands of drunken Mummers. No cop would give him a second look. Dressed in his Strutters outer layer, gold boots, and white face paint, he was indistinguishable from three hundred fifty other guys...on this day only. The Rose had really thought it through, Frank acknowledged. It was surprising someone hadn't tried it before. Frank knew nothing was one hundred percent, but he had to hand it to himself, it had always been a good plan. It nagged him that the Rose found a way to take credit for it.

He walked south on Ninth for seven blocks to Oregon. Turning left, he weaved his way to Fifth street, taking a staggered route, using only the smaller streets now, the named streets sandwiched by the numbered streets—the spaces between.

He continued in this manner as he turned and back-tracked north, while also sliding east until he mixed in with the building crowd of Mummers assembling on Second Street. It was on Second Street where the unofficial—some would say *real*—parade would take place after the officially sanctioned march at City Hall. Frank was able to blend into the swelling sea of wenches. He found a porta potty and locked the door behind him.

A porta potty on New Year's Day is not a place you want to linger. Even at this early hour, it was already filling with vomit and waste. Frank thought it was too risky to try to use a bathroom in one of the clubhouses. It was tight quarters, but Frank took off his boots and wrestled off his Strutters suit, revealing the costume beneath. He switched hats, placed the Strutters hat and bag inside the second black and white satchel, and put his boots back on—his *work* boots. He emerged from the porta potty a Yankee Clipper.

When Frank finally reached Morris Street, he turned left and continued his winding route, circling back to the neighborhood. He was starting to breathe hard but couldn't slow down now. He had an appointment to keep and couldn't afford to be late. He pushed creeping doubts out of his head and checked his Casio watch—7:30, plenty of time. His target had a reliable schedule. His blind trust in Frank would be his undoing.

His bag was strapped crossways, and he held it close to his body to keep it from swinging with the weight of the revolver as he increased his pace. It made a rhythmic clicking noise in time with his stride, and Frank had to stop for a second to wrap the flask inside the Strutters hat to muffle the sound. His approach would need to be silent, and the clicking could compromise his advantage. Nothing was left to chance. Even the flask was not super-fluous. Every item Frank carried with him that morning had a purpose. He felt an adrenaline rush that could only be described as the sense of immortality that comes with wielding the power of life and death over another human being. Frank felt some rising agita in his chest and throat and regretted the glass of orange juice. *I should have doubled up on my antacid,* he thought. He rubbed his chest and spat out some of the rising acid, lest he vomit.

Nick sat in the kitchen of his grandmother's house. Other than Vecchio, it was the last property remaining to be sold to close out the estate. He had purposely drug his feet on this one. The little rowhome was chock-full of childhood memories, and more than a few ghosts. Every utensil was in its place, frozen in time. Nick pulled out a wooden spoon and laughed to himself. It was the chosen weapon of every Italian grandmother, and Nick knew this one intimately.

It was worn unevenly after decades of stirring in pots and pans by Nick's grandmother. He wondered how he could possibly sort and box all the utensils and knickknacks. Each one seemed more a talisman than a tool, and he would hate to throw them away. He knew what Grace would say. Let them go. Hold them for a moment, acknowledge their existence, and then leave them in the past, along with all the other things holding you back. Maybe there was something to Grace's mysticism. She was at peace with herself, which was more than Nick could say. He vowed to try things Grace's way once he returned to Lauderdale.

Nick finished his coffee and washed out his cup in the sink. New Year's Day was always a big day at the Caffé. Nick was never really fond of the parade. Sure, he marched in his younger days, but it soon lost its luster, like most other things from his youth. He'd hung up his golden slippers long ago, never quite understanding how other guys made the leap of converting it into a religion. That's how seriously they took it. Nick moved on. Grace would have approved, he thought to himself.

He had parked his car on a garage pavement directly across from the rowhome. The two garages sat side by side on the narrow street and had been owned by the Di Nobile family since the twenties when they were stables. Parking was tight on the street, and neighbors made use of the pavements when there were no spots to be had. In the past, neighbors shared parking spots and simply knocked on one another's doors if they needed a car moved. Now, the Parking Authority patrolled on blocks where they had previously feared to tread, and new neighbors called the police for every perceived slight.

Nick put on his coat, grabbed his keys from the old candy dish that never held a sweet, and took a long look around the old rowhome. He breathed in deeply as he closed his eyes for a brief moment. He walked into a small vestibule that became downright claustrophobic as he closed the stained glass door behind him. The vestibule floor was tiled in a black and white pattern Nick had seen somewhere else a long time ago. He hadn't noticed it previously, as his grandmother kept it covered with a runner that had obscured the pattern. For no cognizable reason, the tile filled Nick with a vague sense of dread. Sensing the foolishness of such a notion, he dismissed it as best he could and walked out into the cold New Year's morning.

He carried two bottles of homemade wine in a brown paper shopping bag in his left arm and held it close to his chest as he turned to lock the door behind him. The storm door rested on his hip as he performed the maneuver.

At the bottom of the steps, he clicked the remote to unlock the car door and switched the bag to his right arm, reaching for the car door handle with his left. As he stood for a moment in the crook of the partially opened door, Nick sensed movement in his peripheral vision as a figure approached from the rear of the car.

Frank kept the pistol low by his side. It felt a bit slippery in the cotton glove's grip, and he made a mental note to use something with a rubberized grip next time. *What next time?* Frank thought. *This is my last rodeo.* It's strange, the things that go through a man's head at a time like this.

They say your life flashes before your eyes when you face death. What most people will never know is that a similar phenomenon occurs when you're about to take one. He picked up his pace and moved like a veteran waiter, swiftly but not so quick as to appear to be running. He held the flask to his lips and actually took a quick sip. If anyone saw him approaching, or any nosy neighbors were looking out their windows, they would be looking at the flask at his lips and not the gun at his side. Hell, you could shoot a gun in the air on New Year's Eve or Day and get little more reaction than a head shake. 911 operators were inundated with calls of random gunshots that might be fireworks. Most of the cops on duty were assigned to the parade route, and Frank doubted the remainder would even respond to another call for shots fired. He was counting on it.

Two shots. That's all it would require. One less, or a few more, each carried their unique risks.

Frank was only a few feet away, but the target was moving as he put his right foot into the car. This was the moment of vulnerability Frank was striving to time precisely. Something made the target pause his movement into the driver's seat, resulting in the first shot striking closer to the right ear, causing him to spin. It must have been the swoosh-swoosh sound made by the legs of Frank's satin suit. The bulk of the redundant costumes, together with his thermals, was causing the inner legs to rub together. Frank must have grown accustomed to the rhythmic swooshing, especially as it synched up to his rising heartbeat.

His target was stunned. It would take him a few seconds to realize he had been shot.

The Rose didn't get to see much beyond the dawn of 2019. The first shot had spun him, and he was facing Frank as he raised the pistol again. Frank saw the moment of recognition in his eyes in that split second when he put it all together. *Good,* Frank thought, *I want you to know it was me.* He had to give the prick credit; he actually managed a smirk in those last moments. A large chunk of his right ear was missing, and it was gushing blood. Together with the sneer, it gave him a crazed look. Maybe it was the first shot still ringing in his ears, perhaps the first bullet had compromised the Rose's speech, but Frank could only lip-read him mouthing, "You mother—," when he delivered the second bullet into Bobby De Rosa's left eye.

"Fucker." Frank finished the phrase for him as he fell back into the door and slumped down. The back of his head became wedged between the door and the pillar in a weird way that left his body propped up. Frank just kept walking. He put the gun in his bag for the moment and held the flask in his left hand. As he approached the corner, he continued to walk briskly, adding a little side-winding sway to his gait—just another drunken wench late for the parade.

It wasn't precisely how Frank had planned it, *but it never really is, is it?* He had hoped the first shot would have caught the Rose in the back of the head while he eased himself into the driver's seat, allowing Frank to deliver the second shot while he was seated. That way, he wouldn't have to shoot through the window and could simply swing the man's legs in and close the door behind him. It turned out a bit messier and would likely be discovered sooner. *Fuck it,* Frank thought. He stuck to the plan, weaving north and east, still using the little streets, making his way to the staging area, where he would blend back into the Brigade and strut his way back. *Nascosta in piena vista.*

He ducked into a non-descript, *old man's bar* along his route to do a quick change in the bathroom. Plus, he really did need to take a leak. The bar hadn't changed much since Frank left. It wasn't quite in the neighborhood, but not quite in Center City either. It was one of those shot-and-a-beer bars on the fringe that catered to drinkers at both ends of their drinking careers. The Bamboo Tavern also did a brisk underage business, hosting an unofficial "teen night" on Fridays in the back room. Once upon a time, it served Chinese takeout. The kitchen operated only for the occasional burger hastily cooked on a flat top to satisfy an inspector and preserve the license to open on Sunday. No one bothered to change the name, and no one cared. Numbers, horses, and small loans supplemented the day trade. An assortment of hardcore drinkers hastened their journey to Holy Cross Cemetery. The place was purgatory for alcoholics. A portrait of Pope Pius XII hung over the door. Mussolini's picture kept watch over a Dodge City video poker machine in an alcove next to the beer box.

Real estate was booming in the surrounding area, and Frank was surprised the relic hadn't been sold and flipped already. It still had what used to be referred to as a "ladies entrance." It was a throwback to the days when it was considered inappropriate for a lady to be seen walking into the front door of a South Philly bar. Nowadays, it primarily served as an underage entrance for the Friday night crowd. The bar was close to Broad Street and would be crowded by now, with the parade crowd stopping in for takeout or a quick celebratory shot.

Frank slipped in through the ladies entrance. The bathrooms were in the back, and Frank tried the men's room door. It was occupied, and Frank waited until one of the regular drunks stumbled out. He didn't give Frank a second look. The smell of early morning bleach was sickening. Frank stared at himself in a broken mirror. He was sweating profusely from his scalp, and the white greasepaint glistened. He wanted to rub it off with the rough C-fold towels stacked neatly on the sink but still needed it for the march. His heart was beating wildly from the combination of the long walk and adrenaline. His reflux was out of control, and he vomited into the toilet. He wiped his mouth on his sleeve after alternately sipping from the sink and spitting out the taste. He wrestled his way out of the Shooters suit and pulled down the Strutters suit enough to take a piss. He folded the Shooters suit and shoved it together with the flask into the Strutters bag. He kept the hat off for the moment and fixed his hair as best he could with his fingers. Looking down at his shoes, he noticed that the gold was speckled with drops of red, resembling two ghoulish Easter eggs. He wiped them with a handful of wet C-fold towels, smearing them enough to obscure the droplets, then flushed the towels down the toilet. He would dispose of everything else, along with both suits, later today in the Delaware River. The effort made Frank lightheaded, and he had to jerk himself upright to stop the tiny room from spinning.

Frank walked out of the bathroom and decided to take a seat at the bar to compose himself. He ordered a Rolling Rock and a shot of V.O. No Stoli Elit here. Frank smiled at the random thought.

The sudden pain in Frank's chest was crushing. At first, he just figured he had injured his shoulder during the effort, but the suffocating chest pain was unmistakable. "I'm having a heart attack," Frank managed to gasp to the bartender before he collapsed forward, sending the shot and beer crashing across the bar.

SS UNITED STATES

Nick turned to see Joey approaching as he stood in the crook of the open car door. Nick smiled at him, wondering for a moment what he was doing outside his house so early on New Year's Day. His smile faded when he saw the gun in Joey's hand, and he contemplated the unthinkable.

"Get in the car, Nick." Joey moved to the passenger side, and they got in the car together. "Drive," Joey barked. His head was spinning like an owl, and he kept the gun down across his lap.

"Where to?" Nick asked while glancing down at the gun. The shopping bag with the wine bottles sat on his lap as he steered off the pavement. Joey was looking out the rear window as they drove down Mountain Street. He lowered the passenger window as they approached the corner, his right elbow propped on the door frame. Nick noticed that the hammer on the revolver was cocked.

"You might want to ease that down, kid," Nick said.

Joey lowered the hammer carefully as they drove north on Ninth.

"Wanna tell me what this is all about?" Nick asked.

"It's Frank," Joey said. "He's working with the Rose. They're trying to kill you."

Nick laughed. He wanted to kiss the kid. "And you were going to do what?" Nick asked.

"I don't know, shoot the motherfucker I guess."

"You truly are your father's son," Nick said. He was torn between dressing the kid down for his foolishness and hugging him for his brazen loyalty. "Just put that thing away for now. We'll talk about it more at the Caffé. You can shoot Frank later if you still feel like it."

Nick could see the relief settling over Joey's face. Getting himself in that place where he was ready to take a life had taken a toll on him, and the rush of adrenaline was draining from his body. His hands started to shake as he leaned forward and tucked the pistol in his waistband.

"That's normal," Nick said. "Better they shake now. But listen to me, Joseph, those hands were meant for greater things. Besides, it's not what your father would have wanted for you."

Joey's jaw was clenched tight, and the muscles alongside pulsed in protest as he struggled to hold back his emotions. "Well, he should have lived long enough to do something about it," Joey said. As illogical as that sounded, Nick understood.

Nick started to speak but stopped himself, and the two of them drove in silence the rest of the way to Vecchio. He was about to tell Joey that he had it all wrong, that it wasn't his father's fault, that his father loved him—that *Nick* loved him—but he realized the kid needed his moment. He reached over and gently ran his hand over the boy's head instead, and that seemed to express everything he wanted to say.

As they pulled up to the Caffé, Gary was waiting for them outside. His arms were folded in front of him and his forehead was creased with worry. They parked and walked up to the Caffé together.

"Anything you want to tell me, slick?" the big man asked.

Nick feigned shock and lowered his head. "Okay. That time the Fleetwood got stolen in '83 and they found it in Cherry Hill with two flats? It was me." Nick smirked.

"Oh, you got jokes now? Well, here's a knee-slapper for you. The Rose is dead."

"What?" Nick hadn't expected that.

"Yeah. Somebody lit his ugly ass up as he was getting in his car. Sure you ain't got nothing you want to tell me."

"Maybe you should ask Wild Bill here," Nick said as he jerked his thumb toward Joey. He should have felt a sense of relief, but an errant thought stopped him dead in his tracks. "Wait. Where's Frank?"

"Marching in the parade or some such bullshit, I suppose," Gary answered. "Why?"

"Nah, couldn't be… forget it."

They sat at one of the tables and Gary opened a bottle of 1999 Tommasi Amarone.

Joey turned on the TV and it was all over the news. A sheet was set up covering the car, and cops were milling around. One plainclothes officer laughed like he just heard the funniest joke, and the camera cut away to a reporter. The heavily bundled woman was probably pulled away from parade coverage and had nothing substantive to report. The chyron below her read *New Year Shooting*. The wild speculation and obligatory greatest hits recap would follow in the days and weeks to come. The years would pass, and the murder would remain unsolved.

Gary poured three glasses of the magical blend of dried Corvina, Rondinella, and Molinara grapes that had become the de facto signature wine of the Di Nobile family.

"We celebrating something?" Nick asked.

"Nah, man, just something me and your pops would do every New Year," Gary said.

They clinked glasses, and Nick noticed Joey's hands had stopped shaking. They drank from the little glasses favored for drinking in your own house. Tony himself would drink from a repurposed jelly jar with cartoon characters on it. Nick could still picture Bam-Bam and Pebbles on a ruby red background of homemade wine.

Gary leaned over the jukebox, and Nick used the remote to shut off the TV. Levi started singing about "Standing in the Shadows of Love." A few paradegoers walked through the door but froze up a little at the sight of Gary snapping his fingers and moving side to side in a Motown two-step. Nick stood up to welcome them in. He turned on the outside light to confirm the Caffé was open for business. They had a little boy with them, and he was wearing the unmistakable look that he was about to piss his pants. Joey directed the boy to the bathroom, and Nick poured his mom and dad two glasses of Amarone, finishing off the bottle.

"Nick, there's something I need to tell you," Joey said.

"Join the club, kid. It seems like everybody has something to tell me these days."

"It's bad, Nick. It's about the Rose. I think he was a rat."

"Ya think?" Nick answered. "Let me confirm it for you, Joey. He's been on Team America since the eighties."

"You knew?" Joey looked like he was searching for a way to say something painful.

Nick felt terrible for his friend's son. He looked lost. Nick remembered Jimmy had that same look when he was struggling with *his* problems.

"There's more, Nick. The Rose paid Frank to kill you. He wanted me to—"

Nick stopped him. He put his arm around Joey and pulled him close. "Frank would never have gone through with it. He was scamming the Rose the whole time. And you, Joey, you would no sooner hurt me than your father would." Nick looked at the kid. He thought of himself at that age. "Look at me, Joey. I'm not blameless either here. I should have been here for you all these years. So what do you say we start fresh? Deal?"

Joey put out his hand to shake on it. Nick scooped him up in a crushing bear hug and then kissed him on top of his head.

Nick's phone rang. It was Virgil.

"Hey, Nick. Happy New Year. Listen, I think I know where your father stored my kayak."

"That's great, Virgil. Listen, can this wait? We're kinda in the middle of something here."

"Sure, Nick." The painter sounded disappointed.

Nick relented. "I'm sorry, Virgil. Where is it?"

"He said he was storing it at Old Port. Do you know where that is?"

"Yeah, I know where it is. I'll pick it up the first chance I get."

Gary had taken a call of his own and was waving at Nick as he moved for the door.

"I gotta go, Virgil." Nick ended the call. "What's up, G?"

"It's Frank," Gary said as he put on his coat.

Nick and Joey followed him out, and all three jumped into Gary's car.

"What's going on?" Nick asked.

"Frank had a heart attack."

"Is he dead?" Joey spoke up.

"He's alive. He's in ICU at Jefferson."

"Fucking Marlboros." Nick sat back. He knew Frank wasn't in the best of health, but he wasn't expecting this. His thoughts went back to the day he'd received that fateful phone call about his father. "*He's gone, Nicky.*" That's when it had all become clear. There would be no tearful reunions, no clarity, no closure. Just regret.

"Wait, G. You're going the wrong way," Nick said. "I thought you said, Jefferson."

"Gotta make a stop first."

"Stop? Where? Frank's fucking dying."

Gary kept driving. "Bamboo Tavern. Got a call from James, the bartender. Something there I need to pick up."

Nick gave up. He knew there was no sense arguing with Gary. Besides, if he thought it was more important to stop at the Bamboo before the ICU, he must have a good reason.

Turned out he was right.

James spotted them as soon as they walked into the old watering hole. He looked at Gary, pointed toward the back, and stepped out from behind the bar. Gary followed him, and Nick grabbed Joey by the collar of his jacket to stop him from going with him, which James wouldn't appreciate. Gary returned carrying a red and gold satin bag.

On their way to Jefferson, it was like a contest between Nick and Joey to see who could hold out longer before asking, "*What's in the bag?*" Except, Gary still wasn't driving toward Jefferson. Gary continued toward Columbus Boulevard and the waterfront. He pulled into an Ikea parking lot before they reached the street South Philadelphians still referred to as Delaware Avenue, owing to its prior title, its location parallel to the Delaware River, and mostly, out of stubborn pride. They parked and got out of the car, following Gary across Delaware Avenue to a pier that jutted out into the river. The pier housed a stevedoring company but was notable for the ancient, hulking ocean liner that was docked alongside.

"That's the SS *United States*," Nick said to Joey as they walked along the pier. "When she was built in the fifties, she was the fastest, classiest ocean liner to cross the Atlantic. Now she just sits there rotting."

"What happened?" Joey asked.

"Jets," Gary answered.

"He's right," Nick agreed. "She became obsolete almost the minute she was built. She broke the speed record in fifty-two, hung in for a while, but ultimately, everybody moved over to plane travel. She's still got the pedigree, though. Just look at those lines."

Joey tried to imagine it, but he couldn't see past the rust.

They walked the length of the pier as far as they could until they were stopped by a fence. Gary reached into the bag, using a hat he found inside to grab the revolver. He took a quick sniff from the end of the short barrel. It had been recently shot. Then he heaved the gun as far as he could into the Delaware. It made a nice splash when it hit. The ripples spread out on the filthy surface but eventually faded away.

They walked back to the car, and Gary drove north up a backstreet that ran along the shopping center, stopping every so often at a dumpster to dispose of the contents of the bag. The realization of what Frank had likely done sank in. Each man was processing it independently, but none of them mentioned it on their way to the hospital.

Nick identified himself as Frank's nephew and was told he was in intensive care. He was allowed into the unit alone and presented himself at the nurse's station. The nurse at the desk said Frank had suffered a heart attack but was stable. She allowed him in but warned that he could only stay briefly, as they may be taking Frank out for some test or procedure soon. Nick stood beside his uncle's bed. Frank was hooked up to the usual array of machines, with the tubes and wires that sometimes shock family members. Nick looked at his face, which looked even older than usual. Maybe it was the remnants of the hastily removed greasepaint that still clung stubbornly to his eyebrows and chin. It had the effect of negating his tan and giving the old Crab a strange, streaky complexion. He was still out of it, maybe from the medication, and looked like shit, but Nick had a feeling that he was gonna make it. Nick spoke softly to him.

"Yo, Unc. Don't worry about anything. We took care of the bag. Just get better so we can go back to Florida together."

Frank opened his eyes just a sliver. It looked like he was mouthing, "*Nick*," but no sound was coming out.

"Take it easy, Unc. You don't have to say anything. Just rest."

Frank seemed determined, though. He gathered his strength and willed himself to speak in a raspy, barely audible voice. "The money in the apartment—make sure my son gets it."

Nick had no idea what he was talking about, but said, "Sure, Unc, no problem."

"Did you find the painting?" Frank whispered.

"No, Unc." Then Nick added for reasons he wasn't sure of, "Not yet."

"Nicky." Frank was struggling a bit to keep up the conversation but seemed determined. "I was never gonna hurt you."

"I know that, Unc. Stop now. You need to rest up and get better."

"No, you don't know. I had another plan."

Nick was starting to feel really guilty about some of the things he had said to his uncle, along with some of the things he had thought. He humored the man and played along.

"Yeah? What was that, Unc?"

Frank strained to open his eyes as wide as he could and was trying to lift himself up off the pillow. The tendons in his neck were sticking out from the strain, and one of the machines started beeping more rapidly. "Take it easy, Unc, please." Nick tried to gently ease him back on the bed.

"I was … I was just going to kill myself." Frank collapsed back on the pillow in relief as if he had just unburdened himself of some grave sin in confession—and maybe he had. Nick considered it as he gently smoothed back his uncle's hair and dabbed away his tears with the cuff of his shirt. Nick looked up to see a man at the door.

"Excuse me," the man said. "I'm Frank Valletto. I'm his son." He nodded toward Frank.

"I'm sorry. I'm Nick Di Nobile. I'm a friend." Nick walked over and shook his hand.

"I remember you," Frank Junior said. "From the Caffé. Tony's son."

"Yeah, from the Caffé. Tony's son," Nick echoed. "Listen, he's gonna be fine. He's a strong guy. I'm gonna leave you guys."

Nick started to leave and watched as Frank Junior walked over to his father's bedside. He seemed unsure of what to do but took his father's hand in both of his. Frank Junior collapsed onto the bed and buried his face into the pillow next to Frank's head. He started sobbing uncontrollably. His words were muffled by the pillow and his crying, but Nick easily made out the phrase he kept repeating.

"I love you, Dad."

Frank managed to pull his hand out of his son's grip and slipped it behind his head, where he stroked his hair, easing his cry like a little boy who'd skinned his knee.

Nick felt as if he was intruding and quietly slipped away. As he walked out of the ICU, he whispered a silent prayer for Frank, and at the end, he added a little message of his own, figuring it couldn't hurt. *I love you, Dad.*

Joey and Gary met him in the lobby. "How is he?" Gary asked.

"Better than the Rose," Nick stated succinctly.

It was all over the news now. In the waiting room of the ER, the huddled masses, yearning to be seen, sat watching the coverage with rapt attention.

"Let's get out of here," Gary announced.

SHALLOW GRAVE

The older brother became angry and refused to go in. So his father went out and pleaded with him. But he answered his father, 'Look! All these years I've been slaving for you and never disobeyed your orders. Yet you never gave me even a young goat so I could celebrate with my friends. But when this son of yours who has squandered your property with prostitutes comes home, you kill the fattened calf for him!'

'My son,' the father said, 'you are always with me, and everything I have is yours. But we had to celebrate and be glad, because this brother of yours was dead and is alive again; he was lost and is found.

Luke 15:28

"**I** feel like we should open a bottle of champagne or something." Gary was rooting around behind the bar for a suitable bottle.

Nick wasn't really in the mood for celebrating, or drinking for that matter. The past few days had been something of an alcohol whirlwind, and Nick was considering giving drinking a break for a minute. Besides, as much of a scumbag as Bobby De Rosa was, Nick didn't feel right about toasting to his death. "I think I'll pass if you don't mind, G."

"Suit yourself, pretty boy," Gary said as he popped the cork on a bottle of Veuve Clicquot.

Nick looked around the Caffé as if for the first time since he came back. The paintings, the bar, the jukebox. It felt confining all of a sudden. Tony looked down upon them all from his perch above the jukebox, glass raised, a twinkle in his eye. *The Prodigal in the Tavern.* He couldn't have chosen a more appropriate scene for Virgil to place him in. Nick kept staring at the painting, trying to picture his own face in the image, glass raised, Angie sitting on his lap, and realized he needed to get out of there. Out of the Caffé, out of Philly. Back to the Tiki . . . back to Grace.

"Hey, Joey," Nick said. "Feel like taking a ride?"

Joey shrugged. "Sure, where we going?"

"To get Virgil's kayak." He looked over at Gary. "Okay if I take the truck?"

"Help yourself," Gary answered as he tossed the keys to the pickup they used for catering jobs and grabbing supplies. "It's out back."

Driving had always been a form of therapy for Nick. The events of the day, between Frank's heart attack, Joey's misadventure, and the nonstop coverage of the Rose's demise, made a leisurely ride on the Atlantic City Expressway seem like the perfect antidote. Get away from the city for a while. Spend some quality time with the kid. *He must feel overwhelmed*, Nick thought, *and I haven't been there for him.*

Nick fired up the trusty Chevy C10, and they crossed the Walt Whitman, headed for the shore. Joey had calmed down a bit. He tried to fill Nick in on the machinations of the Rose, which he had become privy to. Nick cut him off. That hardly seemed important now given De Rosa's present circumstances, plus, the kid already felt bad enough, and Nick wasn't about to put him through a debriefing. *What's important,* Nick thought, *is that he knows I'm here for him from now on.*

Nick drove while the kid messed with the stereo. It felt good to Nick, natural. His thoughts wandered back to all those rides back and forth to the shore with his father. Before they drifted apart, before Jimmy's death, before even Angie. He was just a boy then, and his father's voice contained the collective wisdom of the universe. Then, like every young man before him, he began to suspect that his father was wrong about everything. And all those stories that had been so endearing began to sound worn and trite. He had become wiser than his father. How long before Joey would feel the same way about him?

They got off at Exit 2, took West End Avenue across to Ventnor, pretty much avoiding Atlantic City altogether. It was high tide, and the bay at Beach Thorofare was starting to flood the road. Nick had always loved the shore this time of year. The summer crowds were gone, traffic was nonexistent. He and Angie would often abandon the city to slip away to some local bar for the afternoon. They would talk about their plans. *That's when things usually start to go sideways,* Nick thought, *when fate catches wind of your plans.* Maybe that's why he had avoided making plans with Grace. Or maybe, he thought, he was just making excuses.

They pulled up to Old Port Marina just as Joey had tuned in to a Bobby Womack number, so they sat there idling for a few minutes in deference to the song, "If You Think You're Lonely Now."

"Let's go find Virgil's kayak," Nick said when the song ended.

They got out of the truck and walked over to a storage building where George kept supplies and equipment. The door was unlocked, and Nick flicked on the lights. Some gear was stashed over in the corner: a few fishing rods, a flying gaff, and a kayak paddle. "It's gotta be over there." Nick pointed toward a blue tarp. They pulled it back, and there was Virgil's kayak, just as he described it. Nick was surprised something finally showed up where it was supposed to be. If only they'd had the same luck with the painting. He had to remind himself it didn't exist.

They carried the kayak and paddle to the truck and tossed it into the bed. Nick found some rope lying around, and Joey jumped into the bed to tie it down for the ride home.

"I'll be right back, Joey. I'm going to see George for a minute." Nick looked over to the *Tony Rome* and could see that George was working on the boat. An orange extension cord was draped over the stern, and Nick could hear the sound of a power tool coming from the cockpit. He climbed the ladder and called out for the old man, not wanting to sneak up on him. One "uncle" with a heart attack was more than enough for one day.

He was hunched over an open fish box compartment in the middle of the deck. The engines in the Bertram are situated a bit forward and were accessible through their own deck boxes. As a result, she had a huge open cockpit, allowing for plentiful storage below deck. He was grinding away at the built-in fish box, cutting out the bottom. *Probably to enlarge it*, Nick thought. He hadn't heard Nick call out to him over the grinder's noise, and was surprised when he turned to find Nick standing over him.

It was nothing compared to the shock Nick experienced when he realized it wasn't George at all working the grinder and cutting out the bottom of the fish box. It was his old friend Tommy McKenna.

Tommy leapt to his feet at the sight of Nick, dropping the grinder to the floor.

Nick smiled at him. Despite the absurdity of the scene, he was momentarily glad to see him. "Tommy, what are you—"

Tommy shoved a gun in his face, and Nick didn't have to finish asking.

"In the cabin, Di Nobile." Tommy pointed with the barrel.

"Tommy, stop. Are you out of your fucking mind? Think about what you're doing. You're a fucking cop for Chrissakes."

"Retired cop." Tommy confirmed his seriousness by nudging Nick in the back of his head with the barrel." Nick complied and walked down into the cabin, his legs a little wobbly.

"Tommy, think this through. Whatever you're up to here, it's not worth it." Nick turned to face him. Maybe the idea of being in the cabin of the *Tony Rome*, his father's boat, *his* boat now, where they had such great memories, caused him to feel a little indignant. That, and maybe the idea of being shot in the back of his head.

"You know what, fuck you, Tommy. You would shoot your friend over some painting, over *money?* Then do it. Because you're more lost than I ever was, and you'll never get to spend it cause they're using you. And then, when they have what they want, they'll kill you."

Tommy might have felt bad, but he was firm. "I ain't working with nobody. Not the Rose, not Del Ciotto. I'm in it for me and me only."

"Yeah," Nick said, "Angie told me. You're a bigger fool than I ever was, Tommy. What happened to all that 'Mickey loves you' bullshit?"

"That wasn't bullshit. I do love you, Nick. You just weren't supposed to be here, that's all.'

"So you were the one helping my father with the fiber-glass work. And what? You came up with the idea to hide the painting down there?"

"That was your dad's idea. I just built the false bottom."

"He trusted you, Tommy. And this is how you repay him?"

Tommy motioned for Nick to have a seat in the cabin.

"Do you even know the story of the Prodigal, Nick? I mean the biblical one."

"I think so, but I've got a feeling you're gonna tell me anyway."

"Damn right I am." Tommy stood in the doorway of the cabin, blocking out the light and hovering over him. Nick couldn't stop staring down the barrel. "You see, no one hardly mentions the other brother in the story. You know, the one who stayed back, worked, did the right thing, all while the prodigal ran off and blew his inheritance. That brother? He confronts the father. He asks him why the fuck do you have a party and slaughter a calf for him, and you never did that for me, the one who stayed and did right by you?"

"It says fuck in the Bible?" Nick cracked.

"You get the point, Nick. Why should you reap all the rewards after running away and I get stuck with what? My pension?"

"Oh, I get it. You're the other brother in this story, right? You really are delusional, Tommy. You get nothing? How about Angie, you dumb bastard? And me. I was your friend. I would have split it with you. Are you really that blind?"

"I'm not blind, and I'm not stupid. I didn't leave Angie. She's in for a piece once I get clear. You're the blind one, Nicky."

Nick heard the click of the hammer being pulled back. So did Tommy.

"Put the gun on the table." It was Joey. He had watched what transpired in the cockpit, crept up the ladder, and slid over the gunwale and into the cabin, nimble as a cat. He had a cocked revolver behind Tommy's ear.

I fucking love this kid, Nick thought. Tommy had no choice. For all he knew, it was Del Ciotto or one of the Rose's men on the trigger, not some nineteen-year-old DJ. He put the gun on the table. Nick grabbed it, and Joey came down hard with the butt of his gun on the top of Tommy's head. The Irishman crumpled to the ground like a drunken department store Santa Claus. Nick stood over him in disbelief, unsure what to do with the hulking mass now taking up most of the cabin floor.

"Is he dead?" Joey looked distraught. Whatever balls he had grown in the past few minutes were now firmly retracted up into his body. *God bless this kid*, Nick recited to himself.

"Nah, he's just taking a nap," Nick answered. "But he's gonna be plenty angry when he comes to." Nick thought back to something Tommy had told him that night in the Paradise: 'Don't trust anyone, Nick. Not even me.' *No shit.* "Help me roll him over, Joey," Nick said.

They rolled him on his back and Nick frisked his friend all the way down to the empty holster on his left ankle.

"What are we gonna do with him?" Joey seemed like he was about to puke, so Nick tried to lighten the atmosphere.

"Cut him up and throw him in the bay, I guess. There should be a serrated knife in the drawer next to you. I'll go get the tarp in the shed."

Joey leaned against the bulkhead and blew out a forceful breath. He reached for the drawer.

"I'm fucking kidding, Joey. Are you nuts?" Nick started to laugh. "This fat fuck might have pointed a gun in my face, but he's still my friend. Besides, we're not killers, are we?"

Joey looked at Nick and shrugged, like he wasn't sure anymore, and Nick immediately regretted fucking with the kid like that.

"My bad, kid. Too soon to joke, I guess. Help me get Kris Kringle here into the V-berth."

Getting Tommy up onto the cushions was like wrestling a giant Bluefin tuna over the transom. "We could use a block and tackle," Nick quipped. "That's thirty years of graveyard shift donuts lying there."

They finally maneuvered him into the berth as best they could, just as he started to groan. Nick grabbed a few zip ties from a tackle drawer and secured the Irishman's hands behind his back and around his belt, doubling them up and making an extra loop.

"This should slow him down enough," Nick said, but took off Tommy's sneakers as an added handicap and threw them out of the boat. In the middle of this whole scene, Nick couldn't help looking at the New Balance 624s Tommy had undoubtedly bought at Walmart and wondered how the hell he had landed Angie. Then he remembered what Tommy said about her being in for a piece of the action and it all made sense. Nick also had the presence of mind to check the compartment where Tony had kept his pistol. It was empty. Nick had a closer look at the revolver Tommy had tossed onto the table. He thought it looked familiar.

"Son of a bitch." He turned to the groaning man, who was now writhing like a fish in a cooler. "You were going to shoot me with my father's gun?" Tommy just groaned in response. "Keep an eye on him, Joey. I'll be out in the cockpit."

Nick examined the deck box. Tony (with a bit of help from Tommy) had glassed over the main fish box with a false bottom. It was a professional-looking job, complete with gelcoat and a diverted drain, except it appeared about half as deep as it should be. It was better suited for a flounder than a tuna. Tommy had managed to cut away three of the sides before Nick had interrupted him. Nick picked up the grinder and made quick work of the remaining edge. It collapsed downward, and Nick was able to lift it by sticking two fingers into the drain and pulling it up.

Beneath the false bottom was a cylindrical object wrapped in a blue tarp and secured by bungee cords. Nick lifted it out of the box. He hollered over his shoulder to Joey. "Everything alright in there?"

"All good," Joey answered.

Nick walked to the cabin door with the object under his arm. It resembled a giant blue burrito. "Let's get out of here." Joey walked out of the cabin. Before he closed the door, Nick peered in. Tommy was still lying in the V-berth, and Nick spoke to him calmly.

"Tommy, listen to me. This thing is bigger than you and me. Just let it go. I have a feeling the people looking for this wouldn't have let you go with a bump on the head."

Tommy groaned a little more clearly, and it sounded like he was in agreement, so Nick took it that he understood. "Look, let's just write this off as a misunderstanding. I'm gonna pretend like it never happened. I can't afford to lose you too, Tommy. Remember? *Rocky* at The Colonial?"

This time, Tommy didn't groan. He didn't say anything. He just closed his eyes and nodded twice.

Joey climbed down the ladder first, and Nick passed him down the blue burrito. Nick climbed and they walked to the truck. Old man George was walking the other way, and they stopped to talk.

"Happy New Year, Nicky."

Nick returned the greeting and introduced Joey.

"I'm sorry, George, we're in a bit of a hurry. Just came by to pick up that kayak." Nick nodded toward the pickup.

"Whatcha got there, Nicky?" George pointed at the tarp Joey was carrying.

"Oh, that's just a rug for the cabin, George, but it turned out it didn't quite fit."

"That's probably best, Nick. You wouldn't want to cover that beautiful teak and holly sole with a rug. Besides, I have good news. I think I have a buyer for her."

Nick put his arm around George as they walked toward the truck. "She's not for sale, George. Not now, not ever. Just keep fixing her like my dad wanted. And don't worry, I'll make sure you're paid in full for all your work."

George smiled. "I knew you wouldn't sell her, Nick. Will you keep her here?"

"Nope, she's going south." Nick smiled back. "By the way, George, a friend of mine is sleeping off a bad hangover in the cabin. It would probably be best to steer clear of him until he sobers up."

"Sure thing. I'll start back up on her tomorrow."

Nick and Joey got in the truck. Joey propped up the tarp between his legs and angled it back a bit on his shoulder. It barely fit between the floorboards and the headliner.

"Should we have a look at it, Uncle Nick?"

Nick paused for a moment, savoring the first time Joey called him uncle. "I don't think so, nephew. Call Gary, tell him we're headed back. Tell him to close up and, most importantly, make sure he has Virgil there."

"Okay, Unc." Joey called Gary with the instructions.

They pulled out of the marina and headed back to the Caffé.

EMPTY TABLES

Nick parked out back of Vecchio, and they carried the blue burrito through the kitchen and into the dining room. Gary laughed as they maneuvered it through the swinging doors.

"What's so funny?" Nick asked.

"Nothing. You two just reminded me of a scene from *The Godfather*, that's all."

"*Godfather II*," Joey answered for Nick.

"Nicely done," Nick complemented the kid. "How's Frank?" he asked Gary.

"He gonna be just fine. Might need a surgery, but he ain't dead yet."

Nick made a quick sign of the cross and kissed his hand. He cleared off four tables with Joey's help, then fit them all together forming one big square. They placed the burrito on top as Gary walked to the front door to let Virgil in. Virgil was still sporting his lipstick-smeared mask but pulled it down around his chin when he saw what they had lying on the table.

"Santa Lucia," Virgil exclaimed as he strode over to the table. "Is this it?"

"That's what we about to find out," Gary answered. He looked at Nick. "Well, you wanna do the honors?"

Nick stood over the tarp for a moment. After all he'd been through since he got back, he couldn't believe this moment had arrived and that the elusive *Prodigal* could possibly be real. After decades of his father's bullshit and braggadocio, they were about to discover if there was ever any truth to any of it. Nick paused. He wasn't sure he wanted to know. He called Joey over.

"You do the honors, kid. You earned it."

Joey gently undid the bungees and carefully unrolled the tarp. Gary took it, folded it up, and tossed it to the side. The contents were encased in a plastic bag. Joey cut the bag open with a steak knife and withdrew an industrial-sized cardboard shipping tube. Gary stepped in to slice off the duct tape securing the end cap as Virgil looked on nervously. Joey popped off the lid and pulled out two giant silica gel packets. The middle of the tube was filled with a cheesecloth type material, and Virgil helped Joey pull it out.

Virgil took over and delicately placed his hands inside the tube, applying light pressure and a counterclockwise twist to the canvas rolled inside. Virgil prayed the painting was rolled with the paint facing out and didn't want to damage the surface. He slowly extracted… a blank canvas.

Nick let out a groan like he'd been gut-punched.

OCEAN ABODE

Ralph was sipping a Tito's extra spicy Bloody Mary at Surfside 11, an oceanfront bar in Deerfield Beach. The Surfside was a nice little getaway for Ralph when he wanted to escape his usual haunts in Lauderdale and Boca and was conveniently located right between. The cocktail came with a crispy piece of apple-smoked bacon. Ralph immediately devoured it and placed the jumbo shrimp on a cocktail napkin. He slid it over to Vinny, who was on his second Michelob Ultra.

He had been trying to reach Frank on the burner since ten. Ralph got the word about the Rose and read the early news articles from back home. Frank was supposed to check in with him one last time and then get rid of the phone. It wasn't a good sign that he hadn't called, and Ralph was starting to get worried.

"You okay, Mr. C? Want me to get you a cigar or something?"

"No thanks, Vinny. I'm trying to cut back."

"That's a good resolution, Mr. C. I keep telling you to come to the gym with me. I can train you," Vinny tried to add helpfully and threw a little jab.

"I didn't say it was a resolution, kid. I don't make resolutions at my age. And I appreciate the offer, but what I forgot about training you'll never know. No offense."

Vinny looked a little hurt, but said, "None taken, Mr. C." He raised his bottle and clicked Ralph's Bloody Mary. "Salute."

Ralph raised his glass back. "Salute, kid. Thanks. You never know; maybe I'll take you up on it."

Ralph's phone rang. He picked up on the first ring. "Yeah?" There was silence for a minute while the person on the other side of the call spoke. "Is he gonna make it?" Another pause. "Okay. Thank God. Talk to you later. Ciao."

"Everything okay, Mr. C?" Vinny asked.

"Everything's fine. Let's take a ride down to Lauderdale. You ever been to the Tiki?"

"Fuck yeah," Vinny replied enthusiastically. "I love that place."

"Good," Ralph said as he got up from the table. "Andiamo."

Ralph handed the waitress two hundred, and they walked out to the valet stand.

"You drive, Vinny," Ralph said as the valet handed him the key. "I'm gonna sit back and enjoy the view."

"No problem, Mr. C, relax. I got this."

They drove down A1A along the beach. Ralph enjoyed the view as they made their way along the Hillsborough Mile. The yachts docked on the Intracoastal side belonged to the owners of the gated oceanfront mansions situated on the other side of A1A. It was one of the rare instances where a property had both private beach frontage and docking on the waterway. There were only about sixty private residences on the small barrier island. One of the palaces had recently been purchased by a Swiss holding company for twenty-five million. Ralph was pretty sure the actual owner was Dmitry. He thought about his old friend Frankie the Stone Crab, how he loved this drive. He said a prayer that he would live to see the view again.

Vinny pulled up the driveway of the Ocean Abode Resort, home to the Tuscan Tiki. Frank loved the place, but Ralph had somehow never been there. The hotel was on the ocean, but the Galt Ocean Mile veered off from A1A, where it was located. As a result, you would probably blow right past it without ever knowing it. It was also technically in Lauderdale-By-The-Sea, a small town just north of Fort Lauderdale and the better known, swankier hotels.

Nonetheless, the place did a pretty good business with spring breakers and budget-conscious families and was something of a local legend. Ralph had also heard the Di Nobile kid had a good thing going with the Tiki and thought it was as good a time as any to check the place out. Ralph remembered Tony Di Nobile as a good man. A bit of a bullshit artist, but overall a stand-up guy. He also had a particularly vivid recollection of an event that took place long ago and involved a scrappy little kid from Mountain Street.

The Tiki was packed. Ralph didn't quite get the Italo-Polynesian mashup, but he was the only one if the crowd was any indication. Vinny ordered another Ultra, and Ralph opted for a Tito's and club. The music was blaring and the big screens on the underside of the hut were primed for the bowl games. The whole place was literally steps from the beach, and Ralph could understand why Frank loved the place so much.

"*Madone*." Vinny made a low whistle as a dark-haired waitress walked by.

"Watch your manners, kid," Ralph chided him.

She was a little older than the other wait staff, with an exotic look and a dynamite smile. Ralph pegged her right away for Di Nobile's girl, and he paid Nick a silent compliment. *Nice work, kid.*

Vinny was scrolling on his phone when he came across a news notification about a murder in South Philadelphia. Being from Staten Island, Vinny didn't recognize the name, although it was referred to as a "gangland slaying."

"Hey, Mr. C," Vinny said as he handed his phone to Ralph. "You know this guy?"

Ralph took the phone and breezed through the article. He handed the phone back to Vinny. "Never heard of him."

Vinny didn't believe him, but he got the message and dropped the subject. The sun was shining, and there was no shortage of bikini-clad women filtering through the Tiki on their way to the beach.

A stool had become available, and Vinny held it for Ralph. "Another day in paradise, huh, Mr. C?"

"You got that right, kid." Ralph took a seat at the bar and thought, *I could get used to this place.* And in that instant, the Tasker Morris Brain Trust found their new meeting spot.

CARPATHIAN SURPRISE

Special Agent Del Ciotto woke on New Year's Day in a small but tidy East Kensington apartment. Kensington was a rough neighborhood and was still relatively early in its gentrification metamorphosis. New construction townhomes sat astride vacant lots. The rooftop decks provided views of the Center City skyline to the south and open-air drug markets to the north. Sid couldn't figure out why Donna insisted on living there. He wrote it off to youth and her adventurous nature. In reality, she had seen conditions in Ukraine that made Kensington look like the Hamptons.

Heroin, and later, fentanyl, had taken a sad toll on Kensington, and Philadelphia in general. There was a brave outreach effort underway, but the streets in parts of Kensington resembled scenes from a zombie apocalypse. Lost souls wandered through tent cities. Heartbroken parents trolled the perimeter, looking for sons and daughters caught up in the plague. Donna would occasionally feed them, talk to them. She made up toiletry kits that she would hand out to some of the harder cases. She remembered what it was like to live in the streets.

Sid played along. He pretended to care and praised Donna for her charity but was fundamentally incapable of empathy. At best, Del Ciotto thought all junkies suffered from a character flaw that prevented them from overcoming their addictions. At worst, he figured they deserved it.

He couldn't believe his luck when he hooked up with Donna. He had been separated from his wife for about a year. The kids were out of the house and finished college, so Sharon Del Ciotto finally felt she could leave with a clear conscience. She'd known her husband was a narcissist when she married him, but she could no longer tolerate his "eccentricities," as he liked to call them, which had become increasingly less discrete since the kids went away to college. First, it was the mechanic at the Jiffy Lube, which he tried to explain as "just goofing around." She packed his bags, though, after discovering him with a rather hirsute barista in his "man cave." She'd caught them in the middle of what could be described in quite a few ways, but "goofing around" was definitely not one of them.

At first, she didn't feel comfortable going back to Starbucks. But eventually, her desire for a Caramel Macchiato overpowered her shame, and she gave in. Then the strangest thing happened—she and the grunting barista became unlikely friends and yoga partners. He turned out to be a sweet kid, and they bonded over poetry and old movies. He helped her transform the man cave into a library. The kids liked him too.

That was another reason Sid felt so invigorated with Donna. On top of impressing all the guys on the Avenue, including that fucking Di Nobile, she wasn't squeamish about his proclivities. Once, he even thought he caught her snapping a picture of him on her iPhone during a particularly vigorous session with one of the neighborhood street urchins, as he referred to them. Because, although Del Ciotto wasn't very sympathetic about their plight, he wasn't totally against a bit of charity here and there.

Sid was awoken by the roar of the illegal dirt bikes and ATVs that seemed to have commandeered the streets of Philadelphia of late. He constantly worried that one of the wheelie hoodlums would crash into his Mercedes, which was parked in front of Donna's apartment.

Donna walked into the room with his herbal tea. She was wearing a black bra and panties, topped off with yellow kitchen gloves. She placed his tea cup and saucer on the nightstand.

"Excuse the gloves, my love. I'm doing a little cleaning and don't want to ruin my manicure."

Sid couldn't argue with that. Donna kept a spotless apartment. It was so clean, sometimes it hardly seemed like anyone lived there.

"No problem, *amore mio*," Sid answered.

"Would you be a prince and go out for some of those delightful biscuits?" Donna asked. "We seem to be out. After you finish your tea, of course."

Sid really didn't feel like going out. He hated going to the coffee shop and dealing with the Mexicans or Guatemalans or whatever the fuck they were that ran the bakery. It was three blocks away, and it was probably freezing out, but Sid could hardly complain. Donna was a certified dime piece. Here she was, prancing around the apartment in her underwear, cleaning and making him his favorite tea. Besides, he was still feeling a little bad about his performance (or lack thereof) the previous night.

Donna had been on top of him, rocking rhythmically. He had tried to imagine one of his urchins, or even the barista, all to no avail. Sid couldn't seem to focus on anything but the three interlocking medallions dangling from her necklace and swaying to and fro. He asked her to take the chain off, but she politely declined. Come to think of it, in all the time he had been seeing Donna, it was the first request she had ever refused.

He gulped down his tea. Donna had introduced him to her special blend of Ukrainian rose hip, juniper, and elderberry, which she swore were harvested from the primeval Carpathian forest of her homeland. The way Donna described the forest was so enticing. Sid would sip the tea and imagine the dark, inviting woods. She promised to take him there one day. She also told him of another tea called Chifir that Russian prisoners would brew to induce a narcotic-like high. Her father had passed down the recipe. Donna called her proprietary blend *Carpathian Surprise*. Whatever it was, Sid was hooked.

"You're like a mad scientist," he would joke.

"Yes. Something like that," she would answer.

Del Ciotto walked out into the cold New Year's morning. He checked his burner cell phone for a message from Bobby De Rosa, but there was none. Sid was beginning to tire of the Rose's constant demands. *Who does he think I am? One of his flunkies?* Once the painting was recovered and in his hands, he would show him who's really boss. But first, he had to get the photos the Rose had insisted he was "*holding in safekeeping*" for him.

Sid had a plan, and it didn't involve splitting any money with Bobby De Rosa. Once Nick Di Nobile was out of the way, he could begin to put it into play. Sid glanced at his Rolex, noting the time. *And that should be very soon*, he thought, as he hustled along the squalor-filled three blocks to the bakery. *Who knows, maybe I'll go away with Donna when it's all over and visit Kyiv.*

The combination of the cold air and his quick pace began to make Sid feel queasy. He was sweating profusely, and worse, he felt like he was losing control of his bowels. Sid hastily sat on a bus stop bench. He stared straight ahead at the overgrown vacant lot directly across from the bus stop. He imagined it was the Carpathian Forest, beckoning him to enter. He began to foam at the mouth, shit his pants, and slipped into a coma.

The sight of a person overdosing on heroin or fentanyl was an all too common occurrence on the streets of Kensington. So much so, three people walked by without a second look. Then, a kindly looking older woman stopped pushing the shopping cart full of her worldly possessions long enough to check for a pulse and found none. She was gagging from the smell, but stuck around long enough to relieve Sid of his Rolex as a wolf pack of dirt bike riders thundered by.

Back at the apartment, Donna pulled on sweats, grabbed a prepacked carry-on out of the closet, and headed for the door. The apartment was spotless—like no one had ever lived there.

The EMTs hit Special Agent Del Ciotto with two shots of Narcan before declaring him. The cause of death was determined to be an overdose of fentanyl, as the medical examiner lacked the sophistication, or motivation for that matter, to detect the Novichok that actually did him in. Donna had carefully sealed up the perfume bottle containing the Russian nerve agent in one of her ziplock toiletry bags and tossed it in a construction dumpster on her walk to Kensington Avenue. There, she called an Uber to take her to the airport. Donna could hear the sirens as they pulled away. "Surprise, kozyol," she said under her breath.

The FBI conducted its obligatory investigation, but all in all, it was a seedy affair and the Bureau was anxious to distance itself from the stench, so to speak. The email and attached video, sent from a Ukrainian internet café, didn't help matters. Del Ciotto wasn't very well-liked to begin with.

It was bad enough Del Ciotto turned out to be a junkie. But a *sexual deviant* junkie was apparently a bridge too far, even for an agency that named a building after J. Edgar Hoover.

The file on the death of Special Agent J. Sidney Del Ciotto was swiftly and unceremoniously closed.

ROAD TRIP

But while he was still a long way off, his father saw him and was filled with compassion for him; he ran to his son, threw his arms around him and kissed him.

The son said to him, 'Father, I have sinned against heaven and against you. I am no longer worthy to be called your son.'

But the father said to his servants, 'Quick! Bring the best robe and put it on him. Put a ring on his finger and sandals on his feet. Bring the fattened calf and kill it. Let's have a feast and celebrate. For this son of mine was dead and is alive again; he was lost and is found.' So they began to celebrate.

Luke 15:20

"Take it easy," Virgil cautioned Nick as he continued to carefully extract the canvas from the tube.

I should have known, Nick thought. *Just when I started to believe.* This was Tony's final trick, after a lifetime of puffery and misdirection. All the frustration Nick had tamped down over a lifetime of filial disappointment began to simmer on its way to a rolling boil. Nick concluded in that moment he was right to have left the city all those years ago. Angie's betrayal and Tony's seemingly bottomless well of bullshit only confirmed that his instincts had always been correct. In a strange way, it gave Nick the beginnings of closure and a sense of peace he didn't realize he had been seeking.

And then Virgil began to peel back the canvas.

Someone had taken care to cover the painting with a second protective canvas. It wasn't a perfect solution, but it didn't seem to be damaged beyond repair either. Colors began to reveal themselves. The canvas beneath began to take on texture and form. Figures appeared. First, the ancillary subjects. Almost cartoonish in the "original," they leapt off the canvas in all their humanity. It was still heavily varnished, suggesting it was early in the restoration process when it was stolen. Virgil's eyes danced in delight at this revelation in the hope the varnish and grime had offered a degree of protection. Nick, however, still wasn't convinced.

Virgil carefully unfurled the remainder of the canvas across the adjoining tables, revealing the prodigal son kneeling before his father, who embraced him with forgiving arms. The father's coat was a brilliant ochre, and his face shone with beneficence.

"Well?" Gary posed the question to Virgil.

Virgil answered Gary's question but was looking at Nick. "It's either a Rembrandt or the greatest forgery I've ever seen."

Nick stood over the painting. It was stiff from the varnish and the memory of having been rolled up. Virgil, Gary, and Joey were carefully holding it down across the tables. This was the painting that had brought his father to tears. If genuine, it was probably worth half a billion dollars. But all Nick could think of was all the heartache it had caused. He gazed deeply at the face of the Prodigal's father, trying to find a connection to Tony Di Nobile. He didn't even realize he was crying until his tears fell onto the canvas.

Nick straightened up, wiped his eyes, and looked over at Virgil's painting of Tony hanging over the jukebox. His father was smiling and seemed to be toasting their success.

Virgil draped an arm around Nick. "Now, do you believe?"

Gary motioned to Nick and pointed to the bar. "We gotta talk." Nick followed him as Joey helped Virgil cover the painting.

Gary opened two Peronis. "Congratulations, slick. I always knew you would find it."

"I got lucky, G. If I didn't stumble over Tommy, *The Prodigal* would be in the wind."

Gary was looking at the Mummers Parade on the TV. Hundreds of wenches strutted around like whirling dervishes. "You did him a favor. He wouldn't have gotten very far."

Nick agreed with Gary's assessment, but perhaps for the wrong reasons. "How do you mean?"

"I mean, I believe in coincidence up to a point, but shit's been happening behind the scenes to make sure you lived long enough to find it. You lucky, pretty boy, but you ain't that lucky."

Nick thought about that. So much had happened over the past few days, it was hard to sort out the events. A few things had come into focus, though. He *wasn't* selling the Caffé. Gary deserved at least half of it. He damn sure wasn't selling the *Tony Rome*. Perhaps more than the painting, she was his strongest connection to his father. And lastly, he needed to get back to Grace and make things right with her.

"What exactly are you saying, G?" Nick asked.

"I'm saying you got a guardian angel or two watching your ass."

"Oh yeah?" Nick responded snidely. "And who would that be?"

Gary shut off the TV, took his time walking over to the jukebox, and played a song. He walked back over to the bar and opened two more Peronis for Virgil and Joey, who had finished securing the painting and taken seats at the bar.

"You a smart boy, Nick. You'll figure it out on the ride."

A Pitbull song began playing on the jukebox.

"Yeah?" Nick laughed. "Where we going now?"

Gary broke out into a little salsa step before answering. "Miami, baby. The Magic City."

"I'm in," Joey declared.

"Me too!" Virgil was nodding his head enthusiastically, if a little out of time with the beat.

"Fuck it." Nick was too weary to ask any questions. He raised his beer. "Miami, baby."

The four of them clicked bottles and toasted in unison. "*Miami, baby.*"

Above the jukebox, Tony raised his glass in approval.

SOUTH OF THE BORDER

Nick and Joey went home to pack. Gary put Virgil in a Lyft and agreed to stay at the Caffé until Nick returned. They resolved one man should stand guard over *The Prodigal* until they made "the exchange," as Gary described it. The big man took the first watch. They moved the painting to the office and Gary sat at his desk, a .38 in close reach.

It was just after 2:00 p.m. when they reconvened. They piled into Gary's Yukon and secured the painting in the back, wrapped in a comforter. They made a quick stop so Gary could hastily pack a bag.

"I'll just buy whatever I forgot down there," Gary said as he came out with a backpack in record time.

They picked up Virgil, who had packed some extra surgical masks, and were on 95 south by 2:20 p.m. Nick took the first leg. Joey volunteered for the second shift so Gary could try to get some sleep. Virgil confessed that he didn't know how to drive, not that any of them were about to trust him behind the wheel.

Traffic was light, and they made great time out of Pennsylvania. Gary and Nick both needed to take a piss, so they pulled into a travel stop so they could fill up the Yukon at the same time. Joey only briefly acknowledged the fleeting déjà vu that accompanied his visit to the unlikely location twice in a matter of days. With all that had transpired, it barely moved the needle.

Joey took over for Nick after they navigated the Washington, DC beltway. Gary snored loudly in the back. Nick tuned the Yukon's satellite radio to a '70s channel and turned up the volume on "Stumblin' In." Nick found himself mindlessly singing the lyrics. He was jolted out of his reverie when Virgil chimed in with the Suzi Quatro part of the duet. Joey busted out laughing at Virgil's surprisingly soulful vocal. Gary was roused from his slumber. He pulled his hoodie over his head and muttered, "Crazy motherfuckers."

Gary took over in North Carolina. By the time they passed the tacky monstrosity of the *South of the Border* motor inn and roadside attraction, it was going on 10:30 p.m. They agreed it would be best to stop for the night. They pulled over in Florence, South Carolina, went through a late-night Wendy's drive-thru that left Virgil perplexed, and checked into two rooms at a Day's Inn. Joey bunked with Virgil. Nick, Gary, and *The Prodigal* took the other room.

They were back on the road by 7:30 a.m. after fueling up and grabbing three Venti coffees from Starbucks. Virgil insisted on ordering a Cotton Candy Frappuccino from something called "the secret menu." The Yukon's GPS showed nine hours left for Fort Lauderdale, their first stop before the Magic City. Joey took the first shift. Virgil had called shotgun, leaving Nick and Gary in the backseat.

Gary filled Nick in on everything he knew. How Tony had entrusted Leo with the memos Tommy gave him. Leo's father and uncle were some of the earliest victims of Bobby De Rosa's campaign of disinformation and treachery.

"Leo reached out to me because your father made him swear to keep you out of it."

Gary explained how Ralph Cappello was collateral damage in the Athens Hauling case. The Rose had thrown him in the mix for no discernible reason other than jealousy. Raphael "The Rifle" Cappello was a handsome young middleweight being groomed for a shot at the title. Instead, the Rose and the federal government conspired to take him off the streets.

"So, how are Ralph and Leo connected?" Nick asked.

"Ralph looked out for his old man, Al Manos, while they were in Ray Brook together. The Rose hurt a lot of good people. Guess he never thought they would eventually figure it out."

Gary called Beto to check in. Everything was good back at the Caffé. Frank was stable and recovering from surgery. *Thank God*, Nick thought as he overheard the conversation. Nick couldn't wait to see Frank back at the Tiki, *Daily Racing Form* spread out on the bar. He had to remember to order some Stoli Elit for the old aristocrat.

Nick texted Grace. *I'm on my way home. Can't wait to see you. I have so much to tell you. Miss you.*

What time does your flight get in? I'll pick you up. Miss you too! Grace texted back.

No flight. We're driving. Nick realized how crazy that sounded right after he sent it.

Uh, OK. Lol. What time should I expect you?

I'll be at the Tiki tonight. I'll explain everything then.

OK, Nick. Be safe. I love you.

I love you too, Nick replied.

Gary turned to show Nick his phone. "Look at this."

It was an article about Bobby De Rosa on a gossipy underworld website. The headline read, *The Rose was a Rat!* The story covered the shooting and cited anonymous sources who revealed that Bobby De Rosa was a longtime informant for the FBI in the Top Echelon program. Nick was starting to feel a little sick about tossing the Rose that chunk of Reggiano in front of all those people.

Virgil said, "I told you; the eyes of St. Lucy see all."

Joey said he felt good, so he drove straight through Georgia. When they reached the Florida border, Joey exclaimed, "We're almost there."

It was a bit premature, and Nick and Gary exchanged a knowing look. It was a rookie mistake but forgivable. Nick remembered the first time he made the trip, driving straight through. He couldn't help feeling energized back then. The citrusy signs for Florida had made him feel like he had arrived at his destination though there were still miles to drive. Three hundred sixty, to be exact.

Nick was driving when they finally arrived at the exit for Commercial Boulevard. He was exhausted. Virgil had his head out the window like a golden retriever and was transfixed by the sights whizzing by. Somewhere in that beautiful mind, he was assembling the rough material for his next painting.

It was a little after 5:30 p.m. They had stopped four times since leaving South Carolina for a combination of fuel, restrooms, and fast food. Nick wanted to sleep in his own bed, Gary wanted a good meal, Joey wanted a Michelob Ultra, and Virgil just wanted to paint a palm tree.

Ralph texted Gary with the location. Gary offered to map the route to the meeting spot, but Nick knew the place well enough.

 Blaine's Tavern was tucked into a side street just west of Federal Highway in Oakland Park. It might have only been a mile or so off the beach, but it was as fundamentally removed from the party scene of Fort Lauderdale and the so-called beautiful people who inhabited it as you could get. It was a dank and dreary affair, even by dive bar standards. No Taco Tuesday or "rosé all day" here, no promotion whatsoever. It was situated between a discount mattress store and a psychic. The interior hadn't seen the business end of a paint brush since Teddy was a Blue Note. It was a place where the hard-core drinker could slowly kill himself without being disturbed by spring breakers. Blaine's wasn't a place where dreams went to die, it was where they went to get cremated. In short, it was the perfect place to handle their business.

Nick and Gary got out of the Yukon. Joey wanted to come in too. "No, Joey, you stay with the painting." Nick thought about it for a second and added, "Better yet, just keep circling around the block until you see us come out." Gary nodded like he thought it was a good idea. Virgil wanted to go to the psychic for a "spiritual reading," but Gary convinced him to go to the frozen yogurt shop across the street instead.

Gary opened the door and walked in first. The contrast between the cheerful Florida sun and Blaine's crypt-like interior was too much for Nick's eyes to adapt to. All he could see were a few figures and spots before his eyes. A pool table light and a Budweiser sign behind the bar seemed to be the only illumination in the whole place. They walked over to the bar and had a seat while Nick's vision adjusted, which wasn't necessarily a good thing. The bartender leaned forward in a low-cut top and made a big production of squeezing her breasts together. Far from being sexy, it just accentuated the wrinkles and sun damage of a spring breaker who'd lingered a few decades too long. Blaine's didn't have a jukebox, but if it did, Nick would have played Connie Francis's "Where The Boys Are."

"I'm Cathy. What can I get you boys?" Nick knew better than to say something theatrical like, *we're here to see Ralph*, so he just said, "Two Budweisers?" while looking at Gary, who shrugged in response. "Two Buds," he repeated to low-cut Cathy. She placed the sweaty Buds on stained coasters and returned to checking her Tinder profile.

They were soon joined by a young kid in a tight tee shirt. "Ralph sent me over. He would like to see you in the back. Would you like another drink?" Vinny repeated it exactly like Ralph had instructed him to say it. *None of your Hollywood ad-libs*, Ralph had added.

They picked up their Budweisers and walked into a room that seemed to be set up for card games. Round tables were spread around the room, and a few decks of cards were still littered about. It smelled like a combination of stale cigar smoke and bleach, with some notes of vomit.

Gary broke the ice. "Nice place you got here."

Ralph rose from his chair, and the two men embraced like old friends who hadn't seen each other in years, which is precisely what they were.

"Ralph," Gary began, "this is our boy, Nick." Ralph flashed a smile that threatened to light up the place and looked at Nick like he was a winning trifecta ticket.

"Good to see you, kid."

"Nice to meet you," Nick responded.

"Oh, we've met before, Nicky," Ralph stated.

"Really?" Nick decided to test him a little. "The Fontainebleau?"

Ralph looked pleased. "Touché, kid." He paused and stared off a bit. "Nah, this was a long time ago." He patted his belly with two hands. "I was a middleweight back then."

"One of the best," Gary added and raised his bottle.

"Eh, that's ancient history. Have a seat." Ralph gestured to a table and they sat. Low-cut Cathy came back with fresh drinks for the three of them. "Sorry I can't offer you something to eat, but this ain't exactly Vecchio." Ralph pointed to an old hot dog machine that was taking two petrified hot dogs for an endless ride on the world's saddest Ferris wheel.

Gary put his hands up. "I'm good."

"Sorry, I don't get here much," Ralph said by way of explanation. "But it's the first place I bought when I came down here, so I keep it going for sentimental reasons." Ralph got right to the point. "So, that brings us to the business at hand. Did you bring it with you?"

"You know how that works," Nick answered. "It's close by."

Gary and Ralph shared a proud look and a smile, like they were witnessing a child who'd finally learned how to ride a bike without training wheels.

'You don't understand, Nick. You're not here to give the painting to me. I don't want anything that doesn't belong to me."

"It doesn't belong to anyone," Nick stated. "My father has just as good a claim to *The Prodigal* as anybody."

"He did, Nick, and you'll be compensated for that, believe me. But you're wrong about it not belonging to anyone. Someone placed that painting into the museum's care before he died. And that someone had a brother."

"Frank said they bought the guy off after the theft."

"That's because that's what Frank was told. He was better off not knowing the truth. The owner was killed before he could see a dime."

"And what is the truth?" Nick asked.

"First, let's have a look at this painting that's caused so much trouble."

"I'm not sure that's such a good idea," Nick said.

Gary looked on but didn't interrupt. Nick needed to handle this on his own.

Ralph stood up. It wasn't that he was such a big guy or scary-looking or anything, but the man had an undeniable presence. He motioned Nick over to a small secondary bar set up in the corner of the back room. "I want to show you something."

Ralph took down a black and white photo from the wall behind the bar. It was of a handsome young boxer crouched down in a fighting stance. "I told you we met before. This picture was taken around the same time. Do you remember now?" Nick looked at the photo. The boxer was obviously Ralph, albeit a great deal younger and lighter.

"I'm sorry." Nick didn't want to hurt his feelings. "I don't remember."

"It's understandable. You were just a boy, and I went away soon after that day. But do an old man a favor. Take a closer look."

Nick looked closer. It was still pretty dark in the room. There was some writing along the bottom of the photo. *Raphael "The Rifle" Cappello – Middleweight – 10 wins, 0 losses.*

Nick's memory clicked back to that day on Mountain Street. He could picture the silhouette of the boxer in the photo standing in the doorway of the garage.

"You're the Rifle." Nick said it like some fan seeking an autograph.

"You see, kid, I saved your ass a long time ago. I wasn't going to let that rat fuck get to you … and neither was your uncle." Ralph stopped his story for a second. "How is he?"

Gary answered. "He's gonna be just fine."

"Good," Ralph answered. "Because I got a feeling he's about to come into some serious money. Ain't that right, Nick?"

Nick didn't hesitate for a second. "Absolutely."

They walked outside, and Gary signaled for Joey to pull over when he rounded the block. Gary popped the lift gate on the Yukon, and they gave Ralph a well-deserved peek at *The Prodigal*.

Ralph took it in and smiled. "Nice work, kid."

He gave Nick the instructions for the final leg of the trip, adding, "He wants to see you, and you alone, Nick. I'll meet you tomorrow. How 'bout at that Tiki bar of yours?"

"Sounds like a plan," Nick said.

Ralph and Gary hugged. Joey ran across to the frozen yogurt shop to retrieve Virgil.

The Rifle kissed Nick on the cheek. "I knew you could do it, kid. Frank said you were special." He placed both of his hands on Nick's shoulders and looked him directly in the eyes. "Your dad would be proud of you, Nick. Hopefully, he's looking down on us and smiling."

Nick thought of the painting above the jukebox and said, "I believe he is."

Joey took Commercial to 95 and pointed the Yukon south toward Miami. Nick sat in the front so he could direct Joey and talk to him on the ride.

"Joe, have you ever really looked at the painting of *Christ in the Storm* on the back wall of the Caffé?"

"I'm sure I have," Joey responded. "I DJ right there."

"Everyone in the boat is running around, looking terrified. Except Christ. He's sitting there like he knows everything will be fine. It reminds me of a fishing trip I took with my father when I was about twelve. We hit a real bad storm coming back in from the twenty-eight-mile wreck where we had been sharking. I was terrified. But I looked at my father at the wheel. He was all business, working the throttles and keeping our bow into the waves. I felt like crying, but I didn't want him to know I was scared. He pulled me close to him, and I held onto his waist for dear life. Eventually, the storm passed, and we made it back just fine."

"That's a great story, Nick. I wish I got to know him better."

"Me too, Joey, me too. But that's not the end of the story. Years later, he was at the bar with a few guys gathered around, trading fishing stories. He didn't know I was close enough to overhear. He told the story of that day. How scared he was. Not just of the storm, but of losing me. You understand?"

"I think I do," Joey answered.

"All I'm saying, Joey, is that I think sometimes we expect too much from our fathers. When you're a kid, you think he's Superman. But as you get older, and presumably smarter, you come to find he's just as flawed as you—and that's a tough realization for a young man, glimpsing his own mortality. So maybe you do whatever it takes to escape the same fate, to avoid becoming like him."

"Are we talking about you or me now?" Joey asked.

"Maybe a little of both, Joey. I'm just saying that your father would be proud of you. And I'm proud of you."

Joey pursed his lips and blew out a slow breath. *Just like Jimmy*, Nick thought.

"Thanks, Uncle Nick," he said.

Gary leaned forward from the backseat and whispered to Nick. "You starting to sound like somebody I once knew."

Nick took that as the highest compliment.

MISHKA

They pulled into Miami around 7:45 p.m. Joey parked at the loading dock of the fish market like Ralph had instructed. Nick was beyond exhausted. His hands were shaking and his legs almost gave out from under him as he stepped out of the Yukon. The loading dock area was dimly lit.

"You good, slick?" Gary asked.

"I don't know, G, am I?" Nick asked, meaning something slightly different.

"If Ralph says you good, you good. You want me to handle?"

"No. This is for me to see through."

"Okay," Gary said. "We'll be right here."

Nick gathered himself as he walked along NW North River Road to the restaurant, also like Ralph had instructed. Coastal Cayenne was a swanky lounge-restaurant on the Miami River. At night, it transformed into an exclusive club of bacchanalian proportions. Bottles flowed freely, and the DJ orchestrated the gradual transition from Sunday brunch to pulsing nightlife. *Joey would do great in here.* He was seriously underdressed for the place he realized as he approached the hostess stand.

"Dmitry, please." That's what Nick had been told to say. The hostess's eyes lit up, shifting from the disdain of her suspicious gaze as Nick had approached. She was predictably beautiful, but exceptional even by Miami standards. She could have been Russian, Columbian, or even Italian, for that matter. Some women reach a universal apex of beauty where ethnic distinctions fade away. Nick was surprised to find himself so transfixed.

"Dima," she chirped cheerfully. Not to Nick, but to a bouncer standing off to the side. "Ramon will escort you if you please." Her eyes lingered on Nick, who snapped out of his stupor and managed to wrangle a hundred from the creased pocket of his jeans. She smiled, thanked Nick, and the fever broke as she went to the next guest. *Fucking Miami*, he thought.

Nick turned to Ramon, who was whispering something into a small headset microphone while holding the earpiece in place. It looked like someone had tried to wrap a suit jacket around a mountain, and as he moved his hand away from his ear, it revealed an impressive cauliflower. Nick heard him whisper, "Putah," under his breath, apparently about the hostess. Nick sensed that she wasn't supposed to take his money, and he took some comfort in that notion. He also reminded himself that giving someone a sense of comfort was often a prelude to something else and resolved to keep his guard up. His exhaustion was working against him in that regard.

He walked through a crowd of well-heeled party people. Waitresses weaved through in a bottle service procession of skin and pyrotechnics. They were carrying a magnum of Ace of Spades champagne aloft like a golden calf. The scene was basically Gomorrah on the Miami River. Nick scanned the tables for someone he thought looked like the Russian from the Fontainebleau and wondered how they would have a conversation over the pounding bass.

Situated on the river, Cayenne, as it was commonly referred to, had the added feature of boat access. Boats jockeyed and rafted, and Cayenne even provided the service of a tender to transport guests back and forth. The consensus being that the real parties happened on the yachts. As Ramon cut a path through the crowd, Nick followed closely on his heels. The sea of swaying bodies parted dutifully, and Nick could make out his destination.

Nick recognized the vessel. The name *Mishka* sparkled backlit above the blue underwater lights. The stern appeared to be suspended on ether. Ramon boarded first and extended a helping hand to Nick. Nick felt like he was shaking hands with a grizzly.

Dmitry was seated in the salon and rose to meet Nick. He grasped Nick's hand with both of his. "Welcome, my friend." His voice was warm, with a pronounced Russian accent.

"Nice boat," was all Nick could manage. His head was still spinning from the ride and now the lights and music and scene at Cayenne.

"You know what means mishka in Russian?"

"I think it means bear?" Nick phrased it as a question, not wanting to appear either presumptuous or ignorant. He couldn't help glancing over at Ramon as he said it. The grizzly stood at the cabin door, facing out, his paws folded in front of him.

"Excellent, Nikolai!" Dmitry now grasped him by the shoulders lightly. "I'm sorry, you don't mind I call you Nikolai? It was my brother's name, and I mean it only with respect. My father named him after the writer."

"Gogol?" Nick ventured.

"Exactly, my friend. Forgive me, may I get you a drink?" Dmitry asked, but had already moved to pour two glasses of vodka. He gestured to an enormous seafood platter that had been set out on the salon table. "Please, you've had a long drive." Nick noticed the ice had barely started to melt beneath the largest stone crab claws he had ever seen.

Nick was starving but passed on the shellfish tower. He clinked glasses with Dmitry.

"*Za nashu druzjbu*," Dmitry said first.

"Salute," Nick said in return.

Dmitry knocked back what had to be a triple shot at least, and Nick reciprocated. It burned for a second but soon filled Nick's chest with the familiar warmth.

"No *cent'anni*?" the Russian quizzed Nick.

"Do you know many happy hundred-year-olds?" Nick retorted.

Dmitry paused to reflect on this, then burst into a booming laugh.

"This is good point. Excellent, Nikolai! I will never say again." With this, Dmitry poured them two more glasses. Nick doubted he could keep up this pace and was eager to be done with business and get back to his Tuscan Tiki … and Grace.

Nick looked around at the yacht. It was spectacular. Every appointment was custom, but it wasn't gaudy in the least. If anything, it had a minimalist aesthetic. *I wonder what this guy would make of the Tony Rome*, Nick caught himself thinking. Nick watched as a launch shuttled partygoers from boats rafted alongside one another back and forth to the club, much like the *Mishka* would eventually shuttle guests back and forth to the mega yacht Dmitry was having built. The table they were seated at had an impeccable gloss, and Nick carefully placed his glass onto a coaster.

"I'm parked at the loading dock, just like Ralph told me."

"I know. It is already unloaded," Dmitry said with a steely certainty.

Nick had a sick feeling in his stomach as he imagined the worst-case scenario between Dmitry's men and Gary, Joey, and Virgil.

Dmitry continued. "You are a man who appreciates beautiful things. I can tell this. Not like a certain *kozyol* who saw only dollars."

Nick wasn't sure if he should be relieved or worried. In truth, he was so exhausted, he just wanted to get to the point and be on his way, but he didn't want to insult the Russian. For one, Dmitry had been nothing but hospitable to Nick. Second, Nick knew what Dmitry was capable of—the Rose could vouch for that. Nick was relying on the fact he was no threat to the man and, in fact, had proved himself indispensable. He was happy to finally be free of the painting, which had brought grief to so many.

Dmitry watched Nick closely. On some level, he probably knew what Nick was thinking. A man doesn't get to Dmitry's level without possessing such a skill. Dmitry had risen from the slums and juvenile colonies of Volgograd and Leningrad's prison to the rarified air of the oligarchy.

"I have something for you." Dmitry raised his eyes in Ramon's direction. The grizzly who had appeared to move oafishly through the Cayenne crowd must have shape shifted into a panther, because he was at Nick's side before he could turn around. To Nick's relief, he only had a hockey-sized duffel bag over his shoulder, which he placed gently on the teak and holly sole next to Nick.

"There is four million dollars in there. Half is for you, half you give to Mr. Ralph. No?"

It wasn't really a question, but Nick responded in the affirmative just in case.

"May I ask you something?" Nick couldn't help asking.

"Of course."

"Why pay me anything?" Nick was starting to think he must be delirious, but he continued anyway. "I mean, I don't own it. I barely found it. I probably couldn't sell it, and if I tried, I'd probably get killed. You're clearly holding all the cards, and I have absolutely no leverage here."

Dmitry looked at him not so much quizzically but with a certain satisfaction. Like Nick had lived up to some expectation he wasn't aware of. He paused to pour himself another vodka. *Thank God he didn't pour one for me*, thought Nick.

"You do not disappoint me, Nikolai. Mr. Stone Crab was right about you."

Nick wasn't sure what he meant by that, but he silently thanked his uncle for the compliment.

"Do you know what is the most famous painting in Russia?"

Nick had no idea but took a shot. "Is it a Kandinsky?"

"No, but is a good guess. That is, if you like abstract garbage. But I apologize. I did not mean to trick you. It is not matter of taste but popularity."

Dmitry knocked back his vodka and made a satisfied *aah* sound.

"It is *Morning in a Pine Forest* by Shiskin. It is bullshit painting of some bears in the woods, but every Russian child knows it because it is on a candy wrapper. We called it Mishka Kosolapy. You would say, Clumsy Bear. So, as you have learned, value is relative. Maybe you remember something a certain way from your youth. Maybe it is real, maybe it is a shadow. Maybe a little bit of both. You understand?"

Nick sensed that Dmitry was lapsing into some previous, inferior version of English. Dmitry was capable of perfect English grammar, but occasionally found himself using an earlier iteration of his voice. Maybe it was the drink. Maybe it was just some nostalgic pride.

Without sarcasm or hesitation, Nick responded, "I believe I do." *And if I didn't before,* Nick thought, *I definitely do now.*

"Yes, I believe you do, my friend. When I was a boy, we were very poor. We didn't have many things, hardly enough food. I stole. I did not feel guilty then, and I do not feel guilty now. I did what I needed to do to survive. Now, the game is larger, but it has not changed. Still, I do what I need to do, but now I am responsible for many. You understand?"

Nick simply nodded, realizing Dmitry was determined to tell his tale.

"One day, when I was ten years old, I went to the State Museum, the Hermitage, for something called 'cultural enrichment.' It was mandatory for the children in my school. I had never been to such a place and did not know what to expect. St. Petersburg was still known as Leningrad then. We toured the museum and I saw many things that day: the treasures of Egypt, Greek sculptures, the Italians, Da Vinci and Michelangelo, Picasso and your Kandinsky."

Ramon suppressed a chuckle at Dmitry's mention of Kandinsky. *Suddenly, everyone's an art critic,* thought Nick.

"Last were the Dutch works. I was bored and angry by then. I was used to being outside, and I was still wearing my coat, so I was sweating. I was thinking of what I could steal next before I returned to my gutter. I had no father. He killed himself with this." Dmitry gestured to the bottle of vodka sweating on the table. "It was no loss. He was worthless and beat my mother. I found him dead in the snow on St. Catherine's Day and I did not shed a tear."

Dmitry was standing now. He was facing away from Nick. Not disrespectfully, but gazing out the salon window at the river. Dmitry was in that state of trance where a person is triggered by a memory of a time or place. He continued, but was now talking as much to himself as he was to Nick.

"That is when I first saw *The Prodigal.* The father's face—his rich coat—the son's dirty bare feet. I did not know why at the time, but I started to cry. My little friends laughed at me, of course. We were just filthy urchins, delinquents, you would say. I thought I was going crazy. My teacher became angry and reprimanded me. But my cry was uncontrollable, and I buried my face as best I could in my arm. Had we not been in the museum, surely she would have struck me. I knew the story from the bible, but before then, it meant nothing to me. I thought the boy in the story was a fool and his father a bigger fool for taking him back. I remember thinking that if I was the brother, I would have killed them both on the spot. But looking at the father's face that day, as Rembrandt rendered him, I understood. I understood what I did not have and would never have—the love of a father. On that day, on that spot, I vowed to escape my gutter, no matter the cost. Eventually, I made my way here."

Dmitry made a sweeping gesture that indicated that "here" meant not only Miami, not only the US, but referred to all his fortune.

"My poor brother died before he could see all of this. Before he could see his painting returned. And now here I am, and I learn from Mr. Frank of another man. I do not know him. He lives a world away from that filthy little urchin, and yet, he sees the master's true work, the original, uncorrupted by the hands of others. I picture him gazing at the face of the father, and he cries. He doesn't think of riches. No, he cries. I think to myself, I was not alone that day in the Hermitage—other souls feel as I did. I apologize, my friend. You asked me a question, and that was the best I could do to answer it. That is why I do not seize what surely I could. The money is meaningless to me, but I hope it is helpful to you ... that man's son."

Nick sat stunned. It was almost too much to take in. The powers of fate that reached across time and oceans were too much to fathom. *Surely there are greater forces at play here*, Nick thought. *If there is not a God, there certainly is a universe that mimics one.*

They both sat quietly for a while, absorbing the weight of such a force.

"I don't want the money," Nick finally said.

Dmitry smiled. He sat back down across from Nick, leaned back in his seat, and placed his hands flat, palms down, on the table between them. He had the pleased looked of a man who has just finished a good meal.

"Mr. Frank said you would say that. But I'm afraid it is the one condition that is nonnegotiable. It is the thread that binds us, you and I. It is not much, but I know you will do good things with it. Besides, your friend Ralph would be disappointed."

Nick thought about it and realized he didn't have an option.

Dmitry's men walked into the cabin. They both looked like UFC fighters. One was carrying the blue burrito. They unfurled it at Dmitry's feet. Dmitry Ivanov stood over it like the Colossus of Rhodes. Vodka was poured all around. Even Ramon joined in. Dmitry raised his glass, and Nick felt compelled to join him.

"To my brother, Nikolai. You can rest now. *The Prodigal* has returned."

Nick knocked back the vodka and fought to keep it down. He was beginning to feel a bit claustrophobic in the cabin. He turned to Dmitry. "Do you mind if I get some air?"

"Of course not. Treat the *Mishka* as if she were yours."

Nick's first act as co-owner was to speed walk out to

the cockpit and hurl over the side. The crowd on a nearby Azimut, which included two topless women, whooped and cheered at the sight.

As he righted himself, a woman was quickly at his side with a towel. Nick used the towel to wipe his face, and the woman retreated just long enough to get him a bottled water.

"Here," she said. "Drink it." She wore a crocheted cover-up over a white bikini. Three interlocking rings swayed on the chain around her neck.

"Donna?" Nick was transfixed by the unlikely sight of the woman he had last seen in Vecchio a thousand miles away and seemingly a lifetime ago.

"My name is Anastasia, but you can call me Donna if you like. And you are the famous Nick. I enjoyed your Caffé very much. It reminded me of my favorite restaurant in Kyiv."

"I'm glad you enjoyed it. But I don't feel so famous," he said as he rinsed with the spring water and spit it over the side. "So what happened to Del Ciotto? You guys still hot and heavy?"

"It's a sad story. I tried to help him, but in the end, I could not save him from his demons."

Demons?

She must have seen the puzzled look on Nick's face, because she pulled up a news article on her phone and showed it to Nick.

Decorated Special Agent J. Sidney Del Ciotto of the FBI found dead of apparent overdose.

It all came together for Nick, and a chill ran up his

spine. Suddenly, he felt quite sober. He handed her back the phone.

Ramon came out into the cockpit with the duffel bag over his shoulder. "Dmitry says I should help you take this to your car. He begs your forgiveness for cutting your meeting short and says he would very much like to resume the conversation one day soon."

"Tell him I would like that too," Nick managed.

Anastasia looked disappointed. "Just when we were starting to get to know one another. Perhaps we can have a drink sometime?"

"I think I'm gonna take a break from drinking for a while," Nick answered.

"Yes. I understand, Nick." Then she added somewhat cryptically, "But I'll keep the kettle on for you just in case you change your mind."

"Kettle?" Nick said, thinking it must be a Russian thing. "I'm not much of a tea drinker."

"No," Anastasia said. "I didn't think so. That's probably for the best," She kissed Nick and bit him hard enough on the lower lip to leave a mark.

Ramon laughed and reached out a paw to assist Nick, while balancing the duffel bag on his shoulder. They walked together back to the seafood market, where the Philly crew waited patiently. Nick reached for a few bills to tip Ramon, but he shook his head no, and Nick wasn't about to wrestle him for the privilege.

Nick tossed the duffel bag in the back of the Yukon. Turns out four million is pretty heavy. He remembered something Tommy McKenna had said—*Don't trust any-*

body—and unzipped the bag. It was all there.

"Well?" Gary asked as they drove away.

"Looks like we'll be eating good for the foreseeable future," Nick answered.

"*Cool Hand Luke.*" Gary grabbed him around the neck and shook him playfully.

"Joey," Nick said, "get us to Lauderdale."

"You got it," Joey answered, and they were back on 95 in no time.

GRACE UNDER PRESSURE

They pulled into Lauderdale around 10:00 p.m. Nick directed Joey down A1A across Oakland Park Boulevard and into Lauderdale-By-The-Sea. They entered the underground garage of Nick's high-rise. They took the elevator to his condo on the southeast corner condo of the thirty-first floor. Gary carried the duffel bag, and Joey shouldered as many of their bags as he could.

Virgil opened the sliding doors and stepped out onto the balcony overlooking the ocean on one side and the lights of the city of Fort Lauderdale on the other.

"This must be beautiful at sunrise, Nick. I would love to paint it."

"No problem," Nick answered. "We'll get you some supplies tomorrow."

"It's really nice, Uncle Nick. Mind if I get a shower?" Joey said.

"This is your place, Joey. Make yourself at home."

"Thanks, Unc."

Gary opened the refrigerator, took out a Yards Pale Ale, and turned on the TV. The way he settled back in the recliner suggested he wasn't going anywhere else for the night. Nick stashed the duffel bag in his bedroom closet.

He would settle up with Ralph tomorrow. All he wanted to do right then was brush his teeth and get to Grace.

He brushed and did his best to rinse the taste out of his mouth. He took the elevator down to the lobby and walked out the exit to the beach. He stepped out onto the sand, having decided to walk the short distance to the Tiki along the ocean.

Grace was slammed at the bar. One of the bartenders had called out. *Probably still hungover from New Year's Eve,* Grace thought. She was doing her best to keep up with the onslaught of mixed and frozen drink requests but was deep in the weeds. She felt someone at her side. It was Ronnie Cruz, Nick's friend from back home. He was one of the best bartenders they had, although a little temperamental.

"You okay, sweetie? I got this," Ronnie said, gently moving her aside.

"But you're not on tonight." Grace was puzzled.

"I got called in, baby. Heard you needed some help."

"Thanks, Ronnie, I do. This crowd is crazy tonight. I'm about to cut a few of them off."

A big local gator boy was bellowing for a beer from two deep at the bar.

"Keep your fucking pants on, bubba," Ronnie shouted. Ronnie was short in stature but quick with his hands, as well as a blade back in the day in the Badlands of Philly. He was long retired from the game, but he still barked orders like the crew boss he once was. Bubba backed down. "Go, mami. Take a break. I got this."

"Thank you, Ronnie." Grace wasn't about to argue with him. She gave him a kiss on the cheek, walked out from behind the bar, and had a seat on the ledge overlooking the beach.

The Tuscan Tiki was just three buildings down from Nick's condo. He took off his loafers, held them in his hand, and walked down to the water's edge. The ocean looked both familiar and exotic in the moonlight, just like Grace. He wet his feet as he walked along. The rivulets felt so enticing that he waded a bit deeper. The water felt warm and soothing and magnificent. He was almost at the Tiki when a rogue wave caught him off guard and knocked him over. He emerged from the foam laughing and spitting up the salt water that had gone up his nose. His phone was probably toast. *Fuck it*, Nick thought as he dragged himself out of the water, still keeping a death grip on his loafers, which he had somehow managed to keep dry. He had the sensation of being newly baptized—born again.

Grace was looking out at the water. A lonely boat was suspended on the horizon. Its green starboard light gleamed across the surface. From the corner of her eye, she detected some fool frolicking in the waves like a lunatic. *Good lord*, she thought, hoping it wasn't someone she'd served who would end up drowned and washed up on the beach.

She turned to get Ronnie's attention, but he was as buried as she had been. She got up off the ledge and walked down just far enough to make sure it wasn't one of the Tiki regulars.

Grace could hardly believe her eyes. Was it really Nick walking out of the ocean? As happy as she was to see him, the shock of seeing Nick emerge from the surf like a drunken Poseidon upset her a bit. So when she tried to say

I love you, it came out as, "What the fuck are you doing?"

Nick was soaked and had some sand stuck to his face. He was laughing, partly because he was so relieved to finally be back, partly because he never heard Grace speak to him like that.

"I told you it was my turn to swim to you."

"What happened to your lip?" she said.

"It's a long story. Have you ever heard the Italian phrase *nascosta in piena vista*?"

Grace shook her head no and started to cry.

"I'll tell you all about it later," Nick said as he kissed her. Her tears mingled with the salt water on his face and disappeared.

Grace jumped up on him, wrapping her legs around his waist and kissing him all over his face. Nick's legs were still a little wobbly, and he fell back onto the sand with Grace on top of him. They lay there and kissed like two teenagers.

Ronnie Cruz whooped and hollered "¡wepa!" and the crowd at the Tiki joined in.

VECCHIO SOUTH

The next day, they all met at the Tiki. The Rifle was on his way with the Tasker Morris boys.

Joey had taken Virgil to pick up some painting supplies in the morning, and the *Mad Painter of Rittenhouse Square* had set up his easel by the beach.

"What's up with the masked painter?" Ronnie asked.

"He's alright, Ronnie. He's with us," Nick said.

"Cool," Ronnie said. He whipped up one of his signature pina coladas, poured a shot of rum into the straw, and ran it over to him.

Nick introduced Grace to Gary, who stood and kissed her hand gallantly.

"Enchanté," the big man said.

"Oh, you speak French now?" Nick joked.

Gary pulled Nick over to the side. "Look here, slick. There's something I been meaning to talk to you about."

"If it's about the Caffé, don't worry. I'm never selling it. It's as much yours as it is mine, and I'm having Leo take care of that right away."

"Thanks, Nick. Really. That means a lot. I loved your father like he was my own dad. But that's not what I want to talk to you about." Gary took a long look around at the Tiki scene, the ocean, the sand, and finally, his eyes came to rest upon Grace, who was seated at the bar, laughing with Joey. "You know I think of you as my younger brother and—"

"I know, G, I feel the—"

"Would you stop interrupting me and let me speak?"

Nick laughed out an apology. "Sorry, big man, please go ahead."

"What I'm trying to say is, I see this fine woman you got here, and I know that painting wasn't the only lost masterpiece you was chasin' back in the city. You feel me?"

"I feel you," Nick answered.

"Do you? Good. Cause some shit needs to *stay* lost, else you might lose what you got chasin' something that never existed."

Nick thought about it. He knew what, or rather *who*, Gary was referring to, and knew he was right. Yet, somewhere deep down, he still had a hard time accepting it.

"You know," Nick said, "that would make a great lyric to a song."

"What's that?"

"Don't lose what you got chasing something that might not exist."

"I don't recall sayin' 'might,'" Gary corrected him.

Joey walked over and interrupted. "This place is great, Unc. You maybe looking for a guest DJ?"

"Absolutely," Nick said.

WHIZ KIDS

It was Monday, March 18, 2019. Twenty-nine years to the day of the Isabella Stewart Gardner Museum heist. Despite a ten million dollar reward, the crime remained unsolved, and the stolen works remained in the wind.

Ralph picked up Frank at the airport. The old man was on the mend and wasn't looking half bad.

"Still can't kick these things, though." Frank had a pack of Marlboros at the ready.

"We all gotta die of something, Frankie," Ralph answered.

"Ain't that the truth."

"I got you something. It's in the glove box."

Frank opened it and pulled out a large envelope.

"There's fifty thousand in there. I'm holding another fifty for you. Don't hurt yourself."

"I don't know what to say, Ralph."

"That ain't all." Ralph handed him what looked like a credit card. "I figured one of us should be official." It was a membership to the Royal Palm Resort and Club in the name of Frank Valletto. "Just don't go crazy. Tasker Morris is paying for it, and I don't need Abe breaking my balls."

Ralph pulled the Rolls out of the airport and took Federal, turning right on 17th Street.

"Don't you have a meeting to get to?" Frank asked.

"Fuck it, Frankie. Let's take the beach."

Clearwater, Florida – Whiz Kids Tavern

Ronnie Cruz made the trip across alligator alley and up to Clearwater in four hours. He was transporting a special delivery in the trunk. He felt naked, but Nick had insisted he not take *cariño*, his trusty blade, with him.

Ronnie walked into the Whiz Kids Tavern. The Phils were at the Cardinals in a spring training matchup, and the game was on every TV. He ordered a Corona from the bartender, a heavyset guy who looked a little like Santa Claus.

"Hey, you're from Philly, right?" Ronnie asked him.

Tommy McKenna sized him up and figured right off the bat, *this guy is gonna be a problem*. "What makes you say that?" Tommy snapped.

"Nothing, bro, take it easy. Just, this is a Phillies bar, right?" Ronnie gestured around at all the Phillies memorabilia that filled the room."

"Yeah, this is a Phillies bar. What about it?"

Ronnie downed his Corona and left a twenty on the bar. "Hey, man, I'm sorry if I said something wrong. I ain't looking for no trouble. I'll be on my way." Ronnie got up from his stool.

Tommy picked up the twenty, tossed the empty corona bottle in the trash, and wiped the bar where it had been.

"Let me ask you one question though."

Here it comes, Tommy thought as he reached under the bar for his Louisville Slugger.

"You ever see the movie *Rocky*?" Ronnie asked.

Tommy didn't give an inch. "Never heard of it."

"That's too bad," Ronnie said. "I was gonna ask you, what was your favorite part?"

Tommy barely restrained himself and was about to come over the bar.

"Don't you want to know *my* favorite part?"

"Don't tell me, the part where Rocky forgives Mickey," Tommy finally conceded.

"Exactly. And this is for you," Ronnie said as he put a backpack containing one hundred thousand dollars on the bar. "Our mutual friend says no hard feelings, and that you should come visit the *real* Florida sometime."

Tommy looked into the bag. He should have been shocked, but knew Nicky well enough to realize a gesture like this was just like him. He wasn't entirely over being pistol-whipped and zip-tied, but this certainly helped smooth things over.

"Hey." Tommy waved at Ronnie to come back. "Can you tell him something for me?"

Ronnie walked back. "Of course, my friend." The old crew boss had softened his tone.

"Tell him that I lied. Angie—she didn't know anything about it. I just said that to hurt him. Because—in my heart—I knew she was still in love with him."

"I shall tell him. Word for word." Ronnie bowed a little, acknowledging this was a solemn request and must have been difficult for this tough son of a bitch to say to a stranger.

"And tell him—tell him Mickey still loves him."

"Done," Ronnie said and turned for the door. Before he walked out, he put his fist in the air and yelled out to no one in particular, "Go, Phils!"

CHIAROSCURO

Rittenhouse Square – Philadelphia
April 25, 2019

Virgil set up his easel and focused his attention on the sidewalk tables that lined the square. Through the trees, the sun's angle created a dapple effect that caused his brain to fire in that magical sequence that God had ordained. Virgil worked feverishly, racing the clouds to capture the interplay between light and dark. He was employing the *chiaroscuro* technique perfected by Caravaggio and Rembrandt. Virgil's awkwardness faded as he moved with the grace and economy of a ballet dancer.

A secret drama played out as Virgil focused on the woman seated alone at a table. He imagined her as Titian's *Venus of Urbino*. His subject was bathed in sunlight, while the area around her remained in shadow. Virgil burned the image in his mind but moved swiftly to capture her face before the clouds moved in. He framed the scene in a border of sakura pink.

Angie ordered a Negroni and checked her lipstick in her phone. The cherry blossoms were in full bloom in the park, and a few errant petals fell upon her table. She raised a glass, proposing a silent toast to an old friend.

In the distance, Virgil captured the moment in a symphony of light and shadow.

EPILOGUE

Christie's Auction House, New York
Old Masters Live Auction 19739
April 22, 2021

Bidding had stalled at 300 million, and it was starting to look like a sale was imminent. At the last second, a representative for an anonymous buyer in Abu Dhabi raised his bid. That reinvigorated the contest. The gavel finally fell at 475 million on *The Prodigal of Passyunk Avenue*, as it had been cryptically titled by its equally mysterious owners, breaking the previous record of 450 million paid for the *Salvator Mundi*.

Lauderdale-By-The-Sea
June 1, 2021

Nick was working the day shift. Grace was visiting her mother in West Palm.

Nick saw the woman from a distance and watched as she walked up to the bar. A glamorous vision in a caftan, floppy hat, and dark sunglasses. She was no longer blonde, but Nick recognized her immediately. The necklace, with its interlocking rings, reflected the midday sun.

"How are you, Nick? Ready for that drink now?"

"Sure," Nick said. "But I'll pour if you don't mind."

Anastasia giggled. "You're funny. I knew I liked you."

"I see you've dyed your hair," Nick remarked about her brunette locks.

"No, this is my natural color. That was a horrid wig," she said.

Nick poured her a Stoli Elit and a club soda for himself. "So, what brings you to my humble Tiki bar?" he asked.

"I missed you, Nick. You're different. Isn't that a good enough reason?"

Nick entertained the thought for a second, but quickly came to his senses. *Geez, this woman is good.*

"Okay, you got me," she admitted. "I *do* think you're different, but that's not the *only* reason I'm here."

Nick was dreading what was about to come out of her mouth next—and then she said it.

"It's about the painting."

Jesus Christ, he thought. "*The Prodigal?*" Nick had seen the news about the auction.

"No," Anastasia corrected him. "*The Storm on the Sea of Galilee.*"

Nick knew the painting well. It was one of Tony's favorites. The reproduction was still displayed reverently in Caffé Vecchio. Along with Vermeer's *The Concert*, it was arguably the rarest and most valuable item stolen in the Gardner heist.

"Dmitry has tracked it down."

"And?" Nick asked the question, but he already knew the answer.

"It's somewhere in Philadelphia, and he needs your help."

Anastasia stared at Nick as she lifted his club soda from the bar. A chilling grin spread over her face, and she started to giggle as she stirred.

THE END

ACKNOWLEDGMENTS

This book is the culmination of decades of accidental research. The years I spent growing up in South Philadelphia and especially on Passyunk Avenue are the inspiration for this book. Therefore, the friends and associates I met along the way deserve to be acknowledged for their contribution. I hope my fondness for the people and places in both South Philadelphia and South Florida shines through. In many ways, this book is my love letter to South Philadelphia, the amazing people who live there, and the magical places it contains.

I want to thank some people without whose assistance and encouragement; this book would not be possible. If, for some reason, I have neglected to name someone, rest assured, I will thank you in person.

My family, immediate and extended, deserve the first acknowledgment, especially my Mother and Grandmother for encouraging me to read, my sister Janine, for always being in my corner, my Aunt Lenora for buying me The Chronicles of Narnia at an early age, my Father for his quiet example, and a special thank you to Lorraine for being a wonderful mother to our son.

Robert Levant has been a constant source of encouragement and support. I have benefited greatly from his advice and guidance.

Thank you to Ray Driscoll of Protocol Cigars for being an advance reader and reviewing the cigar content.

Thank you to Ralph Frangipani of Frangipani Photography for the back cover photo and website/social media photography.

Thank you to Latte & Melanie Goldstein of River Design Books for the great cover and beautiful interior formatting.

Thank you to Elizabeth A. White for her patience and kindness in editing my manuscript and sharing in my journey.

Huge thanks to David Di Paolo of Maximus Internet Marketing Group for the website and marketing expertise over the years, but more importantly for his friendship.

Thank you to the most generous person I've ever met. My dearest friend, Chris Carvell, unofficial Mayor of the Tiki, for his years of brotherhood and being my guide in Fort Lauderdale. Love you buddy.

This book started as an idea for a screenplay that I shared with a special person through a unique email system. His unwavering support and enthusiasm convinced me to keep going. It was my pleasure to accompany him on his journey to South Florida. To my friend J in Boca Raton, may the gates always rise at your approach.

Thank you to Frank Talerico, owner and operator of the Ocean Manor Hotel and Resort and the world-famous Bamboo Beach Tiki Bar, for your years of hospitality and generosity.

A most special thank you to Lynn Rinaldi and all my extended family at Paradiso restaurant. Lynn made Paradiso an extension of my home and created a loving atmosphere that epitomizes everything good about South

Philadelphia and Passyunk Avenue. Thank you for feeding me and always reserving the corner stool for me. Through that window, I collected the images that would form the imaginary world of The Prodigal.

Thank you to my friends, Frank, Joe, Greg, Spider, and Stevie, for their loyalty and support over the years.

Thank you to Sophia and Santino for keeping our house exciting and vibrant.

To my wife Christine, to whom this book is dedicated. Thank you for being my inspiration, muse, alpha reader, and partner in life. This book would never have been finished without your gentle prodding and careful proofreading. I believe in you and me.

To my son Nick: You were in my thoughts with every keystroke. Being your Father is the highlight of my life. I wrote this book for you to hold in your hands as my legacy and testament of my love for you. I will always pester you to keep reading. Love, Dad.

For exciting updates about the world of Nick Di Nobile and the Prodigal crew, join us in the Prodigal Cabana Club at caudobooks.com. You'll be the first to learn about events, giveaways, bonus material and updates about Revenge of the Prodigal, Book II in the Prodigal of Passyunk Avenue series.

caudobooks.com

📷 @michael_caudo_author
🅵 @caudobooks

Made in the USA
Middletown, DE
21 September 2021